# The Himalay~

*An Affro~*

*By* **SUFI ABDUL AZIZ**

# Blurbs

The Himalayan Politics -*an affront to democracy*, is based on factual events in local elections between the years 1999 and 2022 in one of the UK's major Cities. Some local elections led to massive postal vote fraud, and the victims took the matter to courts and they appointed special commissioners to investigate the fraud. A few elections, after a thorough investigation, were declared void and new ones ordered. The author was one of the victims of the fraud. The author has been a political activist since the age of sixteen. He was honoured to be elected as a City Councillor in 2005. The book examines the background of the electoral fraud committed by the participants in the political process from the South Asian region. It examines how some candidates and activists bend the law and use the medieval clan system called *the baradari system* (an offshoot of Himalayan politics) to steal votes and destroy the opposition candidates' character and credibility.

Although this is a work of fiction, some of the events described are factual, other than those that patently are not. The characters and location of events have been changed. I believe there is much interest in such work as incidents of electoral fraud at a local level are on the increase. Many readers in other countries may also be familiar with the events captured here. The work also examines international politics from a personal perspective considering the Kashmiri and Palestinian issues. The author was born in Kashmir. The state of Jammu and Kashmir borders the Himalayas, China, India, and Pakistan. India occupies two-thirds of it, and Pakistan occupies one-third. The majority of Kashmiris want freedom from both occupiers through self-determination; an inalienable right of everyone to be free.

# Acknowledgements

Himalayan Politics
*An affront to democracy*

Acknowledgements

I thank all my supporters, family, friends and residents who voted for me in the numerous local elections in which I was a candidate and who have encouraged me to write a book about my experiences during the election campaigns. The title of the book was suggested by a friend in Pakistan, Khalil Hussain. The author and Mr Hussain witnessed dirty election campaigns in Pakistan which, in their view, time travelled to inner-city areas of many British cities. I also take this opportunity of thanking my colleague Salim Akhtar J.P. for reading the manuscript and imparting valuable criticisms. I also thank, Mr Khanzada, Publisher from Pakistan for making an editorial assessment of the manuscript and making global improvements to the manuscript.

Sufi Abdul Aziz
16th day of March 2023

# Dedication

*The only thing necessary for the triumph of evil is for good men to do nothing.*

Edmund Burke

*Take no part in the worthless deeds of evil and darkness; instead, expose them.*

Ephesians 5: 11-14

*An Englishman once conveyed a secret to me, though before public such secrets are never laid.*

*That democracy is a form of government in which people are counted, never weighed!*

Dr Sir Allama Iqbal,
Poet and Philosopher.

*This book is dedicated to ALL principled politicians and activists for working hard (often dangerously) to spread truth and justice worldwide.*

# Contents

# Chapter One

"Eh, Sufi are you standing in this year's council election, mane?" Hasan Ali asked me. His first few sentences always sound gibberish as he unsuccessfully tries to imitate the West Indian accent. He was only five feet tall, with a light skin tone, a squawky voice, a fragile ectomorph physique, and a long beard; he looked nothing like a West Indian. Hasan was precisely a foot shorter than I was. We went to the same primary and secondary schools and had difficulties forming lasting relationships like any teenager. Like our parents, we argued passionately about politics and religion, which often culminated in the breakup of our friendship, but only for a short while. Our affection was based on mutual respect and family ties. During the Bangladesh War of Independence of 1971, we were on opposite sides and often came to blows but did not stop talking. My father, a mosque Imam, used to say even the warring parties must not stop talking; that is what differentiates humans from beasts.

Now, in our early fifties, we consider ourselves more mature and able to tolerate each other's opinions. Jokingly, I asked Hasan what he was doing in the mosque now that Ramadan was over. Unlike many Muslims, Hasan and I prayed regularly throughout the year, not only during Ramadan. Our life philosophy was simple: *do what you can regularly and keep out of the rat race.* We witnessed Muslims entering the mosques in drones during Ramadan, but many did not return until the following year. Some carried on with their normal behaviour; lying, cheating and backbiting. Hasan told me that a Japanese friend of his asked him about the benefits of Ramadan. Hasan said he had a holier-than-thou attitude and tried to impress his friend, but Kenzo taught him a lesson that he will never forget. Hasan pompously told him that Ramadan was not only to do with abstaining from food, but the fasting person had a duty to refrain from telling lies, committing fraud, fornicating, and cheating. And fasting Muslims should be gracious to others and give money to the poor and be patient in times of adversity. Kenzo smiled ruefully and told Hasan that the Muslims were lucky to have to do all these things for one month only, when he, as a human being, did all that for the whole year. Hasan

1

said his friend's remark, deeply affected him. He lowered his head in shame and thereafter changed his outlook on life. His ego evaporated, as he recognised the subtle truth behind Kenzo's remark and stopped being part of the Ramadan rat race, and started obeying God in every respect throughout the year.

His wife disapproved of his new outlook on life and their marriage suffered. He stopped cheating, lying and terminated his wife's bogus benefit claims and found a low-paying job. They did manage to live comfortably but it was not sufficient for Alia Begum's luxurious lifestyle. Within months, they were divorced. Now, he lived a solitary life, in the Estone ward of the Cosmopolitan City, occupying a flat on the top floor of the twenty-one-floor tower block on Newtown Road. Estone Ward suffered from severe deprivation with many of its terraced houses, high-rise flats and maisonettes unfit for human habitation with no bathrooms or inside toilets. Ethnically diverse communities lived in the Cosmopolitan City. Over 50% were born outside the United Kingdom, with Asians being the largest community followed by black and white European communities. Of the Asian communities, Pakistanis were the largest ethnic group, followed by Bangladeshi and Indians.

I laughed at my friend's failed attempt to sound like a West Indian and told him that I will contest the election from Estone ward. Hasan was happy and assured me of his full support. He always looked forward to local and parliamentary elections as they gave him an excuse to eradicate boredom. I asked Hasan if he was free to attend a meeting at midnight. "At midnight? Who would be crazy enough to hold a meeting at midnight?" Suddenly, his eyes widened and he threw his arms in the air. "Don't tell me it's the Estone Socialists." I nodded. "Yes, I will come with you. No problem, mate." It was nearly eleven o'clock in the evening. My emergency night duty at the city hospital was due to start at midnight. Hasan was the only one I could trust to go to the meeting, listen to the socialists' plan and report back.

If I accompany him or go on my own, they will recognise me and refuse entry. "So, you want me to attend the election meeting and spy on them?"

2

"Yes," I said eagerly, hoping that he would agree to go alone.

From the thoughtful look on his face, I could tell, Hasan Ali knew why I asked him to spy on the Estone Socialists. Some of their candidates and activists were ever ready to play dirty tricks, often illegal, to outwit the opposition and gain votes that did not belong to them. I thought Hasan would be eager to go to the meeting as he would be curious as to why the Estone Socialists were holding a political meeting at midnight but he insisted that I accompany him. "They'll not allow me to even enter the tavern, let alone attend the meeting," I argued. Hasan said I was worrying for nothing; this election would be different because of the Iraq war and our party will win. Was he trying to change the subject? I could not believe what he said next: "I do not know why you politicians force others to do your dirty jobs. You should go yourself and find out. It is getting dark, I have got to go with them," he said, pointing to his neighbours Ashfaq and Tariq, who had just left the mosque and were going home. "I got to go," Hasan said, and the veins ballooned on his neck, his face turned red and his voice became squawky. Hasan looked worried as he saw his friends going further away from him. He wanted to catch up with them. I told him to get lost and never to talk to me again. He stopped. It was my turn to become angry. I would do anything for him, why was he being awkward? "I can go to the meeting with you or if you send someone else with me. It is too dark. I will not go on my own," he almost screamed. "Dark? You are not a child, are...." I stopped mid-sentence, as childhood memories flooded back. He was only twelve when dacoits kidnapped Hasan and held him for weeks in a dark, confined space for ransom in Bangladesh. As the tragic events unfolded before my eyes, I cursed myself for forcing Hasan to relive the pain. I embraced Hasan and patted his back. "I understand mate. We will have to abandon the idea."

Hasan said he met Yoda Khan in the Punjab restaurant last Friday evening and he boasted that the Estone Socialists will win this year's election outright, despite Muslim voters' opposition to them. The regional officers and activists made similar, outrageous claims. I heard such claims too but could not reconcile them with the ground reality. A private poll showed our Democrats party in the lead with 85% to Estone

Socialists' 5 %; an overwhelming support for us. Opposition to the Estone Socialists, among the Muslim voters, was a resounding 100 %. So why were they making futile claims? I was eager to find out but neither Hasan nor I could attend the meeting. He insisted I come with him. He must have had a brainwave, "I know how you can attend the meeting without discovery," he said suddenly. "Let's sit in the car," he whispered, as the Imam objected to us talking loud inside the mosque. Instead of being community hubs, mosques were like morgues nowadays. The imam discouraged all worshippers from meeting and greeting before or after the prayers. Notices plastered around the walls of the mosque read: *silence in the house of Allah*. I did not know whether to feel angry or sorry for the Imam and the trustees. Which planet were these people living on? The Broadbent Mosque, like other mosques in the Estone ward, opened at prayer times only and for teaching Arabic to children in the evening. In the time of the prophet, the mosques opened round the clock.

"I have an idea Sufi. We can attend the meeting and they will not recognise you," he said and burst out laughing. "Why are you laughing for? I am serious man. We have got to find out what they are up to," I said. I was annoyed at the way Hasan was behaving. "Sufi listen," he said, "You'll have to dress like a woman." I was shocked. "You bastard," I said, "you want me to dress like a woman? What the....."

"You will only need to wear the *burqa*, for an hour or so. No one will be able to recognise you." I had serious reservations about this idea and told Hasan that it was unworkable. I could not walk or talk like a woman. "Okay, in that case, why don't you ask Irfan? He looks half woman anyway," he said. I heard him giggle.

I tried to get out of the car and he pulled me back and said, "Seriously though Sufi you need to find out for yourself what they are up to. Only a handful of them know me.

I will say you are my wife and pregnant and cannot leave you home alone." I lifted my hand to smack him and he quickly said, "Okay sister. You are happy now? At midnight most of them will be half asleep

4

anyway. Trust me." It took me over half an hour to decide. I was due to start my emergency night shift at the city hospital so I rang Jayne and asked her to cover for me. I gave her an estimate of an hour or so. I had to get ready in thirty minutes. Most Asian meetings rarely start on time but this one might, as it was so late anyway. "I will go home now to dress. Pick me up in twenty minutes." Hasan nodded. My wife was fast asleep and I tiptoed to the wardrobe and removed a pair of gloves and the black burqa. Iram only wore it during our pilgrimage to Makkah, two years ago. With the wide hemline, the dress looked like a tent. It naturally ballooned around my chest, which was a good start. Apart from the eyes, nothing of me was visible, so I did not change my socks and shoes. I sprayed the sides of the neck, chest, and inside of the elbows with Chanel Coco as I had seen Iram do every morning. I was ready but was not happy about what I was doing. God forbade men to dress like women and vice versa. True this is the twenty-first century but you cannot change your religion to suit modern times as my Quran teacher, Imam Hatim used to say. He had kicked out, Imam Bohra, his deputy from the Madrasah because what his tongue said his evil heart did not believe. Religion and politics are the roots of controversy, discord and disunity. Holy books teach that cross-dressing and homosexuality are the works of Satan. Under the pretext of teaching children how to perform ablution, Imam Bohra's desire to force children to put his apples into their small barrels overtook him. That was the satanic desire that the Quran warned him against. It was the desire that expelled humanity from heaven. One rotten apple spoils the whole barrel. Tolerance leads to understanding and acceptance of other's viewpoint.

Hasan was already waiting for me. "You look beautiful darling. Don't forget to wiggle your bum," he teased. "Piss off," I said. He could not see my smile and apologised. Hasan asked: "Why were the Estone Socialists holding a political meeting at midnight?" I told him; his guess was as good as mine. I was hoping that attendance would be low as most of their members would be asleep at this late hour.

The meeting place was only a ten-minute walk from the Broadbent Mosque and my house but we decided to drive. It was a cool and blustery early April night. We gazed at the star-studded sky as we entered the Old

Tavern. We walked through the foyer into the meeting room and noticed that it was warm but stuffy. The irritating smell of cigarette smoke and smog enveloped the room, making it difficult to breathe and to recognise people from where we stood. The last row of seats was immediately to our right. I was surprised to see the room full of members, even the elderly and the infirm were in attendance. Old Rahim Khan and Fazal Rehman, both octogenarians, sat in the front row, and we could see no empty seat. I guessed we were the last ones to arrive. We were not members but hoped at that time of the night, they would not find out. There was no security at the door. No one asked for our membership cards. That was a good omen. The shape of the room was like a trapezium, and had four rows of chairs neatly laid out; ten chairs in each row. I thought they could have arranged a further two rows of chairs. A glaring oversight of party management, but after some consideration, I put it down to a lack of chairs. It was safe to sit in the back row as the rostrum was in the furthest corner.

I narrowed my eyes; Hasan was doing the same to see clearly through the haze. We identified over half the attendees. I could not see an empty seat and around forty men, mostly young, stood at the back, leaning against the wall. We spotted Iman Dar, a clinical psychologist, and a good friend, sitting at the end of the last row next to old Haji Bashir. Prostate cancer had made the old man look pale and haggard. The Estone Socialists must be desperate to get an old man out of bed to attend the meeting at night.

We passed a group of four men, standing by the wall, smoking, and chatting; one of them recognised Hasan. "Hasan Ali! What are you doing here? You a member?"

"Ye, what do you think?" he lied. The questioner was Amjad Hussain, old Bashir's son. "What's the meeting about?" Hasan asked him and elbowed me to carry on to the seat. No one noticed me in my black burqa. I did wiggle my bum. Did they all suffer from ED? Most of them were half sleep.

"We're going to destroy the Democrats," Amjad whispered. Hasan walked quickly away from them and shook hands with Iman Dar and old Haji Bashir. They made some space for us. Iman Dar asked a young man sitting next to him, if he would vacate his seat for a lady. I did not recognise him. He immediately vacated his seat. *Good of you Iman Dar and you young man, I said to myself.* Hasan moved to the seat next to Iman Dar and thoughtfully left me the last seat in the last row. I sighed with relief. It was turning out to be easier than I thought. Seeing friends like Iman Dar made me calmer. I was not sure if we could tell Iman Dar who I was but decided against it. Hasan thanked them, sitting on half of the chair, making more room for the old Haji Bashir. Iman Dar asked Hasan who I was and he replied: *"My sister. Couldn't leave her home alone."* Iman Dar nodded and left it at that. He asked Hasan if he knew about the purpose of the meeting. Hasan told him what Amjad had said to him only a few minutes ago; something to do with 'destroying' the Democratic party's selection meeting tomorrow.

"Why are we interfering in other parties' affairs?"

"I give up mate. These morons are determined to win the election at any cost, knowing full well they can't win this one. But It's to do with honour, I think. We kill and maim, our women and children in the name of honour and now we've to win elections because it's dishonourable to lose." Hasan put his hands up. Everyone was talking so loudly that Iman Dar had difficulty hearing Hasan. He was whispering to avoid discovery. Lots of Bangladeshi and Pakistanis who wanted to vote for us had received threats of severe consequences from the Estone socialists.

The meeting was about to start. I took a sharp breath. Raju was asking everyone to sit down. Minutes later, an eerie silence descended on the room. All eighty members fixed their eyes on the speaker, more eager to get the meeting finished quickly than want of paying attention, I guessed.

"I apologise to those standing at the back, it's not an ideal venue for the meeting but that's all we could get at short notice. Our Cosmopolitan City Council local elections will be held on Thursday 6th May, in three weeks from today. We, in the Estone Socialist Party, have already selected three candidates – me, Yoda Khan and Adah Ram. The national party are fielding paper candidates as usual," he giggled. "I understand...."

"I know nothing about your selection. When did it take place?" Iman Dar interrupted.

"Mr Dar, you were probably with your friend Sufi at the time of the meeting. You rarely attend meetings," Raju retorted. I whispered to Hasan that there was no selection meeting. He passed it onto Iman Dar. The regional socialist leadership imposed all three candidates by closing the ward. I seethed with anger. Raju was a liar and a cheat. I cannot stand people like that. I was about to get up and say something when Hasan delivered a vicious kick to my shin. Bastard. That hurt.

"That's not true Raju. I know you hate Sufi but he's a colleague. We both work in the same hospital. You know I attend meetings if invited. I understand this year you three got in through the back door, courtesy of our regional leadership. Very Democratic decision." There was sniggering and cynical laughter around the room. Raju shrugged his shoulders and continued, "I was going to say before I was rudely interrupted, that the Democrats....," he paused and looked towards me. I saw him narrow his eyes. I showed him two fingers. It worked. He turned his gaze away and continued, "are selecting their candidates tomorrow." *We have selected our candidates. Your friend is trying to get through the back door. But he will not*, I said to myself. Iman Dar nudged Hasan with his elbow and whispered, "looks like your information was spot on mate." Hasan nodded. "We can ignore the National Party," Raju said in his gruff, pompous voice. He was even shorter than Hasan but muscular and had the loudest voice.

He did not need the loudspeaker. "As I said, they only field paper candidates and have never been a threat to us in inner-city wards. Our fight is with the Democrats. I can't say 'fairly and squarely,' because we never play fair.

If we did, we'll lose. I guarantee it wouldn't be 'fair'. Their national leader opposed the Iraq war. Our leader blindly supported it. So, our party has lost support from the Bangladeshi and Pakistani communities and others opposed to the war. A local opinion poll gives us only 5% support compared to 85% for the Democrats. Even if we cajole, persuade, or intimidate the undecided 10%, we will still loose, it's as simple as that. It would be an insult and dishonour for us and our party if we lose."

"I don't agree. We should fight fairly and if we lose why is that a problem?" Iman Dar asked angrily. Raju Miah ignored him, shook his head, and continued.

"Let me tell you that Asif Kazak, a Pakistani; Irfan Khar, an Indian and Sufi Sahab, a Kashmiri, are the candidates for the Democratic Party. They don't have a Bengali candidate. The Bengali community are angry about it. We believe the party will confirm Asif and Irfan as candidates, unopposed, tomorrow and they're ready to co-operate with us. Sufi has refused to co-operate. So, we've persuaded our friend Jitu Miah a long-term member of Democrats and our party, to oppose Sufi's selection tomorrow. It's just …"

"Don't ignore me again Raju. How much have you paid him to stand against Sufi?" Iman Dar interrupted again.

"Not much if you must know. Please don't interrupt. As I was saying, it's just going to be a contest between Sufi Sahab and Jitu Miah for the third position. We have Jitu with us tonight, sitting here on my right. He's seeking our help in defeating Sufi tomorrow." *The bastard, I thought.* "And if he succeeds, all three Democratic candidates will secretly support us and collect postal votes for us. We should win all three seats. Sufi is a straightforward person, not a politician. He works hard for the communities, and people come first for him, not the parties. He believes in and holds the seven principles of public life very dear. Politicians don't like him." *You got that right, I said to myself.*

"You lot should learn from him then." Iman Dar said. *Well said, mate. Love you.*

"Please don't interrupt Mr Dar. It's late as it is. We need to finish the meeting quickly." There were murmurs of Aye, Aye from around the room.

"You don't like members telling you the truth?" Iman Dar was angry but not surprised. Out of eighty members, only about five were literate, the rest were first-generation elderly men who could hardly read, write, or speak English. The socialist party exploited this by spreading false information or fake news about their opponents' religion and caste. They also distorted the nationalists' immigration policy in a way that terrified voters into voting for the socialists.

"There's no room for truth in political expediency Mr Dar. As I was saying, no political party wants a person like Sufi. We believe Jitu can defeat him tomorrow with help from us." *Oh, can he? I seethed.*

"How can you defeat Sufi? He's got massive support from the Democrats' membership and the leaders. I would urge you not to bring dirty Himalayan politics into the UK."

"Too late," Raju laughed, "HP is already here. I know he's your friend Iman Dar. Frankly, I don't know what you're doing in the socialist party, join him; become a member of his party for God's sake. Don't interrupt. Whatever you hear tonight about our plan, if Sufi learns about it, then we can rightfully blame you, can't we? It'll be a pleasure to see you expelled from the party." Most members knew Iman Dar to be outspoken and very brave. No one from the audience interfered in the exchange between Raju and him. Some socialist voters did not support the blatant interference in other parties' internal issues.

"For your information, Sufi's at work. He's doing an emergency night shift. He'll be back around 9 am. I won't see him until next week. I'll leave now so I don't hear your half-baked dirty plan. You lot can go to hell." *Again, well said mate. Don't worry I already know what they're up to.*

"9 am? Wow, that should be fun. He'll be half sleep when the selection meeting starts. Victory is yours my friend Jitu," he said smiling.

"Yes, it's best if you leave Mr Dar. Good night." He waited for Iman Dar to disappear through the door, before continuing.

"Democratic party's total membership from this Estone ward stands at eighty," Raju said to the audience, half of them looked asleep and the other half were staring at their phones. Many were forced to leave their beds to come to the meeting. I heard two elderly men whisper in the front seats about annual membership fee. It shocked me to learn that the socialist candidates and activists paid the annual membership fee for most members. So, most attendees were reluctant members. "Last week, the split was thirty to fifty votes in favour of Sufi," Raju continued, "but, we've infiltrated the Democratic party; the twenty-one members sitting in the back row hold dual membership. That's good news for us and our friend Jitu as they'll vote for him tomorrow and we thank them for their co-operation and understanding." *No, they won't, not if I can help it.* "This will ensure that Sufi is out of the contest by 51 to 29 votes." There was clapping all around at their Imagined fool proof plan. Most members, who were only half awake, on hearing the clapping, stood up and joined in.

"Iman Dar mentioned 'Himalayan politics,' what did he mean by that? What is HP?" 'Dr' Iqbal asked. He was not a proper doctor. It was his nickname. He could hardly read or write. He was one of the many with dual membership. Everyone called him *Doctor* because he shared the name with the illustrious poet and philosopher of the East, Sir Allamah Dr Mohammed Iqbal.

"I know little about HP but our friend Yoda is an expert. I'll ask him to shed some light on it. Thanks, Yoda." Yoda received rapturous applause as he approached the rostrum. Iman Dar hated his monotonous voice that put him to sleep.

"Thanks, Raju. Thank you all for the welcome. There isn't much time left to explain HP. It's a bag of tricks used by unscrupulous politicians or clever politicians like us," Yoda said smirking. "There are more than ten deadly tricks that the Himalayan politics teach about winning elections, but unfortunately in the UK we can only exploit the baradari system, use personation, buy votes or destroy opposition candidates' character and credibility by spreading rumours. The exploitation of the baradari system is the major component of this bag of tricks. We'll learn about HP when we start a door-to-door campaign in the next few days. Using personation, we can easily get a few hundred votes. For example, we can vote for people who are abroad at the time of the election and for the sick and the dead people. We can also vote on behalf of the registered voters who have never voted if we can persuade, intimidate, or bribe them to hand over their polling cards."

"How can you vote for the dead?" Asad Khan, a young teenager asked incredulously.

"I saw a practical example of personation in the Jhelum district of Pakistan, Asad, my son. The electoral process in India, Pakistan and Bangladesh is identical to the one in the UK. I saw an old man, Mohammed Sadiq, a *mochi* (shoe repairer), enter the polling station (I was standing in the polling station, observing proceedings, as I was a polling agent for my cousin, Shahid Ali). The old man asked the polling clerk, "has my wife voted yet?" the polling clerk nodded, adding, "sir, she voted ten minutes ago. You've been asking the same question for the last nine years. Why don't you reconcile with her?" The man looked worried. "Ten years ago, my friend Haji Bashir *the massalee* (musician) told me that his wife Ambreen Kausar had seen her voting," he said. "At first, I didn't believe him but his wife confirmed that my wife was standing in the queue in front of her and gave her details to the polling clerk as 'Asimah Noreen, wife of Mohammed Sadiq of Purana Khatna, Dina, Jhelum'. I had to believe that it was my wife. Ambreen Kausar did say that my wife was wearing a burqa (veil) so she did not see her face. So, every year at election time, for the last nine years I've been waiting for her outside the polling station all day and I only vote just five minutes before the polling station closes to make sure that I meet her but every time, I miss her. She always votes between ten and fifteen minutes before me. I have a horrible *kismet*," he said with tears in his eyes. The clerk sympathised and asked again if he had tried reconciliation. "No, we never had a fight or anything. No need to reconcile. We loved each other very much," the man replied sobbing. "The thing is, I miss her very much. She died ten

12

years ago. She comes every year to vote but doesn't come to see me."
The room erupted into laughter.

"I'm glad you find it funny," Yoda said, "but we can cast hundreds of such votes in the UK because many deceased individuals' names and addresses remain on the electoral register until the election office deletes the details, the following year. Even a couple of hundred such votes can make a lot of difference. Its late now friends, most members have already left, so we must end the meeting. Good luck to our friend Jitu tomorrow." *I have been complaining about your tricks to the election office for the last ten years but no one listened,* I said to myself. A round of applause and cheers followed for Jitu. The remaining twenty members shook hands with him and wished him luck and we left the tavern with them. I wiggled my bum furiously, but no one noticed. They looked more like zombies than humans at that time of the night.

# Chapter Two

The next morning, Hasan called; asking me if I was ready for our party meeting. I told him, I just got back from work and would be ready in ten minutes. He reminded me the meeting starts at nine sharp and we may be ten minutes late. "So be it. Did you sort out your Bangladeshi friends?" I asked anxiously.

"Yes, all sorted. They'll vote for you. I'm leaving home now; will be with you in ten minutes."

"I've asked JB to allow a question-and-answer session at the end of the meeting, as you requested," I said.

Just as we entered the meeting room, John Boyes, popularly known as JB, approached the rostrum and asked the Democratic party members to take their seats. It was a tiny room. All eighty members had turned up unexpectedly. JB wanted the meeting to be just a formality. A stamp from members on the decisions already made. Somehow, it did not look as if it was going to be a walkover. The presence of all eighty members, especially that of Sher Dill, was unsettling for him. He did not like Sher Dill, someone told him he was a troublemaker. JB had never met Sher Dill before. I could guess who gossiped about him to JB. Sher Dill was very intelligent and a close friend of mine. JB looked more worried with each passing minute. I asked JB to allow a brief question-and-answer session after his talk and he did not like that. JB was a big burly man of mixed race. He had a West Indian father and an Irish mother. Asif and Irfan had picked him up from the New Street railway station. On the way, he expressed some concern about the question-and-answer session that I had asked him to undertake after the meeting. The idea was for members to ask questions to clarify any issues as the previous regional organiser had not held a meeting for two years. I did not see any problem with that. Irfan invited JB into his house on the way to the meeting for *lamb curry and nan*. Asif said Irfan told him that JB was fond of curry but according to the rumours circulating in the ward, he was fond of Irfan, not the curry. Irfan did not invite Asif into his home but asked him to wait in the car which was not a nice thing to do. Asif felt insulted and complained to me. Asif said when JB came out of the house, Irfan walked behind him with a limp. He seemed in pain and had difficulty sitting in the back seat. Irfan screamed with pain when Asif went over a bump in the road. There appeared to be something wrong with his bum. JB had looked worried and kept asking him if he was okay. I felt that JB must've had more than lamb curry and nan. Whatever he offered to JB in the house, it was not food. If, as Irfan claimed, they had lamb curry and nan at his house, then why did JB, on his arrival at the venue, ask Asif for tea and biscuits? I could see he was a bit peckish as he was dunking two biscuits at a time.

Standing at the rostrum now, he seemed at ease and asked members waiting outside the room to come in and take the remaining seats or stand at the back. This had the effect of making the room more congested and the stuffy atmosphere was worse.

"Good afternoon colleagues," he began, checking the mic by tapping it with stubby fingers.

"I apologize for the limited space but we'll have to live with it for now as this is the first-ever meeting of the Estone ward members of our Democratic party. As some of you know, I am a member of parliament for the Skimmington Constituency in our Cosmopolitan City. The National leader has asked me to re-organise the Midlands regional Democratic Party as a matter of urgency. The existing management committee was dismissed by the national president for failing to implement the party's constitution in letter and spirit. I have now extensively re-organised the regional party and have put new practices and procedures in place which will mean that the local branches will have to hold meetings at least once every three months. I'm aware, many members became disillusioned and left the party. But we've gained a multitude from the Socialist and the National Parties following our leader's wise decision to oppose the Iraq war. I, thank you all for hanging in there through these difficult times. Things will get better, I promise you."

"I don't think anything will get better," Sher Dill Sighed. JB sniggered, ignored the interruption, and continued.

"The local election is due shortly, and we have limited time to select our candidates as nominations will be submitted to the Cosmopolitan City election office by four o'clock tomorrow afternoon. I understand the Estone Socialists selected their candidates last night. Until two days ago we had nominations from only three gentlemen, but as you all know, Mr Jitu Miah has now entered the contest." My supporters interrupted JB and started shouting: 'shame! shame! He's wasting our time.' I thought of revealing the previous night's adventure to JB, and name and shame the crooks, Jitu and Irfan but decided against it as he will only go by what they will tell him. JB smiled and resumed, "So, the nominations now are: Mr Jitu Miah, Irfan Khar, Asif Kazak and Sufi Sahab. Around forty members have now nominated Jitu to replace Sufi. The contest is, therefore, between Jitu Miah and Sufi Sahab. I think we can confirm Asif Kazak and Irfan Khar as the candidates. All those in favour please raise your hands". Only around thirty members raised their hands. JB, Irfan Khar and Jitu Miah looked worried. Their expectation was for fifty-one hands to go up. What was going on in the members' minds? Jitu frowned and his face became contorted when Sher Dill said, "they're not our choice sir but we approve them if you ask." I relaxed, knowing that Hasan and Sher Dill had done their job according to my instructions.

"That's good, thank you. One selection process is out of the way," JB sighed with relief. I knew he was only concerned with Irfan Khar's selection. Asif's selection was a bonus. Who will be the third candidate? Me or Jitu? I guess JB had no real preference. Irfan Khar, however, preferred Jitu Miah to me. I got on well with Asif. A Bengali candidate was a must, but I could not support Jitu, because of his selfishness and double standards. The democrats feared that most Bengali vote will go to the Estone socialists as they have Raju as the candidate, but I did not think so. As a rule, Bangladeshis do not vote Pakistanis. According to some reliable reports received from London, JB's instructions were to ensure my selection to satisfy the electorate's demand for suitable candidates. Secret polls carried out on behalf of the party, confirmed that the Estone residents favoured me, not Asif or Jitu, as the candidate.

Public opinion compelled the Democratic party's leadership to nominate me as a candidate. Irfan asked JB to persuade the National Executive Committee to select Jitu instead of me. JB sent an email to the NEC stating he could not understand why they had directed him to ensure my selection. As things stood with the Enstone Socialists, they had no chance of victory, anyway. There was no doubt in his mind that Democrats will win with flying colours without me. But the NEC had insisted on my selection. Judging from the response from the audience, it was clear to JB that I had the upper hand. Private poll held in the ward showed a comprehensive victory for us.

"Normally, the selection would've been by show of hands," JB continued, "but both candidates have asked for a secret ballot. Our party's selection rules allows that so the selection for the third candidate will be by a secret ballot. Do you want to say anything, Sufi Sahab? Jitu Miah?" Both of us shook our heads. There was nothing to say. Jitu and Irfan were in bed with the Estone Socialists, and I did everything possible to turn the tables on them. Perhaps the NEC suspected them and that is why they demanded my selection.

"No? Ok. In that case, I'll now distribute the ballot paper. After voting for the candidate of your choice, please place it in the ballot box, here, on my desk. I'll then count and announce the result. That'll be the end of the matter. I must warn you gentlemen that my decision will be final. Acceptance of any complaint or appeal is out of the question. Is that understood?" There were some vigorous nodding and mutterings of 'yes sir' around the room. About fifty members stood up and started clapping, cheering, and chanting "Sufi, Sufi, Sufi" to the obvious dismay of Jitu Miah and Irfan Khar. They looked at each other, shocked. Chants of "We want Sufi," reverberated in the room. JB smiled. "Mr Sahab is very popular. That's an excellent start." I noticed Jitu Miah and Irfan Khar hanging their heads in shame. "Our other two candidates will no doubt also do well in the election thanks to our national leader's anti-war policy on Iraq and Afghanistan."

The audience stood up again and shouted: "long live our leader, David Drinkwater." Some members even shouted in *Urdu*: "David

Drinkwater *zindabad.*" Ironically, our Party leader's surname did not match his day-to-day drinking habits, as he drank very little water. His favourite drinks were Guinness and Orchard Thieves. I met David a couple of years ago when he visited Cosmopolitan City, accompanied by Jitu Miah, Irfan Khar and JB. I could not understand why Irfan Khar and JB pretended not to know each other. I dismissed the thought with a shrug. Whatever the problem is between them, it is nothing to do with me. A vicious rumour, linking the two to the LGBT community was circulating in the Estone ward. I left it at that, voted for myself, placed the ballot paper in the box and sat down. The traitors were in for a shock.

Twenty minutes later, JB asked everyone to take their seats as he was ready to announce the result and would also give information about the ward for the benefit of new activists and Asif as he was from a different area. JB approached the rostrum. "Friends, I can now tell you, that all eighty ballot papers have been counted.. Jitu Miah received twenty-nine votes. Sufi Sahab has received fifty-one votes. So, I declare Sufi Sahab as the third candidate. "Oh, Shit! The bastard has turned the tables. Fifty-one was our vote," Jitu Miah hissed. "What the fuck," blurted Irfan Khar. Seventy-eight members gave me a standing ovation and congratulated me on my selection. JB resumed. "I take this opportunity to congratulate Sufi Sahab on his selection and feel confident that his popularity will ensure victory for the party. I want to tell you all a bit more about the ward as some of you, like me, have only recently moved to the Cosmopolitan City from London and other areas. The Estone ward's residents are from diverse communities, most of them are of Bangladeshi and Pakistani origin. There are also European, African, West Indian and Indians belonging to the Kokin and Gujarati communities. "Why do we not have a Bangladeshi candidate, then? According to you sir, two of the largest communities are Pakistanis and the Bangladeshis, so shouldn't we focus on them?" Sher Dill said.

"I agree Mr Dill. Over 80% of those communities come out on election day and vote. I have taken this figure from the last year's marked register. That's good for us. I'm sorry if I'm boring you but you must know the processes and procedures because we believe we have an excellent chance of winning these three seats from the Estone socialists for the first time." Little did he know about the unholy treaty between Jitu Miah, Irfan Khar and the Estone Socialists. *I think Asif Kazak as well*, I said to myself.

"Because boundary changes and election rules", JB resumed, "each party has to field three candidates. So, you're looking at a dozen candidates from the four major political parties and others from the Green Party and independents. I agree with Sher Dill, we've made a mistake by not selecting a Bangladeshi candidate. We've Asif from the Indian, Irfan from Pakistani and Sufi from the Kashmiri communities. There has been a chronic lack of interest in politics from other communities."

"That's because sir no political party's truly representative of all communities," Sher Dill interrupted.

"I agree. I can't deny that. The most plausible explanation for this has come from Irfan Khar and Jitu Miah. They tell me that in the past, people voted blindly for the Estone Socialists in inner-city areas to the extent that a donkey with an Estone socialist label won."

"Ye, it takes one to know one sir," Sher Dill said, and got applause and guffaw. JB smiled and continued, "They also tell me that most Asian immigrants arriving in the UK were told to consume Adams butter and vote Estone socialists. This message has been passed on from generation to generation of immigrants. Most of them have erroneously attributed their presence in England to the good offices of the Socialist Party. Times have changed. Our young generation is well-informed and does not blindly vote for any party. They now look at the candidates, their education, their standing in the community, honesty, and integrity."

"These requirements should rule out Irfan Khar, Asif Kazak and Jitu Miah, shouldn't they, sir?" Sher Dill interrupted and again the hall erupted into a hearty laughter.

JB looked amused and continued without showing the anger that he felt inwardly towards Sher Dill for insulting his friend.

"I hope everyone here will get together to ensure a splendid victory for our party. Thank you for listening and that's all I have to say. I'm ready for questions or clarifications that you may require. Once again, I thank you for your patience. If you want to ask a question, please state your name so I can put a face to a name. I haven't met many of you before."

"My name is Chore Miah, sir. Do you know the names of the Socialist and the National party candidates?"

"Yes. I only found out this morning. They are: Raju Miah, Yoda Khan, and Adah Ram. As I understand, they're from the Bengali, Indian and Pakistani communities. Ignore the national party candidates, they won't trouble you much. Your direct battle is with the Estone Socialists. Be very careful. As far as I've been able to find out, they are experts in Himalayan politics. They will do everything in their power, by legal or illegal means to win this election. As you all know, the Iraq war has seriously damaged their chances of an electoral victory. Not only Muslims but all peace and justice-loving voters have turned their back on them. They're in serious trouble. Some of our supporters think, they're planning some sort of electoral fraud. I don't see how they can achieve that as they need to follow electoral commission guidance and not visit the homes of registered postal voters and they've to make proper use of proxy votes. They stand to lose a lot if caught so I don't think they'll be stupid enough to risk it. But who knows? There are very few safeguards against postal vote fraud."

"Sir, my name is Sher Dill and I would first like to congratulate you on becoming our regional leader. You mentioned HP. Some members have joined us after becoming disillusioned with the Estone Socialists but I fear they may cause discord and divisions within our party too. There are members of our party colluding with the Estone Socialists to help them win. The members have roundly rejected Mr Miah today but I have some inside information that they have nominated him to replace Sufi in the next election. So, by what logic was he allowed to stand against Sufi in this election? Mr Miah can hardly read or write. So, what sort of representation the public can expect from him if he ever, God forbid, became a councillor? Some voters think he's a member of HP40 and this group has a sinister agenda." *That's a very good question, I thought.* I didn't ask him to put that question to JB. Sher Dill has initiative. He spoke English with an accent but the clarity was there. What Irfan, Jitu and Asif didn't tell JB was that they were members of HP40. This group practised Himalayan politics and consisted of forty members. They carried membership cards of every UK and overseas political parties. It was necessary to make JB aware of this highly dangerous group. It was a party within a party.

"He'll never become a councillor. If we win all three seats in this election, we'll lose them in the next if they replace Sufi." Several members shouted, one after another.

JB looked worried. "I understand where most of you are coming from but I promise we'll review matters when we cross that hurdle."

"Sorry, Sher Dill again, sir. Is it true you've nominated Irfan Khar as our party's parliamentary candidate from the Haywood Constituency for the next year's general election? What happened to the selection process?"

"Yes. As we don't have very many Haywood constituency members, the National Executive Committee (NEC) of the party nominated Mr Khar without the need to carry out the selection process."

"I beg to disagree, sir, we've enough members for a quorum according to party rules for the selection of local council and parliamentary candidates. We're not happy with NEC's decision to bypass members for the selection of candidates. It's unacceptable. If we don't have democracy within our party, how can we expect to sort the country out? We're doing what the NEC of the Socialist Party do. They close wards and constituencies and impose candidates of their choice. That's not democracy sir, I call it hypocrisy."

JB was getting frustrated with the line of questioning. He did not expect the largely Asian and Bangladeshi audience to know much about politics or policy or even possess any in-depth knowledge of how the party machine had been manipulated for the benefit of the few. Instead of showing anger, he decided to be more diplomatic.

"Mr Sher Dill, I will take your comments back to London and make NEC aware of your feelings."

"These are not my feelings alone Mr JB but all members." There were mutterings of "Aye, Aye" from the audience. "Talking of feelings sir, how are your feelings for Mr Khar? I mean, how long have you known him?"

The directness of the question shocked JB but he controlled himself and showed no sign of betrayal of his innermost feelings for Irfan. I noticed some excitement in the audience following this question. JB must be asking himself: *how much did they know about him and Irfan Khar?* Unfortunately for JB, Irfan Khar betrayed his emotions at once by blushing and by visibly looking angry and uncomfortable.

JB said calmly, "that's an irrelevant question, my friend. Now if there're no more questions than I bid you farewell. I'm asking the candidates to get a suitable campaign office which should be roomier than this please," he smiled and continued. "I will then come to see how you get on. Keep working hard gentlemen, be united and we will win ALL three seats."

# Chapter Three

A head appeared around the door with the words *Democrats Party Campaign Office*, displayed in large yellow- orange letters on the glass and said, "Hey, Irfan will you hold this door open while I wheel in this filing cabinet?"

"I'll ring you back Rahman. Jitu and Asif are here, want me to open the door for them. Anyway, keep up the good work but make sure your family and friends don't vote Sufi, it's very important. Explain to you later," Irfan Khar spoke quickly and quietly to a supporter. Having replaced the receiver, he surveyed the well-lit large rectangular room overlooking busy Wilson Street. Irfan felt proud of his success in acquiring the room rent-free from Paul Ali for use as a campaign office. Paul Ali called himself an *entrepreneur* but was a well-known brothel owner in Estone ward. Irfan had cleverly failed to inform JB and other regional leaders, of these facts. Had they known, they would've ordered us to move to different premises. Irfan and I had, earlier, created a home for a cabinet in the corner, next to the massive mahogany table which I had placed strategically, in direct view of the staircase to monitor everyone coming into the campaign office. From experience, we knew that spies from other Parties infiltrated our campaign office just as our spies pretended to be activists for the other parties. Some hypocrites, like Naeema, Sadia and Haram Khor infiltrated all parties to gather information and sell it to the highest bidder. Such spies were very dangerous and we tried our best to prevent them from infiltrating our party.

Irfan stood up, ran a hand over his head and thought: soon I too will be bald like my friends Jitu and Asif. Irfan moved quickly now as he realised Jitu sounded out of breath when he asked him to open the door. As there was no lift in the building, Jitu and Asif must have pushed and pulled the filing cabinet to this floor using the stairs at the back of the building. Anyway, better them than me, Irfan thought. He smiled and tucking the pen behind his hairy ear, pulled back the door as far as it would go. The filing cabinet, looking grotesque with bright yellow features, rolled in on its wheels, pushed by the huffing and puffing bald Jitu. With all four drawers open, the cabinet looked more like a Dalek in 'Dr Who' series than a piece of furniture!

"Where the fuck did you find this... this thing?" Irfan asked angrily. "It looks horrible *yar*. Where's Asif? He was with you."

"Asif's gone home. But this is all I could find for the price," Jitu said, still panting from the physical exertion and continued: "It cost me only four pounds man! Sufi told me to look for one in the local second-hand furniture store and that's all I could get," Jitu explained, his voice almost cracking. To appease Irfan, he added, "Think on the bright side *yar*, at least it resembles our Party Colours!" They laughed spontaneously, a harsh annoying sound, more like the braying of donkeys than human laughter.

"Oh, only a couple of donkeys up here, I was expecting a lot more. Where are they all?" Paul Ali asked as he entered the Campaign Office. Both men swung round to face him. They hated Paul but dared not challenge him in case he withdrew his financial support from them. "They must all be asleep yet. Ten 'o'clock is too early for our team", Jitu said sarcastically. Jitu was an expert Himalayan Politics practitioner. Having lost to me in the selection process he got himself appointed as an election agent even though he could not read or write. He had already played dirty by side lining, Asif Kazak. So that he could get maximum praise from JB and other leaders. Jitu did not allow Asif Kazak to play any constructive role in the election and often told him to, "Go home. Don't worry. Enjoy yourself."

This local election in the Cosmopolitan City, scheduled to take place in two weeks was unique as the boundary commission altered the ward boundaries to reflect the demographic changes. Some National and Democratic Parties' regional officers regarded it as gerrymandering but I did not think the electoral commission was biased in any way.

The fact was that immigrants and host communities constantly moved in and out of many areas of the city, creating population imbalance and ward boundaries have to be changed every twenty-five years to reflect this. The boundary changes meant all three sitting councillors from all forty wards were up for re-election. This year, all four main political parties – The National Party, Justice party, Socialist Party and Democrats Party had to select three candidates each for all wards. Normally, only one of the three councillors would be up for re-election, not so this year. In Estone ward, the sitting councillors, Yoda Khan, Raju Miah and Adah Ram were from the Socialist Party. In the past, the Estone Socialists were very popular not only in Estone but also in other inner-city areas of Heartlands, Ashbrook and Northen. Many voters believed any tom, dick or harry representing the socialist party could win in these inner-city wards. But with the start of the Iraq war, this perception changed dramatically. No one considered the Estone Socialists as the party of justice and truth anymore. By removing clause iv, they had also lost their image of champions of the working class. The Prime Minister, and leader of the Socialist Party, had decided (rightly or wrongly, only time will tell) to go to war in Iraq and Afghanistan. It proved to be unpopular decision in the inner-city areas with a large Muslim population. However, the two million who marched against the war were not all Muslims but other peace and justice-loving people of whom there was no shortage in Britain. Among, the protestors against the war were people from different political spectrums and different religions and races. Black people, white people and brown people and different nationalities - Africans, Bangladeshis, Europeans, Indians, Pakistanis and people from the West Indies, all opposed the war. But the government of the day paid no attention to their pleadings, exhortations, and warnings and thoughtlessly plunged Britain into the cruel and uncertain war on the pretext of some shaky evidence for weapons of mass destruction. The outcome was uncertain; the consequences were perhaps, never contemplated. Many Parliamentarians were not happy with the war as the so-called 'allies' had launched it without the blessing of the United Nations security council and ignored international law. Some great Parliamentarians and champions of truth and justice, like Ms Clare Short and Robin Cook, resigned from the front bench. The government must have thought it was doing a great job to rid the world of terrorism once and for all. But no Iraqi or Afghani was involved in the destruction of the twin towers. So why attack Iraq and Afghanistan? Was the Parliament deceived? Was this, as Ms Short called it, an 'honourable deception?' It was the duty of the government to protect its citizens from the deadly terrorist attacks.. But rumours and conspiracy theories gained popularity. The war and the warmongers, the two Bs came under criticism. Critics viewed them as having a little moral fibre because they succumbed to some iniquitous external and internal forces for revenge, having no regard for further innocent loss of life.

Political analysts and experts in psephology - the art and science of fighting elections - predicted a total disaster for the Estone socialists in the local elections, especially in inner-city areas. The National Party never performed well in inner-city areas as voters considered them the party of the rich. And the cunning Socialists helped to ensure the electorate stuck to this belief to maintain their electoral advantage and alienate the nationalists. Many voters in the inner-city wards believed the Estone Socialists candidates had thrown all caution to the wind and were hell-bent on winning the election at any cost. Poll predictions of disastrous results did not deter them and they swore to keep their chance of survival alive. Of the eighteen thousand listed voters in the Estone ward, over 80% were from the ethnic minorities. The Estone socialist used this to their advantage, attacking the nationalists as the party of anti-immigration and the rich. The Democratic party's leaders believed their fight to be direct with Estone Socialists as the nationalists fielded only paper candidates and did nothing to rebut Estone Socialists' lies. The Democratic Party had become very popular overnight, because of their leader's brave opposition to the war in Iraq and Afghanistan.

In Estone ward, the residents were happy to see me selected as the candidate and they supported our party wholeheartedly but they were very quick to notice disunity within our team. Irfan, Asif and Jitu were asking voters for only two votes – for Irfan and Asif. The majority of electorate thought these two were the only candidates. During their door-to-door campaign, they did not mention me. Asif, at the start of the campaign, asked for two votes, for himself and Irfan. He then secretly followed me and saw that I was asking for three votes. Asif felt ashamed and included me in his door-to-door campaigns. When Jitu and

Irfan learned of this unity between me and Asif, they started excluding him from their campaign. We warned the duo that we will report them to JB if they showed further disunity. This warning soon brought them partly to their senses, and they started asking for two votes but still ignored me. This did not unduly worry me as I was confident of a victory if the Estone Socialists played fair. I had recognised from the start that there was not much chance of that happening. Jitu Miah proved to be a troublemaker and asked for only two votes from the Bangladeshi community. After a week of surveillance, Jitu and Irfan did not approve of Asif's loyalty to me and further alienated him by refusing to campaign with him. The problem for our party was inner strife, created by Jitu and Irfan's hatred of me because in their eyes I was more popular than them. During the very first day of campaigning, both men were extremely disappointed to hear many voters tell them they will only vote for the Democrats, 'if Sufi asked us.' The main reason for my popularity was the perception that I was honest and had integrity and a desire to work for the residents' interests and improve their lives by representing them effectively in the council.

Around one hundred and twenty councillors represented the electorate in forty wards with each ward electing three councillors, thus making the Cosmopolitan City council the largest in Europe. I had often criticised the makeup of the council. I had argued for changes in ward boundaries to reduce the number of councillors and for the elections to be held every four or five years instead of every year. Such a course of action will save the council a fortune which could be spent on providing extra school spaces and financing other projects. But short-sighted council leaders ignored my pleas. When the general election coincided with local election, it confused the voters. The language barriers made it difficult for them to understand the complex election rules. To make matters worse for them, every household received two or three election leaflets from all political parties. Unable to read them, the voters binned these leaflets, especially in inner city areas. Translations in Urdu, Punjabi and Bengali did not fare any better because many voters could not read or write in their native languages. Voters did not like Irfan and Jitu. Many refused to open their doors to them during door-to-door campaigns.

This made them even more mad at me and they began telling lies about me. Some residents, through my team's campaign, learned about Irfan and Jitu's tricks and they warned them not to intimidate or blackmail me and Asif. They told them there was no room in the UK for dirty Himalayan politics. This made them even more frustrated and their determination to 'teach us a lesson' increased.

Adil, a highly educated resident of Estone ward, a rare species, saw some money (he was certain it was a £20 note) change hand between a postal voter and Jitu on Tenbury Street. I asked Adil to report it to the election office. Adil also warned Jitu and Irfan to refrain from such illegal and immoral acts so they do not lose the trust and confidence placed in them by the public. Candidates, elected to the council or parliament are not expected to be angels but must display a sense of responsibility and a degree of morality that sets them apart from those who do not qualify to hold any public office. The question that most voters in Estone ward wanted answered was: *What would the elected representatives do to improve housing, employment, clean streets and make Cosmopolitan City a popular place to live?* I believed in accountability. Politicians must display an air of care and concern for the public and be accountable to them for their actions, which would usher in an era of true democracy.

# Chapter Four

Even their close family members and political associates did not know the extent of the emotional involvement of Irfan and JB. They had known each other since Irfan was thirteen. They met at a house party given by Irfan's uncle who joined the Democrats in 2000. John Boyes, or JB as everyone called him, except Irfan who called him Mr Johnny, took an instant liking to the teenager as he displayed distinct feminine features and an attractive face. Irfan remembered, JB calling at his uncle's house on a Sunday afternoon, three years after the tragic death of his parents and sister in a multiple-car crash on the M6 Motorway. It was love at first sight. JB had asked him to sit in his lap. I am told their first conversation went something like this:

"Is your name Irfan?"

"Yes, how you know?"

"Your uncle told me."

"Oh!"

"Happy thirteenth birthday my boy."

"Thank you Mr johnny. How do you know?"

"Your uncle told me."

"Oh."

"D'you go to Broadbent School?"

"Yeah, how you know?"

"You're wearing the school badge", JB told him, pointing to Irfan's framed picture on the wall.

"Oh!"

"D'you like science at school?"

"Yeah! How do you know?" This surprised Irfan. Mr johnny seems to know everything, Irfan thought. Pointing to a pile of books in a corner of the room, John Boyes said: "I guessed because you've loads of Physics, Chemistry and Biology books there".

"Oh!"

A minute later, Irfan, still seated in JB's lap, asked innocently: "D'you work in a garage, Mr Johnny?"

"No! Why do you ask?"

"I can feel a Jack under me!"

Red-faced, turning to Irfan's uncle, JB attempted to conceal the real meaning of Irfan's last statement. "Nawaz, my friend, your nephew will one day climb to the top. Please allow me to teach the young Boy ins and outs of politics." Irfan's uncle readily agreed to this suggestion and promised to send him for private tuition in politics to JB's house every Sunday evening. During these 'political education' sessions, JB told Irfan that after becoming a politician, it was highly likely that he would become filthy rich.

On his seventeenth birthday, Irfan discovered that the pursuit of money, fame and power with help from JB was not free from pain. JB took Irfan to his home and threw a party in "his honour", as he told him. Just before midnight, JB asked Irfan's uncle if the 'young man' could stay overnight. Irfan's uncle granted the request hoping that his nephew would soon get on top of the political ladder with tuition from his friend. JB wanted Irfan to get on top of something but it was not the political ladder, not yet anyway. JB was determined to extract maximum benefit for his investment in the young man before allowing him to ascend the political ladder.

Since the tragic death of his parents, Irfan's care passed to his uncle, Nawaz Khan, as guardian. He tried to bring up his nephew to the best of his ability. The only impediment was, he hated spending extra money on his nephew.

He asked everyone not to interpret such actions as miserly, because he had five children of his own, and his capacity to buy clothes and other necessities for Irfan was limited to the amount of money received from the government in benefits, for him. So, Irfan received no birthday, Christmas or Eid presents from his uncle or any other family member. Irfan received expensive presents from JB, every birthday since they first met. On his thirteenth birthday, Irfan had received a pair of trainers and football boots from JB for the first time. For his fourteenth, fifteenth and sixteenth birthday, he received, play station, an iPad and a Samsung galaxy watch to his delight and the obvious annoyance of his cousins.

For Irfan's seventeenth birthday, JB decided to make this a memorable birthday for him and Irfan. JB arranged a discotheque and invited around twenty of Irfan's sixth-form mates to the party and presented the most expensive gifts to him in their presence. He received a Breitling endurance watch, Dior low-top sneakers and a cotton-terry tracksuit. His friends sang, 'happy birthday' and 'for he's a jolly good fellow so say all of us' for full five minutes; Irfan felt very proud and repeatedly thanked JB and offered to do "anything for him". "Oh, I hope you'll Irfan my boy, after the party. I've got another gift for you", he whispered. At midnight the party ended. Everyone went home. JB surveyed the mess left by the boys in his reception room but he decided to leave the cleaning until the morning for Mrs Brown. Cleaning would make him more tired and that will not be good for what he planned for the night. Had Irfan known what was in store for him, he would have run miles but JB did not spend all that money, effort and time for free. He did nothing free for anyone. "I'm not running a charity", he told anyone who asked for financial help from him.

"Let's sleep, young man. I hope you enjoyed your seventeenth birthday, Irfan, son", he said patting his back. They climbed the stairs together with JB making circular movements on Irfan's bum. From JB's general demeanour and the way, he looked at Irfan, he felt as if he was being prepared to mount a sacrificial altar. Irfan became apprehensive when an earnest question to his benefactor: *what are you going to do to me, sir*, went unanswered. Upon entering the bedroom, JB sat on the edge of the bed and took his shoes and socks off, Irfan did the same. As JB stood up, Irfan smiled, held JB's hands and kissed them. "Thank you again, Mr Johnny," he said with a twinkle in his eyes. JB was dismissive, "not to worry, my boy. You can pay me back."

"I've no money sir, I can't pay," Irfan said, eyes wide open. JB laughed at Irfan's innocent reply. He was very immature even at seventeen. Loss of parents, early in life, and the cruelty of his guardians made him lead a sheltered life.

"Don't worry son, you don't need money. You can trade your stunning body. With a little make up you'll pass as a gorgeous woman."

"Why do men like me so much, sir? Some always look at me as if they want to eat me. Even teachers hug me and kiss me in school. Last year, Mr Black, gave me detention every day after school, even when I did nothing wrong. He used to sit next to me, stare at me and then lean over and kiss me on the lips, every five minutes."

"Ah, that's because you're delicious my boy. I've waited impatiently for this day. Unlike Mr Black, you don't know what herculean power I exerted to resist doing things to you! You're now ripe and ready to eat."

"Thank you, Mr Johnny, for everything you've done for me."

"No need to thank me. What I've done for you is nothing compared to what you're going to do for me my boy", JB said, in a bemused tone and motioned Irfan to the bed.

"I'm going to brush my teeth, Irfan. You make yourself comfortable and take your clothes off. It's so hot tonight." Irfan looked apprehensive. "Oh, just change into a fancy night shirt. You'll find a red flowery shirt in the wardrobe. There should be one your size, and you can keep it." JB said smiling, and sauntered to the bathroom.

Having taken off his shirt and trousers, Irfan noticed his naked body in the wardrobe mirror for the first time as he prepared to put on the fancy night shirt. What he saw, surprised him.

He noticed a slim, athletic build with bulging biceps and strong rectus muscles stretching from his pubis up to the ribs. His entire hairless body boasted smooth skin with distinct feminine facial features - well-formed, bigger-than-average breasts. The tiny size of his gonads showed a lack of development of secondary sexual characteristics which explained the absence of body hair. Irfan had no feelings for girls but he had a potent attraction to boys. In school, girls in his class had teased him about his habit of always sitting next to James and following him around.

Irfan was about to put on the nightshirt when, in the mirror, he saw JB approach him, stark naked. Irfan froze. His body tensed and he shook uncontrollably. JB stopped him from putting his pyjamas on. "No need for that my boy," he said laughing and with a sweeping movement of his arms, lifted him onto the bed. JB pursed his lips as he placed the boy in a doggy position. Terror showed on Irfan's face as he looked over his shoulder and muttered: "Mr Johnny, what have you got there?"

"It's the Jack, my boy, you felt under you on your thirteenth birthday, remember?" JB replied smiling and got on the bed behind him.

"What are you....?" Irfan stopped mid-sentence and screamed. The sound pierced the walls of the adjoining houses. There was banging on the wall, followed by shouts of *'can you keep quiet, its past midnight for God's sake!'*

JB sighed with relief when the bleeding stopped. The horror that had shown on his face subsided. He feared the boy would bleed to death. JB dressed him and cursed himself for using minimum lube. 'Using more wouldn't have made much difference,' he thought. He led the boy slowly, still crying, to the car and took him to the hospital. The AE doctor informed JB that Irfan had sustained an extensive tear and required complete bed rest for at least three weeks. Seven surgical stitches were used to close the tear. Irfan told the nurses and doctors that he sustained the injury from a fall, just as JB told him to say. But to nurse Jennifer, his friend and neighbour, he told the truth. Even hours after the treatment, Irfan was still in agony, and they decided to keep him in the hospital overnight to monitor his condition. Jennifer confronted John Boyes about his friend's condition. "You must be a huge boy to do that sort of damage to him".

"How do you know it was me or indeed that the damage is sex related? What are you insinuating?" He retorted.

"It was you. Irfan told me. He's my friend and neighbour. I've known him since he was five. He's only three years younger than me. You're lucky, he's not underage, otherwise, I would've reported you to the police you bastard."

"It's none of your business, you keep your morals to yourself or you will be in trouble."

JB successfully pleaded with Irfan's uncle to allow him to stay for at least another week. And to placate him and stop him from asking awkward questions, he eulogised both uncle and nephew and reaffirmed his belief that one day Irfan will earn enormous sums of money and will occupy a much-coveted seat in Parliament. JB's philosophy was simple: *flattery gets you everywhere*. Irfan's uncle appeared grateful and contented upon hearing about his nephew's predicted achievements. Irfan's uncle, however, was unaware of his nephew's hospitalisation and the extent of his injuries. He only knew what JB told him: "Irfan has a minor leg injury from a fall in the garden while he played football after some hard academic work. The doctor has advised rest for a few weeks until he fully recovers from his injuries. So, don't worry Nawaz. I'll drop him home next week."

"I'm never worried when Irfan's with you JB. I know he's in expert hands."

"Of course, mate, and thanks."

The Nurse, Jennifer, warned them to refrain from raunchy sessions for at least six weeks to allow healing to occur. JB took no notice, and every night he got into bed with Irfan under the pretext of keeping him company and looking after him. Out of fear and necessity, Irfan learned other ways of pleasing JB and soon discovered his exceptional manual and lingual skills in phallic manipulation. JB used well-thought-out and imaginative tricks to get Irfan to satisfy his carnal desires.

He placed ripe, juicy halves of strawberries at strategic locations on his body, covered with mounds of fresh cream. Irfan loved eating strawberries and licking the cream from JB's nipples, moving down to the navel and sending ripples of excitement throughout his body making him gasp. "Oh, my God, I can't believe you are such an expert at your age, Irfan". At one point, with growing pleasure, JB had become impatient and ordered Irfan to adopt a doggy position but he was horrified and quickly covered his body with a blanket. "Oh, hell. Sorry, I forgot. Don't stop then!" JB yelled, quivering with pleasure. "I think you'll soon have a drink". Within seconds, Irfan began coughing violently and ran to the bathroom.

"Oh, what's matter darling?" JB looked concerned when Irfan returned to bed. Running his hand through Irfan's hair, kissed him on the lips. "Oh, didn't I tell you, I've more presents for you, my boy?" He retrieved two packages from under the bed. "Look what I got for you", he said. Irfan's eyes twinkled and the sight of the packages brought a smile to his face. Grabbing the packages, he sat up in bed, momentarily forgetting his back and throat pain. He tore the wrapping paper and looked questioningly at his benefactor. "Open it and see", JB teased. Irfan's sad face quickly brightened as he held an iPhone worth thousands of pounds and a brand-new Chromebook in his hands. "Wow, I always wanted these Mr Johnny, oh thanks." Even at seventeen, Irfan was not tech-savvy due to a lack of exposure to technology in early childhood. He learned a little about computers at school as he rarely attended school. His uncle made him do house chores and rang school to say he was ill. JB showed him how to use the gadgets and Irfan quickly set about exploring them. Overjoyed to receive such expensive presents, Irfan did what JB asked him without question. He smiled as he thought about his friends and cousins becoming extremely jealous again of his new possessions. There was a danger of his presents surreptitiously passing to his cousins but he was determined not to let that happen again. The new computer, iPhone and other expensive presents were his and in no way, he will part with them. JB's previous birthday presents for him: a watch, Samsung mobile phone and coupons for thirty free driving lessons, had all disappeared and mysteriously ended up in his cousin Aftab's room. Irfan's attempt to get his presents back met with sarcasm and cruel chastisement from his uncle and aunt. They had claimed they bought them for his cousins' birthday. Since then, Irfan regarded his uncle, aunt and cousins as 'enemies' and acted with impunity against their interests. So, from an early age, Irfan had developed an appetite for the acquisition of wealth at any cost and planned to buy a mansion and move away from, what he called, 'his hostile family.'

Irfan's dream of moving away from his 'hostile family,' materialised three years later under tragic circumstances. Out of the blue, on his twentieth birthday, Irfan's uncle announced he had arranged his nephew's wedding with his friend's beautiful daughter in Pakistan. Irfan refused and said truthfully that he was not interested in women. His uncle laughed and told him he was a comedian. Nawaz Khan had arranged the marriage over the phone and promised his friend, Afsar, a police superintendent, that he will bring his only daughter, Robina (Ruby) Akhter to the UK. Ruby, at twenty-three, had completed her Master's degree in psychology from Namal University and wanted to undertake a doctoral study in the UK. Marriage to a British citizen would make her transition to the UK much easier and cheaper. Tuition fees charged by British Universities were extortionate and many middle-class Pakistanis found it difficult to send their sons and daughters abroad for further or advanced education. But Irfan would have none of it. He refused, point blank, to entertain any suggestion of marriage. His uncle tried his best to persuade him but to no avail. Nawaz was furious and grabbed Irfan by the neck. He would have killed him had his wife not intervened. She told him to calm down and go to the mosque and pray for his nephew to change his mind.

After returning from the mosque, Nawaz Khan sat in his armchair disappointed with his nephew and angry at himself for arranging the marriage and making a promise to his friend without first seeking his nephew's view.

After what he had done for his nephew; brought him up when he had no parents, and treated him like his own son, the least he could expect from him is unconditional love and obedience.

"You know *Jan* (darling), this British education somehow affects the minds of our children. It makes them too independent and freedom-loving. They lack discipline. When I was in school, my masterji (teacher) punished me for even a slight misdemeanour. The cane made a whooshing sound as it landed on my hands and buttocks every day. Children taught in British schools have no discipline and no respect for the elders." he told his wife.

"Some children have no respect *Jan*, not at all," his wife corrected him. "You were very naughty *Jan* that's why the teachers smacked you every day. It's not the schooling that has made Irfan disobedient, it's the unnecessary love that your friends JB, whatever his name is, gives to him. He has spoilt your nephew…"

"Oh, you're a darling," Nawaz Khan interrupted his wife, ran into his bedroom and emerged with his mobile phone. Dialled a number, and talked animatedly for ten minutes.

"It's sorted now," he announced happily, "JB is going to persuade Irfan to get married in Pakistan. *Jan,* the marvellous thing is, JB has promised to take care of the financial side too. So, I won't have to spend even a penny on that scoundrel's wedding. I love it when the plan comes together," Nawaz Khan said rubbing his hands gleefully.

In the middle of October 1998, at the height of a mild and pleasant season, JB, Irfan and his uncle all travelled to the Naka village. Nawaz Khan's friend, Afsar and his police cohort met them at the Islamabad airport and drove them to the village. Seven police cars and four motorcyclists brought them to the village with police protocol. A journey of three hours from the airport to the village took only one and a half hours. People lined the streets to watch them as they sped through the bazaars. Hundreds of villagers lined the street as they arrived, and escorted them to the Afsar residence, a mansion situated on top of the Naka hill, overlooking the village in the valley below.

A couple of days later, everyone in the household went shopping. It took two days to complete the shopping as women argued over which attire would suit the bride and the groom. A week later, the wedding took place and JB paid for the lavish wedding celebrations, organised the *waleema* (marriage banquet) and invited the local police officers, magistrates, politicians, doctors and other community leaders. On Irfan's insistence, they also invited poor people from local villages for lunch. The way Irfan walked and talked sweetly, some of his wife's cunning relatives and locals suspected him of being gay. *Gando* is the derogatory label given to a gay person in this part of the world and some thrill seekers started calling him by that name. Local shops were full of young miscreants, they clapped and sang, "*Gando, Gando, Gando*…and laughed like hyenas." Irfan did not understand the Mirpuri dialect and just smiled. A local English school teacher, Master Ghaffar, told him what they meant when they called him *Gando*. Irfan stopped going to the shops on his own. Ruby's numerous *Sahai lees* (girlfriends) teased her for marrying a *khusra* (trans woman). Nailla, Aysha and Iqra defended Ruby when others were critical. Her cousin, Ambreen, was scathing and she spoke to others as if Ruby was not there: "Ruby hasn't had it yet, you know what I mean," she said winking. "My man took me to heaven and back on our wedding night," she boasted, "Ruby has married a eunuch."

Ruby complained to her mother that her Sahailees (friends) were teasing her as the marriage remains to be consummated. She informed her husband, and then Irfan's uncle learned about it. His cruel words pierced Irfan's heart like an arrow. "Haven't you slept with your wife yet, you useless *Gando*? You've brought dishonour upon the family. We can't face even the low castes in our village. Those who respected us, now ridicule us. Everywhere we go, we've to hide our faces. I hope to God, you die. I don't want to see you anymore. Beyond the Naka hills, flows river Poonch, go and drown yourself if you have any pride left." Nawaz said through gritted teeth; "are you telling me, you don't have even the slightest urge when you're near such a beautiful girl?" Irfan remained quiet and just stared at his uncle.

From then on, he did not venture outside his bedroom. He watched movies on the brand new tv that Ruby's parents bought as dowry for her.

The local sociopath, Jamal, loved Ruby and wanted to marry her. As her cousin, he regarded himself as the rightful person to be her life partner. She did not want him. He learned that Irfan was unable to consummate the marriage. This was music to Jamal's ears and with the help of his crazy friend, Rauf, he planned to consummate the marriage on Irfan's behalf. Jamal, through his parents, had many times, asked for Ruby's hand in marriage, but his uncle and aunt (Ruby's parents) refused, telling him that she was going to marry a British citizen. "Over my dead body," Jamal warned and planned to get revenge whenever the opportunity arose. Well-to-do villagers with pretty daughters, perceived him to be poor and refused marriage proposals brought to them on his behalf by his parents. He had accumulated considerable wealth through illegal means. Disclosing it may mean an immediate prison sentence and the return of stolen good to their rightful owners. Some poor villagers accepted marriage proposals, but he refused them, determined to marry Ruby at any cost. Was that love or lust? There is something strange about a few Pakistani cockerels, they crow at any time of the day or night, to show their dominance. The hens like the cock-a-doodle-doo sound rather than the cocks' incessant crowing. But they ignore the Clucks of hens. "I'll not be sinning," Jamal told his friends. "Irfan has failed as a husband and can't satisfy the beautiful creature, and as her cousin, I must make sure she's happy." His friends asked him how he was going to achieve his ambition. Jamal told them, he could not risk entering a senior police officer's house at night and so decided to ambush Ruby on her daily horse rides. For the last three years he had been following her every morning. He saw her watering the horse at the small freshwater stream, an offshoot of the mighty Poonch river, running behind the Naka hill range, which was at least a mile away from the nearest houses. His two friends, one of them a police officer, were well-known thugs in the village. All three-stole jewellery and money from rich landowners. And as the investigating officer, Rauf closed the files and the heinous crimes remained unsolved. They congratulated him and wished him luck as if he was going to ambush some dacoits.

Ruby was no ordinary girl; her beauty not only raised the eyebrows of the local gentry but other things too. She suspected Jamal of being a thug and masterminding numerous robberies that took place in Naka and neighbouring villages. Every morning, before sunrise, she saddled her favourite black horse (one of her father's three horses), called *black beauty*, an Arabian breed, calm and suitable for novice riders, and rode out alone through her parent's vast land with orchards, lush fields, hills and streams. After the marriage, she asked Irfan to ride alongside her but he was terrified of horse riding. Sometimes JB accompanied her, riding the beautiful white mare. He was an accomplished horse rider and offered to train Irfan but he would have none of it.

Two weeks after their arrival, JB, Irfan and his uncle decided to return to the UK. Time passed quickly for JB and Nawaz, but slowly for Irfan. They told everyone they enjoyed their stay in the so-called Azad Kashmir, part of the state of Jammu and Kashmir. One-third is occupied by Pakistan and two-thirds by India. A few days earlier, they had cruised around the surrounding villages and the main bazaar in police cars. Single-story shops, mixed with large two-story buildings, called *the plazas,* lined both sides of the mile-long narrow street, with no footpath. Irfan marvelled at how the scantily dressed drivers, mostly teenagers, drove buses, trucks, tractors, cars, motorbikes and rickshaws erratically and impatiently but skilfully avoided collisions with each other and with men, women and children walking on the road. The drivers steered the vehicles with one hand, the other on the horns. The muezzin's call to prayer could be heard above the shopkeepers' cry for customers. The bazaar was situated in the centre of the U-shaped Naka valley, surrounded by lush green fields, pine and oak trees; the entire area exuded natural beauty. During the tour, Afsar asked Irfan's uncle if he would allow his nephew to remain in Pakistan for at least six months or even a year until the new bride, gets her spouse's visa. Nawaz readily agreed but JB was inwardly worried. He could not bear to separate from Irfan for a year.

So, the following day, he visited the British embassy in Islamabad with Irfan and Ruby and briefly spoke to an entry clearance officer. He told the officer about Ruby and Irfan's plans and the possible danger to their lives. JB passed an envelope to the officer. The ECO spoke to someone on the phone and told the trio that the visa will be issued within a month. JB was not happy and asked for it to be issued within a week. ECO said that he had reduced the time limit from around a year to one month and there was no way he could reduce further.

Just two days before their return to the UK, tragedy struck. As usual, that fateful morning, Ruby, wearing a red shalwar and kameez, an expensive wedding gift from JB, got her horse out, saddled it and rode at a gallop along the pebble-strewn path, down the hill, across the stream and disappeared behind the Naka hill range. JB wanted to go riding as well but Ruby's horse was too fast for his pregnant mare. He slowly followed the path taken by Ruby. Beyond the Naka hills, ran a freshwater stream, where Rubina dismounted and allowed the horse to drink the mountain-filtered water to its heart's content. The clarity of the water was such that Ruby could see the tiny pebbles, larvae, fry and fingerlings swimming erratically and feeding on plankton. She sat on a stone near the stream and saw her face reflected in the water. She noticed the wrinkles under her eyes and laid the blame on the events of the last few weeks. Once in the UK, she thought, things will be ok. As her father said, she could divorce Irfan and lead her own life. She hoped her beauty and serenity will return. She scooped a handful of cool crisp water and splashed it against her eyes. When she opened them, she saw reflections of two male faces and recognised Jamal. Before she could get up, they quickly moved to her left and right and unceremoniously lifted her and dumped her on a small grassy area among the stones and rocks on the bank. Jamal stood over her, contemplating her beautiful body while the other man moved back and stood by their horses.

"I begged you to marry me and now face the consequences for your refusal," Jamal said between gritted teeth.

"I've got the right to marry whoever I like, not a scoundrel like you," she said trying to get up.

"You've no right to refuse me," Jamal said and fell on top of her, pinning her body, ferociously tearing at her clothes, exposing her chest. She could feel his hardness against her body. She tried to fight back but could not move any part of her body. He had her fragile body under his complete control. Three times winner of the village's wrestling contest, Jamal was strong and muscular. Ruby had no chance to dislodge him, though she continued to struggle.

"I take it that Gando husband of yours hasn't even touched you yet, has he?" He asked and laughed mirthlessly. "Wow you are stunning," he said squeezing her small, hard breasts together and swallowing them. She screamed, and he moved his left hand to cover her mouth. It was the sort of mistake; she was looking for. With her right hand free now she frantically searched for a stone and found one that she could just about lift. Ruby tensed and with all her strength she smashed the jagged stone on the back of Jamal's head. He bellowed in agony and then yelped like a dog, his head slumped to one side and a jet of blood shot into the air from a gashing wound, splattering her face. It tasted salty. Seeing the blood gushing from Jamal's head, his friend rode off quickly and did not even look back. Ruby wriggled free, tied the torn dress together to cover herself and stood over Jamal's body with a larger stone held above her head, and let go. She sauntered to the stream, washed the blood off her face and walked towards her horse. Ruby was about to mount her horse when she saw the white mare, tied to a tree trunk not far away. "Father!" She called out several times. There was no response. "Uncle JB!" There was no response but then someone grabbed her from behind and she felt a sharp pain in her right buttock as if she had been injected. She felt her shalwar slip down and her breasts held forcefully. Ruby tried to back kick but 'could not move her legs. What was happening? She tried to turn her face back to see who it was but failed. Someone was exerting a tremendous force, making her bend down and then roughly entering her. She screamed with pain and felt deep and forceful thrusts for what seemed an eternity and felt blood trickling down her legs.

She screamed again, but no sound came out. Sobbing, she asked, "Are you a man or a beast?" She felt her body fall to the ground and a blanket of darkness enveloped her.

Hours later, Ruby's mother spotted the black beauty but there was no sign of Ruby and she called her name several times. "Ruby, where are you? Remove the saddle from the horse *baytee (daughter),*" she shouted. Kulsoom Afsar looked for Ruby in the bathroom and her bedroom and the kitchen. She then went to the lounge and found her husband, JB, Irfan and Nawaz Khan sipping tea and talking. She looked worried and told them about her worst fears.

"Don't worry *Jan,* black beauty has probably decided to come home early. We'll go and find Ruby," her husband said. A search party headed by Ruby's father found the bodies of Ruby and Jamal, drenched in blood. Within the constraints of the Pakistani medical expertise, the post-mortems showed Jamal's death was caused by the broken skull and although Ruby was still barely alive, they could not find a suitable blood donor. The pathologist thought she had been suffocated as her lips were deep blue. They gave her oxygen. Hospital records, where Ruby received treatment, showed that there were three units of AB-negative blood in the blood bank the previous night but were now missing. An investigation revealed that the night-duty medical technologist had sold the units to a private doctor. So, despite their best efforts, they could not save Ruby and they could find no unequivocal cause for her death other than bleeding from a massive vaginal tear, widespread bluish skin colouration and possible suffocation. The pathologist went beyond the call of duty and carried out other tests and concluded that Jamal was not responsible for Ruby's death. Jamal's mother was quick to spread the rumour that her horse defiled Ruby. It spread like wildfire in the village and surrounding areas. When it became a news item on the local TV station, Ruby's mother committed suicide because of the loss of family honour. No witnesses came forward and medical evidence appeared inconclusive, the third suspect, man or beast, could not be identified and so the investigation was closed.

During the flight, Nawaz Khan refused to sit next to his nephew on the aeroplane and told JB he will not allow his nephew to stay with him any longer. It was music to JB's ears. JB let Irfan beg before giving his consent that he could stay with him. Just before landing at the Heathrow airport, Irfan leaned towards JB and whispered in his ear: "I think it was you sir who…who damaged Ruby. Don't worry your secret is safe with me." JB looked away through the window at the murky black clouds through which the plane was descending rapidly. Irfan did not notice JB's bloodshot eyes and face.

# Chapter Five

Irfan's desire to become rich and JB's increasing carnal desire had unwittingly placed them in a risky situation, forcing them to throw all caution to the wind. During the European Parliament elections, JB was a candidate from the Dockland area. The number of seats won by each party was to be assigned under proportional representation. Jitu's job was to print and distribute leaflets. He had begun sorting leaflets after the machine had stopped printing when he heard loud moans. He did not know if anyone else was in the unit. As far as Jitu knew, JB had given him instructions and went home. He left the print room and went round to the office. His mouth automatically opened wide when he saw both men with trousers down, Irfan slumped on the table with his legs dangling down and JB behind him. It took him a minute to recover from the shock but decided against interrupting them or swearing at them. He took a picture instead with his *sharp* smartphone. An hour later Irfan entered the print room, limping slightly. Jitu confronted him, but he denied everything, although his mouth remained open, his face went pale and his breathing became shallow. Jitu showed him the picture. Words stuck in Irfan's throat. By making gestures with his hands and uttering a few incoherent syllables, he begged Jitu not to tell anyone else. "Your secret is safe with me," Jitu said patting his back. Irfan thanked him many times and since then both Irfan and JB had been "nice" to him.

But Jitu reprimanded Irfan for engaging in such 'despicable' activity, despite being a Muslim. They argued against it while folding leaflets into small bundles for delivery. "How can you say that? You sanctimonious bastard, you told lies after touching the Quran," Irfan retorted. Like some party activists, Jitu was a compulsive liar. He had received his political schooling from the most notorious riff-ruffs in Estone ward, like Liaquat Ali, Bashir Mali, Biman Rajah and Fazle Jat. Irfan was referring to Jitu taking oath on the Quran as a defence witness during a trial for fraud, involving his niece, Noreen Asghar, and telling lies to save her from an inevitable bankruptcy or imprisonment. After arguing for over three hours, they still had not reached the conclusion of which action was wrong: *telling lies when taking oath on the Quran or being gay.* Jitu advanced an argument that not only the Quran but the bible and other holy books forbade homosexuality and declare it a satanic act. Irfan invoked science and declared homosexuality to be a genetic anomaly for which the Almighty himself was responsible. "How can the almighty punish people like me when he is behind it all?" Irfan asked angrily but Jitu did not budge. "My Peer Sahib (*holy man*) told me that homosexual desires are satanic and have origins in parental and environmental influences, i.e., nurture, not nature," he said. "And it can be unlearned. Some scientific research has demonstrated that genetics may only have a secondary influence during child development as the primary factors may be environmental which can affect how genes are expressed. So, a male child receiving no love from his father will seek love from other men and display homosexual tendencies. Similarly, a male child brought up in an environment where both parents were abusive and unloving would be bisexual. The holy man also told me that a male child receiving no love but physical abuse from his mother will be a wife beater and (*wait for it*) a female child brought up by an abusive and unloving mother will display lesbian tendencies. As an extrapolation of peer sahib's theory, a young man if sexually abused as a child would turn out to be a paedophile or gay or both. But the point I'm making is that the 'abnormal' sexual tendencies can be unlearned."

"Jitu, what you're saying is Rubbish. Absolute rubbish," Irfan replied angrily. "You can't read or write so you depend on others for your knowledge but I've read widely. Being a gay person has roots in genetics and can't be unlearned. You're relying on mere conjectures. Islam encourages covering up other people's faults. So, I can be a Muslim and gay. There's no scientific evidence to corroborate what you're saying. The theological and scientific argument propounded by some so-called men of learning that people like me have a choice to turn back is not based on logic. And scientific evidence does not support it.

Science argues that those who are androphilic or gynophilic have no control over their sexuality, which automatically leads to gay and lesbian sexual attraction or arousal. Hasn't your peer sahib told you that many men with small penises are either gay or bisexual?"

"Islam encourages debate, you moron. I don't agree with you that gays, lesbians and others have no control over their sexuality," Jitu said. "They can control their urges and this is recognised by the scriptures and that's why they support a heavy *punishment*, as a deterrence. The Quran prescribes a few lashes but the consensus among the learned Mullah is that those engaging in homosexuality should be put to death. The motive behind this approach is to separate those affected by environmental factors from those afflicted with genetic anomalies. So, you're wrong, mate. These are not mere conjectures; these are viable theories or may be thought of as hypotheses in certain scientific circles but there is a close correlation between results and observed facts. What I've said is based on intuitive knowledge given to holy men and validated by prophets over the centuries. I grant you there may be some exceptions to the rule but these are safe deductions."

"So why then do some Mullahs sodomise their pupils?" Irfan retorted. "They know the Quran recognises genetic factors and prescribes light punishment. The Kharijites (puritans) adopted the harsher punishments as they were influenced by biblical declarations and their whims and fantasies. Classical Arabic is used in the Quran and one word can have several different meanings. The book is widely misinterpreted. A broad knowledge of physical, social, biological and mathematical sciences as well as an in-depth knowledge of Arabic is needed to interpret the Quran accurately."

"Oh, whatever Professor Irfan. My theories, well not all are mine as there has been a significant contribution from my friends, Yoda Khan, Romina Shetty and Samir Bagger from the Socialist Party; can't be proved wrong!" Irfan lost his cool and swore at Jitu. "You stupid bastard. Do they know about me? Did you… you tell them about me?"

"No, I didn't. They guessed it from the way you walk and talk," Jitu said.

Irfan stared and hesitated for a moment and then said, "It's not that fuckin' obvious, is it?"

"It is. You exude femininity at every step you take, darling," Jitu teased. Irfan threw a bundle of leaflets at his face and threatened to punch him. Jitu ducked and ran around the office chased by Irfan wielding a bundle of leaflets. "Stop you fuckin' wanker. I'll kill you!"

"You swear too much nowadays, Irfan."

"Haven't you heard?" Irfan retorted, still trying to smash the bundle of leaflets over Jitu's head but missing every time. "Swearing is now part of our Western literature. You win prizes if your literary works are full of vulgar language, historical inaccuracies, lies and innuendos."

"What d'you mean?" Jitu asked and suddenly stopped running, Irfan quickly stepped aside to avoid a collision. "Haven't you read Salman Rushdie's books?" Irfan enquired but did not wait for a reply. "Oh, sorry you can't read but let me tell you, some of his novels are full of glaring historical inaccuracies and foul language; words like *fuck*, *sister-fucker* and *motherfucker* criss-cross the pages of his books like pearls of this Jahil's wisdom for which they appointed him a fellow of the Royal Society of Literature!"

Jitu was incredulous. "What! He became a Fellow of the Royal Society of Literature for writing some rubbish. Not that I know what it means, but it must be a big honour. Does that mean if you write some anti-Islamic claptrap, full of vulgarity, attrition, vindictiveness and historical inaccuracies then you become a fellow of the Royal Society for Literature?"

"Apparently yes," Irfan beamed.

"I don't believe it; amazing; what a prize!" Jitu exclaimed and continued, "What if you write in favour of Islam?" Jitu asked and without waiting for an answer added, "Then you become a terrorist? And you will certainly be admitted to the fellowship of that most prestigious American Democratic institution: *Guantanamo Bay*?" They laughed heartily at what they perceived to be a splendid joke created by their perverse minds.

They harboured useless and vain desires and Jitu whispered to Irfan saying, "We'll use Rushdie's award against the Estone Socialists," and tapped his nose and winked mischievously.

The two mischief makers turned politicians were never really interested in the welfare of their fellow Muslims. Their interest ended in extracting votes or any other advantage, by hook or crook and manipulating the emotions of voters against the Socialist Party, blaming them for the problems faced by Palestinians, Kashmiris and Muslims throughout the world. They were morally and ethically corrupt. They would not hesitate to sell their mother for money, let alone their country. Some Asian leaders faced similar accusations. Irfan was borne in India, Jitu in Bangladesh and Asif in Pakistan. They learned dirty politics from their father and other relatives as they saw them in action as children. They had seen enormous sums of money change hands at election time and beautiful women to warm their beds. Some of these morally bankrupt leaders spent more time with *the Kakias* than on state business. People suffered from deprivation and ill health while they enjoyed life. They took the developing countries to the brink of social and economic collapse but laid the blame at the door of Western democracies. Money, earmarked for scientific research and general development, ended up in the leaders' pockets.

"My brother, Arif, has read some of Rushdie's books," Jitu said appearing more serious, "he told me, he cannot follow his novels; his writing is all over the place – a complex web, woven with intricate, indiscernible rubbish. Arif tells me, there is no authentic story to Rushdie's writing. My brother thinks Rushdie is not only a *Jahil* but extremely arrogant. One of my friends visited India last year and heard a little boy sing this song, which I think aptly describes Rushdie's writing. It went something like this:

O' his Grimus is grimy,

The midnight's children a moral nakamee (failure),

His shame is extremely shameless and

49

The satanic verses are grotesquely slimy,

Oh, God Please tell me why

You sent into the world, such a Shaitan haramee? (The accursed).

Irfan found the poem extremely funny and could not stop laughing. "Oh, he's a pathetic creature, and he knows not who he is? Forget him mate, we better start distributing these pissing leaflets otherwise we may lose this fuckin' election," Jitu said darting around the room and collecting piles of folded leaflets. "You won't be rich if you lose this election."

"Don't you worry son, I'll make me some serious money by hook or crook," Irfan said, making small manageable bundles from folded leaflets and putting elastic bands around them. Jitu began making similar bundles but at a greater pace.

Jitu has said many times, that: "We, politicians, are employed at the mercy of an apathetic electorate and can be made to pack our bags anytime so we have to build a little egg nest for ourselves, by any which way." To the pair's way of thinking, purchasing a second or even a third home from the public purse or plundering it by accumulating grants, or claiming extortionate expenses, was a legitimate act. So where was that trust, democracy and accountability? They did not know the meaning of these words and never tried to find out. "After all English isn't our mother tongue," they kept telling the critics. They also denied knowing the meaning of honesty, integrity and the rule of law....

A week ago, Jitu was dishing out leaflets in the Triangle area of Estone ward, and some residents were surprised to see him. "*Look, that bastard is still desperately trying to writhe his way to the council chamber,*" they said to each other, rather than him. Whether the destination is Westminster or Council Chamber, some politicians try to get there by any means. Joe Public know it! They knew Jitu was illiterate and incapable of effectively representing their interests in the corridors of power. He got a good memory and stored everything he heard but his inability to read minutes of meetings put him at a disadvantage and minimised his effectiveness as a community worker. My view about the qualification to become a councillor was well known.

I believe common sense and an ability to read large documents and minutes of the council's monthly and committee meetings and digest them and respond appropriately was a pre-requisite for seeking election as a councillor. "Holding a degree could be a bonus," I always said, "but not a necessity." Many potential voters had advised Jitu to desist from this elusive ambition and to concentrate on running the social club and the mosque where he was a committee member.

Jitu and his ex-pals from Socialist Party, Yoda, Romina, Adah Ram, Raju Miah and Samir hated me because of my immense popularity and respect among the electorate. The electorate regarded me as a straightforward person rather than an accomplished politician. I never claimed to be an angel but I've always been a stickler for truth and justice; which often brought me into conflict with vested interests. I was aware of the rumours flying about in the ward about secret plans being made by some Estone Socialists and my party activists to destroy my chance of victory by using Himalayan politics. I knew that at least for now, Paul Ali kept Jitu and Irfan in check by repeatedly telling them, "You need him so be nice to Sufi until you win the election".

# Chapter Six

The Democrats' first-floor campaign office had a glass wall overlooking Wilson Street. It consisted entirely of wide glass windows, making most of the street below visible. The other three walls were normal brick built, painted with light yellow paint interspersed with light green patches and displaying many election paraphernalia – three large portraits of the candidates, leaflets, statistical information and street maps of Estone ward.

The election campaign was in full swing. Only a few weeks ago Irfan's friend, Ifti, had arranged an impromptu meeting at his house to drum up support to ensure that I lose this election and are barred from contesting all future elections. Most attendees, apart from Asif and Jitu, were none other than Asif's and Ifti's closest friends - benefit fraudsters and drug dealers. "Final nail in Sufi's coffin, at all cost. Nothing less will ever satisfy us", Jitu and Irfan told their friends. Irfan also held a secret meeting with his friends about me, and Asif. He told them he perceived both of us to be a threat to his future ambitions. Irfan wanted his friends to help him plan to remove both of us, if possible; but I was his priority. With eyes on Parliament, Irfan could not afford to take any chances and did not trust anyone; not even Jitu and Asif. Irfan's policy, ingrained in his mind, as a young man was that of his political master JB: *keep your friends close but keep your enemies even closer.*

They did not see Paul enter the office. "Ring other activists and tell them to get their arse up here, on the double. I've just seen the Estone Socialists out and about, campaigning aggressively. No doubt telling the voters lies about us, while we sleep. We must win this election," Paul barked orders to Irfan, Jitu and Asif as usual and taking the mobile phone from his pocket rang a few party members, giving them a piece of his filthy mind and then turned to the two men, now busy folding leaflets into small bundles and continued with his vitriolic outburst: "Why do you wankers waste trees, effort and money by circulating these leaflets? Estone ward is full of illiterate voters and you know as I do, most of these leaflets will go straight into the bin. There are many knowledgeable voters in Estone ward, but they're fed up with political parties, anyway. You politicians feed them with a pack of lies, half-baked plans and excuses when explaining the lack of investment in the area, high unemployment and poor housing," Paul shouted, "You need to knock on doors, go down on your knees and beg for votes." Their faces showed anger and contempt for Paul but they had no courage to return his insults.

"There's nothing we can do about it. Our bosses insist on delivering leaflets. They tell us that leaflets win elections," they said sheepishly not even looking at him but increasing the pace at which they folded the leaflets.

"Leaflets win elections, my arse! Here in Estone and other inner cities, it's the lies, deception and baradari system that wins elections, just like in the Indian subcontinent," Paul said explosively and picking up a leaflet paced up and down the office, muttering to himself.

As they folded the leaflets, Irfan debated quietly whether to deface my photo but they decided against it. "It will spoil the leaflet, with your and Asif's photos too", Jitu said. "Where is Sufi?" Paul suddenly asked as if reading their mind. They decided that this was the best time to slag me off. "He's not interested in the election you know. We know he takes us all for granted. Residents tell us he's asking voters for a single vote", Irfan said. Asif and Jitu nodded vigorously. The leaflet carried pictures of all three of us – me, Irfan Khar and Asif Kazak under the caption: *your Democratic Party winning team in Estone ward.* The photos showed us dressed in a striped navy suit with a white shirt and yellow tie with light blue stripes. JB attempted to replace Asif with Jitu, after my unexpected selection in the first round. He had tried to do so at the request of his paederast to bring in his friend, Jitu at any cost. I learnt about this plot in time and objected strongly. After some debate, the Democratic party leadership saw sense and reversed their decision. Jitu seethed with anger and swore to teach me a lesson.. He tried, unsuccessfully, to replace me at the selection meeting by plotting to 'buy out' eleven members to vote in his favour. But I reversed that plot too with the help of Sher Dill and

Hasan. I suspect that they will not but make another plan to get rid of me.

Asif is short and fat with light brown skin, in his late forties, having a clean-shaven round face with some old chicken pox scars. He looks much older than his true age. Irfan is in his early thirties; tall, medium built with distinct feminine facial features. With a little make-up, he would pass as a beautiful woman. The light tone of his body and absence of body hair accentuated his feminine features. He looked much younger. Some residents of Estone ward suspected Irfan to be gay but none were certain except me, Jitu and Asif. Some other observant individuals in the socialist party may have also guessed about his sexuality but many were uncertain. However, I often defended Irfan when some residents or party activists made derogatory comments about his sexuality. I told them that being gay was not a crime. Like Asif, I am also in my late forties but of light complexion, boasting a handsome masculine face, an inch shorter than six feet, with an athletic build.

Most Asian voters knew about me being a reluctant partner in this so-called team; it never functioned like a team at all. This was an alliance based on vested self-interests and could not succeed because of Irfan, Jitu and Asif's indiscriminate practice of Himalayan politics, on supporters, voters and opposition alike. They used deceptive information and the baradari system even in internal party politics to alienate members and rival candidates during the selection process. Such petty political manoeuvres often resulted in the best candidate losing the selection and getting no chance to take part in the election. In the past, Irfan and Jitu picked an influential member from each clan and promised to do a lot of favours for them in return for their support in the selection process. This time Jitu failed, thanks to the ingenuity of my friend, Sher Dill.

In the 1960s, jobcentre Plus was called, "labour exchange" and for this reason, many benefit claimants wrongly associated dole payments with the Estone socialist party as its slogan was: *we stand for labourers, workers and equal distribution of wealth*. Later on, it renounced this slogan but continued to pretend to be the Workers' Party and providers of welfare benefits. Estone Socialists gained an unfair advantage from this false belief and they spread other lies among the voters, telling them that if the nationalists or the democrats won, they will stop welfare benefits, just as they have done away with the "labour exchange" scheme and they will deport all immigrants. Most residents of Estone ward belonged to the black minority ethnic group and the socialists led them to believe that the nationalists were against black immigrants, specifically from the African and Asian sub-continent. Some statistics showed that Immigration under the nationalists was higher than that under the socialists. Mass immigration from these continents in the 1950s and 1960s was attributed to the generosity of the Socialist Party and its activists kept reminding voters to be thankful and vote for them. I had heard a Cosmopolitan City leader, Umar Farooq, telling a public meeting held in Holte School in the early 1980s that, *"if the 1981 nationality bill got through, every immigrant will be deported."* That deadline came and went, the bill became law but no one was sent home. In the local election campaign in inner-city areas, they instantly transformed truth into falsehood and vice versa. Some Estone Socialists were good at this. And in this local election, they were ready to play the deadly game, involving Himalayan Politics. They knocked on door after door, telling lies about me, the democrats and the nationalists. They tried, unsuccessfully, to justify the attack on Iraq and Afghanistan. Many voters tore their leaflet and called for the arrest and trial of the socialist leader as a war criminal.

Having used all dirty tricks up their sleeves and realising that they would lose the election, some activists and candidates resorted to taking Himalayan politics to the next level, involving personation and postal vote fraud. Irfan and Paul Ali knew Jitu and Asif were no different and given the opportunity they would resort to any dirty tricks to get votes. Like Socialist party candidates, Jitu cared only for himself. His transfer from Estone Socialists to the Democrats took place amid dubious and extremely controversial circumstances and reputedly involved deception and backstabbing.

One of his friends, Zahir Abbas, accused a prominent local politician of interference in the selection process, calling the Honourable member of parliament a liar which did not go down well with the socialist party hierarchy and Jitu together with his friend got thrown out of the party. Jitu persuaded his friend to stand as an independent candidate and helped him fight the local election, reducing the Estone Socialists' majority of over a thousand votes to a mere fifty votes. At no time did Jitu and his friend ever deny the allegations levied against them by the Estone Socialists; instead, they further accused the honourable member of parliament of carrying out a witch hunt against them and their supporters. Had they admitted they were wrong and apologised for their behaviour, their membership in the party would have been restored. His Himalayan political masters had taught him never to admit anything even in the light of glaring evidence. Like some Socialist party candidates, he could not accept defeat. For Jitu, winning was the only option even if it involved backstabbing his colleagues, electoral fraud, threats or any other unethical method. He would tell his friends: "Let people say what they want about me. What do these silly people know? They would say, "Ha! Ha! He lost again!" or they would say, "Oh, why does he bother?" But these fuckers don't know about the thrill of being called, "councillor sahib".

I did warn the Democratic Party leadership about Jitu's obsession with deadly Himalayan politics. Removing me from the Democratic Party had become Jitu's, Asif's and Irfan's primary aim. Deep down they knew I was a competent and principled person whose election to Council Chamber or Westminster would benefit the communities immensely but they secretly supported attempts at my character assassination to further their political agenda and "erase me from Estone ward's political arena," as they put it. One of the Socialist Party candidate Yoda Khan was also determined to end my political career. But Yoda was shrewd. He never attacked me directly but targeted my most loyal team members. Yoda wanted me to rejoin Estone Socialists so he can finish me once and for all. He tried to persuade my team members to join Estone Socialists and bring me on board. "There is no victory in Estone ward, except as a Socialist Party candidate", he would boast. And some of my team members fell for Yoda's tricks and tried to persuade me to join Estone Socialists. I did not want to antagonise them, so told them to wait until after the election. The Plan to destroy my political career had been made or was being made by some local Democrats and Estone Socialist Party officials with the full agreement of the regional leadership of both parties and the Member of Parliament for Haywood constituency, Adie Gore. They assigned Jitu to play a leading role in my political demise. Paul Ali advised Jitu to keep his emotions and plans secret for the time being as they needed me to win this election. "So don't antagonise him", he repeatedly told him. Although Paul Ali was not my friend, his cautious approach worked in my favour as it gave me time to think and act. Three weeks before the general election, JB persuaded the Democratic party leadership to nominate Irfan as the Prospective Parliamentary Candidate for the Haywood Constituency. JB had confided in Irfan about his plans for him while sodomising him. The good news excited Irfan to no end and he saw Westminster in his mind's eye. He imagined delivering his maiden speech to the house; criticising the war, defending Palestine and saying other popular things that his political masters wanted to hear and their reaction: *That was an excellent maiden speech, Mr Irfan Khar*. Momentarily, lost in his thoughts, despite the mixture of pain and pleasure that he was experiencing, Irfan joyously shouted: "Westminster, here I come!"

"What! Wait," JB said panting, "I'm coming too!"

As Jitu was only interested in becoming a City Councillor from Estone ward, Irfan had no problem with that if he worked hard for him during the forthcoming general election. Irfan knew if Jitu was literate, he would never allow him to stand for parliament even if he had to succumb to JB's carnal desires. I was his only problem now. Irfan knew that apart from JB the rest of the Democratic Party's parliamentary and council group members were impressed with my credentials and wanted me to fight the next election for them. Irfan and his lover, JB did not want that to happen.

To Irfan's credit, however, he had recognised JB's carnal tendencies early and had skilfully directed them towards his backside, thus not only paving the way to JB's bedroom but to his mind and body and from there to Westminster. Irfan knew JB was a wealthy haulage contractor and as the chief benefactor of the Democratic party, he was in line to become the next leader of the Party. So, getting a candidature for a parliamentary seat early, and financial backing for himself, would not be difficult if he occupied a space in JB's heart for the time being and satisfied his erotic desires. However, Jitu and Asif kept reminding both men about being vigilant and fulfilling their political and erotic desires safely and not becoming victims of some clever investigative journalist or any other prying eye. They suspected I knew of their escapades because in Estone ward secrets did not remain hidden for long from my supporters. Irfan's general demeanour and behaviour often gave away his innermost feelings and anyone with a keen eye for detail could know the truth.

# Chapter Seven

Apart from having political ambitions, I also trained in a local hospital as a physician associate, having previously qualified as a biomedical scientist (BMS), specialising in clinical chemistry. Unknown to the public, this breed of health carers, work tirelessly behind the scene, often for a pittance, to assist clinicians in medical diagnosis and monitoring of their patients. I had witnessed the profession develop from performing a repertoire of diagnostic tests manually, to the modern pathology laboratory, where tests were performed far more quickly, accurately and precisely by state-of-the-art analysers. I had worked in many prestigious NHS hospitals' laboratories and met some great people like Jane Brown and Jim Grant; and some racists too, like Dr James Burke, director of pathology services at the city hospital and his assistant, Dr Lorna Scrofa, PhD. They had little or no respect for people of other races or religions. These two openly supported the idea of white supremacy and believed Britain was for whites only and those belonging to BME had no right to be here. Dr Burke was a bald, elderly man with a flat nose and hairy ears and Dr Scrofa was a short skinny woman; skilled in the art of psychological manipulation and pretence. She could skilfully prove a lie as truth and truth as a lie like some politicians, journalists, and T. V anchors. None of the fifty staff members in the department dared to cross their path. Instantaneous dismissal from work awaited those who in any shape or form argued with the dreaded duo! Just after the September eleven events in America, they subjected Dr Aziz, a friend, to a torrent of abuse in the presence of other staff for being five minutes late returning from lunch. Dr Aziz grabbed a sandwich and then read Friday prayers. The imam recited more verses from the Quran that day than usual which resulted in the delay. I made the mistake of coming to the aid of my beleaguered colleague and pointed out to Dr Burke that it was a five minutes delay and he needs to remember that Dr Aziz always started his morning shift fifteen minutes early every day! Most members of staff supported Dr Aziz and me, shook their heads in disbelief at Burke's behaviour. From then on Burke targeted me too and decided to "teach me a lesson". I did not trust Dr Burke or Dr Scrofa because they never hesitated to insult and harass me and Dr Aziz whenever an opportunity arose. "We know Sufi is gay. What about you Dr Aziz? Are you gay or bi?", they would ask and burst out laughing. Dr Aziz would respond calmly: "If we are gay then Margaret Thatcher is a communist!" That response often shut them up for a few hours. They were cunning enough to ensure that no one else heard these remarks and only insulted us at the start of the night shift when they were alone with either me or Dr Aziz. In December 2001, following an interview at Queen's Hospital, Dr Aziz got an offer of work, as a consultant chemical pathologist, subject to satisfactory references. Dr Scrofa persuaded Tony Browne, the divisional manager, to give Dr Aziz a 'bad' reference. The Queen's Hospital withdrew the offer. I helped Dr Aziz to take the dispute to the employment tribunal. Thanks to September eleven events, he lost. The fact that British justice was suspended for Muslims was glaringly obvious. Dr Aziz moved to Australia.

Shabina Anjem, a young Muslim woman, who worked in the Haematology laboratory loved wearing Hijab and for that reason, the deadly duo subjected her to grossly inhuman treatment and referred to her as *Osama's Ninja*. On one occasion, they removed her veil and tore it to pieces, she made a complaint to the personnel department but no one took any action. The pair were skilful at avoiding repercussions for their crimes. The management integrated clinical Chemistry, Blood Transfusion and Haematology into the Blood Sciences or Pathology Department. This department at the city hospital ran a twelve-hour emergency night shift from 8 pm to 8 am. One night, in December 2001, just before Christmas, at the start of an emergency shift, I was horrified to see Dr Scrofa still in her office when she had no business to be there. She smiled at me and told me she sent Tracey Grant home as she felt there was no point in both being there. I became worried, and searched for her motive for her presence and for being 'nice' to me. Her shift had ended three hours ago at 5 pm. Why was she still in the Pathology Department and most important, why did she send Tracey home?

Tracey was on the rota, not her, and there was no indication that the rota had been changed by anyone. Tracey was not ill; so why did Dr

Scrofa send her home? What was she up to? It just was not like her to behave so amicably and stay behind so late. Normally, around 5 pm every day, she went home with her boyfriend, Dr Burke without even speaking to anyone. I asked her why was she there at such a late hour when she was not on the shift rota. Her immediate and calm response was that she had not yet finished the day's work and so she had stayed behind to catch up. I told her, I did not understand why she sent Tracey home because she was supposed to brief me about the state of the work, quality control runs and the analysers. I glanced at the validation list. Nothing was outstanding for the duty biochemist. "Go home Dr Scrofa, your work list is empty," I told her and headed off to the male changing room to get a lab' coat and to change into comfortable shoes and my work trousers. Unknown to me Dr Scrofa followed me after making a call to security. The call was brief: "This is Dr Lorna Scrofa. Please tell Officer Sheila to come to the Chemical Pathology department urgently. Thanks". She entered the male changing room without knocking. I was replacing my normal trousers with a work one. She profusely apologised, pretending to have entered the room inadvertently. As it happened, she planned it all. I had the shock of my life when going down on her knees, she moved swiftly and held my penis. "Oh, you… you… ah… ah… are so big…" and tried to swallow me but I quickly took a step back, still holding my trousers below the knees, with both hands. My sudden movement caused her to slump forward, but she prevented injury to her face and nose by quickly placing her hands flat on the floor and steadying herself.

"You'll pay for this"! She seethed, clenching her fists so that the veins on the back of her hands bulged.

"I don't know what your problem is. One minute you hate blacks and the next minute you want to make love to them. You're sick!" I fumed. At the sound of footsteps outside, in the corridor, she swiftly got up from the floor and held the male changing room door open and shouted, "In here Sheila!"

"Oh, hello Dr Scrofa, what's up?" a male voice said.

"Nothing is up! I asked for Sheila, where is she?"

"Don't know. Jayne couldn't find her Dr Scrofa so she sent me. I'm Mathew. How can I help?"

Mathew saw me putting trousers on and greeted me. "Oh, hello Sufi!"

"Do you know this man?"

"Yes, Dr Scrofa, I know him as I know you; as a member of staff. Not personally."

"Then I want you to call the police and have him arrested for sexual assault on me."

"It's the other way round, isn't it? You've assaulted me. I'm not in the female changing room; you're in the male changing room!"

"Ah, he has a good point, wouldn't you say so Dr Scrofa?" Mathew said looking at the gold-plated sign on the door. "What are you doing in the male changing room?"

"Ah… Ah, he dragged me in here and sexually assaulted me."

I looked furious and was about to say something when Mathew put his hand up and said, "Where were you when Sufi dragged you in here Dr Scrofa? You have your clothes on and I can't see any bruises or any other marks on you, that's why I'm asking."

"Fuck you. All you men are alike, you protect each other. I'll sort you fuckers out," she shouted and stormed out of the changing room slamming the door behind her.

"Sorry mate, we've had so many complaints against her but she survives thanks to Dr Burke. I think we're both in trouble." Mathew sighed.

"I think you're right. I've got to go mate; I think she's sent Tracey home without briefing me. I don't know what's happening with the work situation. It'll take me some time to work it out. And see you, Mathew. Thank God you turned up, otherwise, I was finished if her lesbian friend turned up." Everyone in the department knew that Dr Scrofa was bisexual. She had confirmed this fact herself several times in the tea room at break times.

"I know, you're a lucky fucker mate but don't forget to thank Jayne. Sending me was her idea," Mathew laughed and left the lab'.

'Oh, thank God for Jane. She is a true English woman,' I said to myself. Jane was the only white woman working in the department who was not a racist. Her ideas on race and immigration were fair, well thought out and balanced. There was not the slightest hint of dislike for any non-white person in her behaviour. I remembered Jane planting a lingering kiss on my lips under the mistletoe at the Christmas party. Both Burke and Scrofa had given her a nasty look; she showed them the fingers to the delight of the rest of us.

I checked the analyser and found over a hundred samples still incomplete. The Albumin reagent had run out and the reagent probe was bent; it must have hit the side of the reagent carousel because of a misalignment, a classic operator blunder. It was that or Dr Scrofa probably attempted to run some samples and mis-loaded them. That would explain the damage to the probe as well. She damaged the sample probe last week when she 'forgot' to remove the cap from the sample tube. Jane told the head of the department to think twice before sending a 'PhD' into the laboratory. "The two don't go together, you know. Have you forgotten?" When I examined the reagent carousel, I discovered the reason for the damage to the probe. She did indeed 'forget' to remove the cap from the reagent bottle again. The analyser had attempted to sample the reagent and met with an unexpected obstruction. I replaced the probe and the Albumin reagent and reloaded the samples. Old Mrs Bennett's amylase was raised, I checked the clinical details: "suspected pancreatitis". The abnormally high amylase result made sense, but it was well above the phone limit set by the consultant chemical pathologist so I quickly phoned it through to the ward and then began assessing the amount of work still outstanding. At first glance, it looked as if I will

63

have to go without breaks throughout the night. The day staff left a lot of work, because it was received late from GP surgeries and everyone went home at 5 pm; except one person. Out of three hundred samples still outstanding, Dr Scrofa only analysed ten, and yet the analyser could have happily taken care of all leftover samples unless she broke the probe deliberately. Life may have been slightly easy if the probe was not broken. It would then have been only a small matter of sorting out bits and pieces and I could have taken breaks later. I now knew that sending Tracey home was a deliberate move by Dr Scrofa to get me the sack but thanks to Jane and Mathew, I survived; at least for a little while.

Her actions amounted to harassment and I took the hospital to the employment tribunal but I resisted the temptation to do so following a biased judgment in Dr Aziz's case. Dr Aziz was forced to take the matter to the employment tribunal for the second time following his unfair dismissal. But the employment tribunal, comprising of an employment judge and two lay members representing employers and unions (all three were white) fell victim to the crocodile tears of Dr Burke and Dr Scrofa. After September eleven, emotions ran high against Muslims and the deadly duo took full advantage of the human weakness of judges and cried before them pretending to be bastions of truth and virtue and made Dr Aziz look like the real villain. Dr Scrofa gave a false witness statement but because she was white and most important a non-Muslim, she got away with it. I was also a witness and proved beyond any reasonable doubt, let alone on the balance of probability, that Dr Scrofa's statement was false but the judges, perhaps unable to believe that two members of their race could sink so low, didn't change their mind even in the face of overwhelming evidence. This jolted my confidence in the British Justice system which I had always praised but felt let down. I attributed this to the September Eleven massacre and its aftereffects. It was an irrevocable fact that after September eleven, the civil liberties of Muslims were seriously eroded and I felt that British justice had been suspended for Muslims. I was aware of NHS trusts using Mills and Reeves solicitors to defend them. I learnt that before becoming judges, many worked for this rogue firm. Mills and Reeves were known as *solicitors from hell*. The bundle of documents lodged with the courts by them had a secret sign on the top right-hand corner of the file (two tiny circles, 1 cm apart, joined by a red semi-circle) so they rarely lost a case. So much for the justice.

It is this type of behaviour that sets apart a banana republic from a true democracy. The tribunal's biased decision made a mockery of the justice system. Justice must not only be done but seen to be done especially in the country where justice is held sacred.

To make matters worse for the Muslims, some unnecessary high-profile police raids were carried out, which enabled the racists to vilify the Muslim religion and victimise the entire Muslim community for the acts of a few. Muslims were bewildered and afraid for their future in the light of irresponsible and biased statements from some ministers and other politicians supported by media hysteria and nauseating utterances of the far-right neo-Nazi groups – BNP and EDL. Highly informed and educated Muslims and indeed some peace and justice-loving non-Muslims became utterly despondent and feared that the big brother system, foreseen by George Orwell, had indeed arrived. Double standards in the Western democracies and the American foreign policy were strikingly obvious and helped the extremist Muslims to radicalise some impressionable young men to commit cowardly acts against innocent people. Injustices and erosion of civil liberties created unbearable living conditions for Muslims as some politicians continuously lied, the press printed biased reports and the civil courts, with-held justice.

A few weeks later, I learned that Mathew had been suspended following sexual harassment complaint by Sheila, no doubt at the instigation of Dr Scrofa. I knew it would soon be my turn to face the music orchestrated by Dr Scrofa. She will never give up, until I, like Mathew, was out of the picture. My vows began only a couple of days later, when Harjeet, another lesbian friend of Dr Scrofa accused me of staring at her boobs and made a complaint. She was a plump, dark-skinned, biochemist from India. The complaint speedily proceeded to disciplinary action, and a meeting of the senior staff under the chairmanship of Dr Burke was held and they suspended me. I promptly appealed and the laboratory's clinical director, Ms Taylor, reversed the decision, re-instated me and awarded me four thousand pounds compensation through a compromise agreement.

Over time, conditions at work became unbearable for me. September eleven, it seemed, continued to haunt Muslims like me even years after the alleged slaughter of thousands of innocent people in America and the so-called war on terror. They singled Muslims out for vilification the world over. I became the innocent victim of the racists' wrath. Dr Burke the boyfriend of Dr Scrofa, instructed the Estates Officer, Martin Hall, to break into my locker as in his words: "*Sufi is hiding terrorist material and bomb-making equipment in the locker.*" But apart from a copy of the professional journal, *the Biomedical Scientist*, a pair of trousers and shoes, nothing else was found. But the dreaded trio: *Dr Burke, his deputy Mr Hill and the principal clinical scientist, Dr Scrofa* continued to inscribe insulting graffiti on the door of my locker: *"What are you hiding in your locker, you damn Paki terrorist?"* And *"go back to Afghanistan and Iraq and blow them up, not us."* To my disappointment my colleagues, except the young scientist Jane Foster, remained quiet and did not assist or support me. Jane frequently told the deadly trio to "fuck off and leave Sufi alone. He didn't blow up the twin towers, did he? The deep state is involved in this cowardly act, but your bird brains can't understand this! You're victimising him because he did what was best for him and asserted his rights at work and put an end to your malpractices!"

The trio always responded with a burst of sickening laughter. Nothing seemed to penetrate their closed minds. Six other staff members witnessed this diabolical exchange with racial undertones and looked disgusted with the trio but kept quiet for fear of losing their jobs. Jane nudged me to move away from them: "Fuck them," she whispered. We joined colleagues in the automated section, who were busy analysing blood samples from patients using dry chemistry Vitros analysers. We continued to concentrate on our work, answering phones and validating results.

At union and staff meetings, I often complained to officials, about their failure to bring the profession to the notice of the public. Doctors and nurses appeared to be the only NHS professions visible to the public but biomedical scientists did tremendous work behind the scenes. Unknown to many patients and rarely acknowledged for their dedication and expertise, this breed of hard-working men and women were, like other professions supplementary to medicine, underpaid and overworked. Successive governments made their lives difficult by keeping the pay low and enacting draconian regulations to stifle the enthusiasm for their profession. Originally known as laboratory technicians their designations changed to Medical Laboratory Scientific Officers (MLSO) and then to biomedical scientists (BMS) in the early twenty-first century and were now heading towards being known as HCS or Healthcare Scientists.

Massive technological advances in the development of automated instrumentation led to the production of quick and accurate blood test results and rapid diagnosis and treatment. In the 1970s and 1980s, tests like amylase were performed manually, and it took hours to do which could now be done in minutes with modern automated analysers. Rigorous training and a degree in biomedical science and registration with the Health Care Professions Council were essential prerequisites to practise as a biomedical scientist. I picked up new tasks easily and was able to competently operate Vitros, Advia, Architect and Roche analysers, within hours of encountering them, even for the first time. Paying attention to detail was the cornerstone of my work. Certain principles governed my life, one of them being to fight for truth and justice and work to live; not live to work. Over the years, and particularly after the sickening events of September eleven, I became a stickler for justice and truth and did not tolerate injustice. This principle often brought me into direct conflict with the powers to be and I was bypassed for promotion. They took me for granted, as my political party did, during the selection process.

The principles of equality, justice and the rule of law only existed on paper, not in the minds of the NHS management. I learned, over the years, that in England, at least, behind the façade of democracy and justice, lay the ugly face of imperialism, social injustice and Islamophobia. I had often thought of migrating to either Ireland, Wales or Scotland where treatment of human beings of any colour was above average; where truth and justice prevailed to a greater extent; where a lie was recognised as a lie and truth as a truth. After nine-elven, while working in the NHS, I was called by many nicknames- *Khomeini, Gaddafi* and *Taliban* to undermine my popularity with senior management to subvert any plans for my promotion even though some of my suggestions were implemented, saving NHS thousands of pounds annually. To demonstrate my experience and knowledge as a biomedical scientist, I had consistently shown a tremendous amount of foresight and business acumen which deserved an immediate promotion to band 8 but it never materialised. As a trainee physician associate (PA) I worked in the Manor Hospital's accident and emergency department. They gave unpopular jobs to PAs whereas junior and senior doctors got better pay and jobs and PAs came to be known as *'the doctors' bitch'*. I gave up seeking permanent jobs in the NHS and instead opted for locum work which freed a lot of my time and enabled me to carry out in-depth political research to find out what was happening in Estone ward and around the world.

# Chapter Eight

After September eleven, anyone with sufficient political insight, knowledge and attention would have been able to discern the emergence of a new world order, in which dissent or speaking one's mind, especially as a Muslim, was actively discouraged and one could sense an erosion of civil liberties for Muslims. Feedback from the residents of Estone ward confirmed my analysis that something was amiss and I tried to seek information and clarification which brought me into direct conflict with not only some powers to be but also with unfair systems and institutionalised racism and Islamophobia. I persevered and tried to bring about a change in the provision of services but these were always refused on the grounds of financial constraints. Residents were denied justice and unsurmountable impediments were erected to achieving ultimate solutions. Letters to the Lord Chancellor regarding the provision of a fair and just judicial system went unanswered. Criminal justice appeared to work better than the civil justice system, where judges dished out some disastrous judgements to Muslim complainants. It gradually became clear to me that even Political party leaders favoured those councillors or Parliamentarians who attended meetings but just sat and listened or slept through the meetings, asked no questions and went home. I failed to understand such politicians and their motives for getting elected to public office but had no desire to make ordinary people's lives better.

Estone ward residents trusted me as they believed I was genuinely interested in solving the problems we all faced. They knew, I had no vested self-interest in becoming a councillor and was doing so merely to help them. Poor housing, lack of school spaces, dirty streets, damaged footpaths and roads and countless other economic and social issues needed urgent solutions. They affectionately nicknamed me, *the people's politician.* I believed nature had blessed Britain with many genuine politicians who sat in Parliament and local councils but could exert no control over human destiny, alleviation of poverty, cruelty, tyranny, and social injustice or speak the truth because of political parties' whip system. Honourable Members of Parliament, like Clair Short and Robin Cook, made personal sacrifices for speaking out against misleading parliament over the Iraq war and so-called weapons of mass destruction. They resigned from the government after speaking up against the war. Institutions and systems in place, popularly called *the establishment* resisted changes to the status quo.

Estone ward, was home to many diverse communities - English, Irish, West Indians, Jamaicans, Pakistanis, Kashmiri, Indians (mainly from Gujrat and Punjab), Bengalis, Kokni and many immigrants from the European Union. I had excellent links with all these communities. For unscrupulous politicians like Yoda, Jitu and Asif, such diversity was easy to exploit through the baradari and bribery systems. Unlike Asian communities, where the baradari system took hold of the decision-making process, the European migrants voted free from such constraints. The evidence from prominent community members pointed to some Estone Socialists attempting to giving non-Asian voters gifts to persuade them to vote for their party. They also promised them council homes and extra school places for their children. Many voters recognised false promises and abstained from voting or voted Democrats.

Non-Asian candidates representing the Democrats and the national party in other inner-city wards with a large majority of Asian voters invited me to talk on the baradari system so they can counter the socialist party activists' lies in their wards. I needed time for my campaign, so I condensed the talk and memorised it, dispensed with the notes and saved a lot of time. I was able to tell them everything about Himalayan politics in just twenty to thirty minutes. A basic understanding of the system was required to appreciate its immense exploitative potential in an election context so the listeners appreciated the time I spent with them. The feedback was very positive. Non-Asian candidates found the basic knowledge useful. They used the information to educate the voters against voting based on the baradari system. They encouraged them to vote on party policy.

The language barrier between voters and candidates rendered the explanation somewhat ineffective. Bangladeshi, Indian, Kashmiri and

Pakistani communities' division into smaller clans or tribes made them susceptible to external influences. Under the baradari system, some occupations were considered demeaning, and people who performed these jobs were ranked as belonging to the lower castes, such as the untouchables in India who were open to exploitation by the higher clans like Brahmins. Low-ranking occupations, among the Asians, recognised in the UK were the Kamares (potters), Mooches (shoe repairers), Nahees (Barbers), Lohars (Black Smiths) and Misallies (Musicians). Within the baradari system, these occupations appeared at the bottom of the social ladder. Under this cruel and medieval system, clans disrespected and hated each other. I belong to the Jat clan regarded as the second highest; first prize going to the Rajput clan. I likened this despicable social system to cancer and actively discouraged it. Activists from the Socialist Party and the Democratic Party, like Zahir, Anwar, and Asif encouraged it.

I developed a lasting relationship with everyone and denounced those who sought to divide people because of religion, caste, or race. Selfish motives encouraged some Asian politicians of all political colours to exploit the baradari or Kumis system for their benefit. A few Socialist and Democratic party activists, like Yoda, Jitu, Asif and Irfan, were acknowledged to be the masters of this system. They selected the chiefs of the clans for special treatment in return for the votes of members of their clans. By pursuing this policy, they largely circumvented the necessity of begging for votes individually from voters and knocking on doors. There were deep-rooted divisions within Asian communities living not only in the Estone ward but throughout Britain. Himalayan politics propped up this division, by supporting the formation of branches of overseas political parties in Britain. I opposed such actions and encouraged everyone to join the British political parties. I refused to support or join anyone attempting to set up a Pakistani, Bangladeshi or Kashmiri political party branch in the UK. Some groups with vested interests from the Pakistani and Bangladeshi communities set up branches of Bangladesh Awami League (BAL), Pakistan People's Party (PPP) and Pakistan Muslim League (PML-N) throughout the UK. And many councillors, parliamentarians and so-called influential community leaders (I called them *lotas*) became members of these foreign parties.

Fraud, coercion, vote buying and spreading rumours shaped the electoral process in Asian countries, which has been imported into the UK and practised here. The practitioners of Himalayan Politics often deny electoral fraud in their countries, even against the overwhelming evidence of its existence. The party with an imaginative and versatile bag of tricks always wins in the subcontinent. In Pakistan, military intervention is the norm, and it is often accused of bringing in the party that it likes for its own political and financial gains. Two eminent politicians encouraged the soldiers to refuse orders from the generals to avoid interference in the election process. Their vows began when they were taken into custody and allegedly sodomised. It is not only the military; politicians also play trick of gerrymandering by ordering the election commission to change boundaries.

Activists and members of the main British Political parties from the Indian sub-continent encouraged such divisions as they stood to gain the most from community polarization. Some Pakistani and Kashmiri politicians often travel to the UK to support a candidate of their choice. I often protested this foreign interference at many meetings and discouraged people from going to the airports and welcoming these *lotas*. At political meetings, Irfan and Asif sought to put a dent in the socialists vote bank by telling the electorate about the history of the Estone Socialists which showed it was the master of the "divide and rule" and created the Kashmiri and Palestinian problems. The essence of opposition or support for a candidate in the Asian communities was based on the baradari system and not on party policies or its track record. I was determined to change this. "Humanity and Humanitarian values transcend petty beliefs, like the baradari system," I told the audience during the election and throughout my door-to-door campaigns. Out of over eighteen thousand voters registered in Estone ward, only thirty per cent bothered to vote at local elections and only slightly higher in the general elections. This was democracy at its worst.

It showed voter apathy because of their dislike and mistrust of some politicians. A party that understood Himalayan politics of the baradari system could ensure victory for their candidates in every election in all

72

inner-city areas unless the electorate could be persuaded to vote on basis of party policy.

Jitu was a political scumbag of Estone ward. His arrival in the UK, in the early 1960s at the age of eighteen, meant he could not get conventional education and gained employment as a shop assistant with his brother, Naeem Donumeri. Thus, Jitu remained illiterate and apart from a few spoken words of English, his communication skills showed limitations. But his ability to cheat, deceive and manipulate systems and elections was not diminished. Being immensely popular with the local riffraff, Jitu always picked up around two thousand votes. During elections, he delivered leaflets, climbed ladders to put up election notices on lamp posts and shop windows and folded leaflets with immense skill and enthusiasm and no one could tell that he was in any way incapacitated or disabled. Once the election was over, he resumed his financial dependence on the generosity of the taxpayer.

The pile of folded bundles, containing about a hundred leaflets each and tied with elastic bands, was increasing rapidly next to Jitu as he worked fast while Asif's and Irfan's bundles were less than half the size. They performed the actions much more slowly as they were smoking at the same time. "Put that fuckin' thing in your mouth and suck on it instead of holding it in your hand," Jitu shouted at them. "You can't fold leaflets with one hand...." Irfan interrupted him: "Oh, yar Jitu, tell us the truth, you're annoyed with Sufi an' you're taking your anger out on us?" Jitu instantly recognised the truth in what Irfan said and his anger subsided. After a few moments, he said, somewhat sheepishly, "I think you are right," and then added angrily, throwing a handful of folded leaflets on the pile," Where the fuck is he? It's nearly lunchtime!"

I startled them with my deep masculine voice. I did hear them swearing at me but I did not tell them that. Instead, I said, looking at the blown-up picture of our party logo, "Other parties have a beautiful Eagle, a globe and a scale as their logo and our party has this dead Dodo as the logo. What a joke. It's only with the help of good people that you goons win here in Estone ward, otherwise, this Dodo of yours would be extinct by now." picking up a leaflet I folded it into a bright yellow paper plane. With one smooth movement of the wrist, I propelled it through the open window. The pair did not see me enter the office, neither did they hear me come up the stairs, and I believe, cursed themselves for leaving the door open. I was already by the window overlooking Wilson Street. "Oi Irfan, Asif and Jitu come here, look", I said pointing to the paper plane, which I had just launched, "the fuckin' Dodo is flying!"

"Oh, so it is. That's a good omen, isn't it?" They looked at each other for an answer. As the object soared just above the dark, slated roofs of the rows of shops opposite, it appeared to have been caught in turbulence and made a precarious descent, flying erratically in circles like a kite in trouble. It hovered above the line of cars passing slowly through the busy Wilson Street and eventually landed neatly on the boot of a silver Mercedes and then fell on the road, only to be crushed seconds later by the slick tyres of the black BMW following closely behind the white Merc. "So much for the flight of the dodo, it's a bad omen." I thought it must be a bad omen for me, not them. They went back to folding the leaflets. I remained at the window, now joined by three of my most ardent supporters, Owais, Yahya and Zakariya. Our attention was momentarily diverted to an environmental catastrophe that was unfolding on the streets of Estone Ward. We saw both sides of Wilson Street and the adjoining streets, Broadbent and Berrington, littered with paper, cardboard, fruit skins, pieces of bread and plastic bags; it resembled the street of a bazaar in Pakistan.

"I was in Sutton Coldfield the other day and saw no litter on the streets. You could drop a samosa on the pavement and pick it up and eat it," Yahya said.

"You can't do that here or in Pakistan," Zakariya said, "you'll die of gastroenteritis." We all recognised the truth in what he said.

Owais said that he visited relatives in Pakistan last month and went to the bazaar to do some shopping. He saw a similar sort of rubbish on the street there. There were animal excreta too. Unpleasant odours lingered in the air. A man walked in front of him, eating a banana and threw the skin over his shoulder. "I sidestepped it just in time," he said,

"But a poor man running to catch the bus slipped on it and fell on his right side, fracturing his shoulder as he manoeuvred to prevent an injury to his head."

"It looks to me," I said, "Like the dirty Himalayan Politics, we've imported the rubbish too." They nodded gravelly.

I told them that just before the last year's local election in the Estone ward, I conducted a short survey. I asked residents the reason for Estone ward's streets and footpaths being scattered with rubbish. They blamed the lack of street bins. I did take this issue up with the council to fix bins, at strategic points on the footpaths throughout the ward. They refused the request for lack of funds.

Through the open windows of the campaign office, we now watched the Merc and the BMW drivers attempting to overtake other cars, their horns blaring just like back home in the dadyal bazaar. Both cars belonged to the rich drug dealers of Estone ward. The Merc suddenly and dangerously overtook the cars in front as if aware of the cowardly deed it had just committed by crushing the dodo paper plane and it wanted a quick getaway from the scene of the crime. Soon the BMW joined it too. They sped along Wilson Street, passing a row of grocery shops, a barber's shop, a few estate agents, a couple of takeaways on the right, a combined garage plus Esso petrol station, a row of houses on the left and then stopped abruptly. Two men wearing tight black leather motorbike gear got out of the car and entered the corner house with the black door. "Are they the same drug dealers who shot a fellow dealer last month?" I asked. "Yes, Sufi they are," my friends confirmed.

Only a few weeks ago, I recalled, the police had cordoned the petrol station off after a gunfight between two notorious Estone gangs. Two men, wearing balaclavas and dressed in similar black leather trousers and jackets, burst into the barber's shop and shot a rival in the arm, having his haircut. The victim, a young Asian man, ran to the back garden of the shop, jumped over the wall into the alley, injured his leg in the process and then limped onto Wilson Street, dodging cars and pedestrians and made his way, agonisingly, to the petrol station where the two gunmen caught up with him and shot him again; this time in the chest and stomach, believing him to be dead, left him bleeding and then made a quick getaway in a black BMW. The victim, also a gang member was quickly taken to the city hospital under police protection and survived against all odds. Many Estone residents believed that he deserved what he got. According to rumours that circulated in the ward, the two men later arrested and charged with the shooting were innocent. Jitu, Asif and Irfan told me that two filthy rich drug dealers and brothel owners, brother and sister, in Estone ward, Paul Ali and Naila Fazal, were behind the crime. What angered me was they both never worked in their entire life and yet owned all these properties and the powers to be never asked them about the source of the money. My friend Mirza was arrested for sending twelve hundred pounds to his mother in Pakistan under money laundering regulations but these two urchins had lots of assets and no obvious source of income and drove Mercedes and BMW, yet no one questioned them. A man named Shaban living in Free Road, bought accident-damaged cars, got his son to do a cowboy job on them, using ties and strings where screws were needed and sold them at 200% profit; paid no tax. I received many complaints about him and his son and passed them on to the trading standards but no action was taken against them. The word on the street was: *crime pays in Estone!*

I was aware of the presence of Asian and West Indian-Jamaican gangs, the Panthers, burger bar boys and Johnson crew in Estone and surrounding inner-city wards. Mercifully only a couple of panthers remain, the rest are extinct, and the police pursued BBB and JC criminals after they murdered two innocent and beautiful teenagers, Letisha Shakespeare and Charlene Ellis in 2003 in a crossfire. These gangsters have been engaged in senseless violence, portraying arrogance and egotistical behaviour since the 1980s. Senselessly and brutally cutting down the two young and beautiful flowers before they could disseminate their fragrance to the world. This heinous crime will hopefully mean that the barbaric gangsters will meet their horrible end soon. I met the girls, two weeks before they were murdered. I did not know them personally but wished I had. They had come to my aid following an altercation between me and a West Indian goon. I was walking through the

76

pedestrian crossing on trinity church road, when the goon, driving too fast, stopped inches from me and instead of apologising and accepting his mistake he started swearing at me. At that moment the two girls told him they saw what had happened, and it was his fault and he should apologise and should be ashamed of himself for disrespecting an elderly person. What a humane and kind thing to do at that young age. I could not help saying to them, "Respect to your parents for bringing up such beautiful souls full of humanity and kindness." The following week, I recalled, I saw their pictures in the papers, that some bastards had cut their young lives short.

"Are you ok Sufi?" My friends asked, seeing tears in my eyes.

"Yes, I'm ok, I just remembered something from the past. Let's help those goons with folding leaflets."

# Chapter Nine

Before we could help Jitu, Asif and Irfan with leaflets, I heard someone shouting my name from the street below. I asked my friends to help them and I returned to the window to find out who called my name. I opened the window wide and poked my head out and observed the Street below.

It was a sunny April Sunday afternoon, a week before the election and many shoppers were out on Wilson Street. Mirza, a young Arabic teacher at a local private school had seen me standing at the window and shouted something. As I was preoccupied with my thoughts, I did not hear him. Now, I saw him standing in front of the *mystery goods* shop, one of many shops and Mini supermarkets on Wilson Street. An elderly Afghani man owned it. "Are you ignoring me Sufi? Don't tell me you've got the KPS up there with you. When is the election?" He was still referring to Jitu, Asif and Irfan as KPS. *He'll never change.* I told him the three scoundrels will kill him if they ever found out what the initials stood for. It did intrigue me when Mirza mentioned KPS three times, during a meeting last month. Mirza had anticipated my question and whispered: *'Keratinized Pieces of Shit.'* "Keep it a secret for the time being. I'll tell them myself one day", he told me.

On hearing Mirza's shrill voice, all shoppers, around fifty, stopped in their tracks and looked to the first-floor windows. "No, I'm not ignoring you. Just busy. *Eh Mirza kaifa Halak bro,* (how are you brother)?" I asked in Arabic, remembering how earnestly Mirza asked me last week to speak to him in Arabic. "Always talk in Arabic to me, bro. I've heard your Arabic is good. I need to practise. No one speaks Arabic at home." Mirza Jut was born in Birmingham, the second largest British City but remained in Cosmopolitan City after he graduated from Cosmopolitan City University in 1998. In January 1999, he went to Yemen and learned Arabic there. After his return from Yemen in September 2001, he was arrested by the police on suspicion of being indoctrinated into terrorism. He was released a week later. I did notice a dramatic change in his attitude and outlook as he was more at ease with himself and gave an impression of a man on a mission rather than a lazy young man who used to sleep till midday and did not give a toss about anything and lived on social security handouts, drank alcohol and slept with prostitutes. Now, besides teaching Arabic, he had become a keep-fit enthusiast overnight. He was more into Islam now and regularly prayed five times a day at the Broadbent Mosque; stopped drinking and visiting hookers. Virtually every evening after school, he went to the gym and engaged in strenuous work. His protruding stomach had receded and looked much flatter and overall, he looked more muscular. The only negative thing about him was that Mirza became more argumentative and emotional during a religious or political debate.

Jane Grant, Mirza's neighbour, noted the same change and told me that she will monitor him in case he blew himself up. I assured her, "I don't think Mirza would do anything like that," but I asked her to remain cautious as my friend's new outlook on life was a little disconcerting. I was confident Mirza will not resort to violence, as he voiced his opposition to extremism frequently. Abdullah, a brilliant young Islamic scholar from Yemen and a firm supporter of the Saudi Arabian regime ran the private Arabic school, where Mirza was a teacher. I called Abdullah and mentioned Jane's concerns about Abdullah to him, but he assured me that Mirza had no violent tendencies. He told me, "Not to worry". As far as I could remember, Mirza praised Saudi rulers for making life easier for the pilgrims by overseeing tremendous improvements to the two holy Mosques. I saw Mirza antagonise the Kharijites militant group by shouting: "Saudi Arabia is a true Islamic State and we must all follow it". I would have worried if Mirza was a member of the Kharijites outfit, but he had considerable enmity against the group. The Kharijites hated the Saudi State and everyone else who supported it. They regarded the Saudis as American and Zionist puppets. Last month, they unceremoniously threw Mirza out of a special meeting convened by the extremists to censor the Saudi state.

He stopped attending their secret meetings after the Home Secretary banned the group. A middle eastern cleric known as Mullah Yaseen led this extreme militant group. Neither Mirza nor I ever held the same views. Speakers from this group also spoke, at fringe meetings, against the Saudi state accusing it of apostasy. At one such meeting, before the group was banned, a speaker, a Saudi Arabian national, opposed to his government said, "Contrary to popular belief, Saudi Arabia cannot be construed to be an Islamic State...". Mirza interrupted him and shouted: "Where's your evidence?" These meetings often turned nasty when verbal confrontation metamorphosed into a physical one. Both of us were often assaulted and forced out of the meeting room. "Thanks for throwing us out 'brothers', now we know how much tolerant you are of others' views". We always bombarded the speakers with complex questions and encouraged by our boldness, most members of the public followed us out of the venue.

Senior members of the Kharijites outfit were acknowledged to be the masters of political intrigue as they combined fact with fiction - spreading conspiracy theories and blaming Western powers for the plight of the *ummah*. They cleverly included Fromkin's book, *the peace to end all peace* as evidence for the destruction of the Ottoman caliphate by the Western imperialist powers and for carving the middle east into smaller satellite states. Many impressionable young Muslims all over the world, accepted the extremist version of history and took it upon themselves to avenge the excesses perpetrated on Islam and *the Ummah* by the West. Their mistaken belief translated into a sharp increase in terrorist activity around the world. The Kharijites group wrote to various British media groups asking them to stop blaming Muslims for international terrorism. "It's not Muslims", they wrote, "it's *thou shalt do war by deception* brigade. Don't you see?" My composed and affable manner had a soothing effect on Mirza's general demeanour and he kept calm in my presence. A raised voice from the street suddenly interrupted my thoughts. I had forgotten what Mirza had asked me. "*Eh kaifa Halak bro* - how are you brother?" Mirza repeated. "You haven't replied to my questions yet."

"*Alhamdulillah ana bekhair, Shookrun* -I'm ok thanks. Just sorting election leaflets." I smiled as I heard Jitu, Asif and Irfan grunt angrily. "Yes, I have the KPS with me and the election date is the fifth of May, a week from today."

"Okay, thanks Sufi. Let me know if you want any help with distributing leaflets." I waved goodbye to my friend and a few other shoppers interested in the election date, who asked me some questions and went about their business as it had begun to drizzle. I could not stop noticing that more people were interested in politics this year than before which was a positive sign for democracy and political awareness.

"So much for the flight of the dodo," I said turning away from the window and facing others. "You know the damn thing did fly, so it's a good omen and I think we will snatch these three seats away from Estone Socialists but I must warn you three not to use filthy Himalayan politics in this election. Let Estone Socialists use it if they want to," I said, waving my index finger close to their faces to emphasise the importance of what I was saying. "We've got to work hard against Estone Socialists, forget Nationalists as JB has said, they've no hope in Estone ward. Our major rivals are the three Socialist candidates." I reminded them all about my previous election attempts in 2002 and 2003. I fought elections from the same ward, gaining over two thousand votes, considered by Democrats, Estone Socialists and nationalists to be an excellent achievement. So, each party sought to recruit me as their candidate. I preferred the nationalists, but gaining votes in Estone ward under their banner was extremely difficult, if not impossible. Residents of Estone hated the nationalists because the Estone Socialists and Democrats always presented the nationalists as the party of the rich and anti-immigration. To my disappointment, the nationalists did nothing to repudiate these lies and merely fielded paper candidates in this and other inner-city wards.

I felt the Socialist and Democrats' local leadership were jealous of my popularity in the Estone ward and were ready to do anything to destroy me. Residents and activists like Noori, Sher Dill, Salman, Sharma and Sala Anaree had advised me to join the Democrats as the Socialist leader's decision to go to war in Iraq had damaged them beyond repair. Their leader was rightly or wrongly labelled as a warmonger and an American poodle. The door-to-door election campaign revealed the total absence of support for the Estone Socialists. A vast number of voters in all inner-city wards no longer considered them as the party of Justice and Peace.

We heard explosive laughter and loud voices from the street below and then footsteps on the stairs. A dozen men of varying ages and races entered the office.

"These guys have agreed to help us deliver some leaflets", I said looking at the blown-up version of the Estone ward map fixed to the wall. "*At least the bastard has a lot of friends so we don't have to go out in the rain to deliver these fuckin' things,*" Jitu muttered under his breath to Irfan. "What was that?" I asked. "Oh, nothing," they both said. I knew what they were thinking. I had planned a surprise for them. First, I sent them to retrieve rucksacks and carrier bags from the filing cabinet while everyone else watched and then got them to put three bundles of leaflets and a much smaller map (about five streets) of Estone ward in each of the seven rucksacks and carrier bags. "You all know what to do guys," I said handing a bag full of leaflets to each team. Noori and Salman insisted (as pre-planned) that Jitu and Irfan should accompany them, under the pretext that they were not familiar with the Newtown and Hockley areas of the Estone ward.

"What do you say, Jitu and Irfan?" I asked.

"The bastard has got us", Jitu whispered to Irfan and then said loudly, "We thought these guys will deliver the leaflets and we three should go knocking on doors."

"Well, that was the plan but Noori and Salman are not familiar with certain areas of the ward but it's important to leaflet those areas. So, Jitu you go with Siddha and Irfan you go with Keota. That's it off you go. Oh, don't forget to return to the campaign office for refreshments and tick the finished streets on the wall map here," I said cheerfully pointing to the ward's wall map.

"What are your plans then Sufi? Are you going to relax?"

"Relax? You idiots! You know there is no time for relaxation. If you must know I will accompany our party leaders, Todd and Jack on a door-to-door campaign. Any more questions?" They were about to open their mouths when Paul dragged Jitu and Irfan away, holding them firmly by the arms and whispered in their ears: "Don't you fuckin' waste your time arguing with him. We will deal with him after the election. You need him now, so piss off and do as he said; deliver those leaflets! I don't know why you bother. No one reads them!!"

# Chapter Ten

The front page of the leaflet showed our pictures and an article attacking the Estone Socialists for ignoring inner-city areas and for taking illegal action in Iraq and Afghanistan. The primary purpose of the article was to persuade Muslim voters and those on the left of the political arena and those opposed to the war to boycott Estone Socialists and vote for Democrats. With only a couple of days before the election, there was no doubt in anyone's mind that in Estone ward, the battle was between Democrats and the Estone Socialists with the nationalists completely out of the picture. A close examination of the nationalists' values shows an uncanny similarity with those held by a majority of Asian voters. I could not understand the failure of nationalists to exploit this, and explain their policies to the Asians and other communities living in the ward. I felt a sincere effort by them could lead to their victory in inner-city wards within a short time. But it was not for me to tell the nationalist leaders how to do their job.

Holding a bundle of leaflets in his left hand, Jitu wearing a light blue striped suit, matching shirt and tie rang the doorbell of every house in Newton and Hockley areas, moving quickly and methodically from house to house. His clothes were rapidly getting wet in the rain and he refused to put on a raincoat or use an umbrella because he wanted to look smart. He kept in touch with Irfan via mobile phone and ignored other teams of activists working on our behalf.

Most Asians closed the door on Jitu when they recognised who he was and threw the leaflet back at him. Jitu lived in Estone ward for forty years and did his best to deceive people by making false promises to get votes. The residents caught up with him and did not trust him anymore. They also found out about his dubious grant applications from the City Council and other grant-making bodies pretending to use the money to ease poverty and deprivation in the ward but the money ended up in his clandestine property deals. He was careful to insert the names of his family members as buyers and not his own to avoid charges of corruption or political embarrassment in the future. Drug dealing, credit card fraud and insurance fraud were the other preoccupations that he indulged in daily, without being caught but officially pleaded poverty and depended solely on dole payments from DWP. In the not-too-distant past, during local and general elections, Jitu had been collecting hundreds of postal votes either by begging or through intimidation from his friends and acquaintances and then selling them to the highest bidder. Having stitched up his colleagues in the Socialist Party, he joined the Democrats. Party politics or Party loyalty or loyalty to anyone else was not Jitu's cup of tea. In the Wilson area of Estone ward, he had business relations with Paul Ali and his sister Naila Fazal. They were very rich proprietors with dubious or illegal sources of income and owned a brothel and fifteen other properties in and around the centre of Cosmopolitan City. The brothel, called the *den of iniquity* was in Estone Ward close to Wilson Street.

Jitu took great care to post the leaflets. He wanted the side bearing our photograph to fall facing up in the hallway. Some residents, hearing the letterbox being pushed, opened their doors and at the sight of him, started cursing him and unceremoniously tore the leaflet and threw the pieces on the pavement. But instead of getting annoyed, he immediately got into the begging mode. With extreme humility and politeness, he beseeched the voter, often touching his or her feet, to vote for his friend Irfan and Asif. And in the same breath, asked them not to vote for me. Some voters told him to "piss off". He then switched to cursing the Socialist Party leaders for killing Men, women and children in Iraq and Afghanistan. Under different circumstances, those who knew him would have simply ignored him but such was the hatred for the socialist party and its leaders that they just nodded in the affirmative or gave him the thumbs-up sign.

Other residents like Jamil Sahib, a straight-talking car mechanic, were more adventurous. Jamil heard about his benefit frauds, his ties with the grant mafia, deceiving local council and corruptly gaining funds to run fictitious projects, so he had no hesitation in relating these facts to him and then told him to *get lost*. Jitu was inherently a shameless and thick-skinned son-of-a-bitch politician and simply bowed to him, thanked Jamil, ignoring the abuse and hoped that he would vote for his friends.

"Not on your Nelly you crook! Only Sufi will get my vote", Jamil retorted and again got profuse thanks from him. In the morning, Jamil rang me and complained about Jitu asking for only two votes. He also said that socialist activists threatened him to hand over his postal vote although he had already filled it out and posted it. I was worried about the threats that many of my supporters were receiving from some activists so I passed them on to the election office but they took no action. Jamil warned me: "Something is brewing, Sufi, but I don't think it's tea. Be careful mate."

Having completed leafleting of the areas assigned to him, Jitu turned into Pudina Road and headed for the *den of iniquity*. This was a large building, comprising two, three-bedroom terraced houses, converted into a massive ground floor room; used as a discotheque and a bar. There were six bedrooms and two bathrooms upstairs. Punters, mostly taxi drivers, used the amenities upstairs seeking relaxation with prostitutes for a half-hour or an hour, depending on the amount of money they were willing to spend. An old man, Ali Baba, who lived on the opposite side of the den told me he saw many Muslims and others, so-called *pillars of society*, go into the den day and night to visit prostitutes. Ali Baba was a retired medical doctor and a student of comparative religion. He called himself a 'student' but he was a master teacher, a highly learned man who kept himself to himself, saying that he gave up on the Mullahs and Muslims as they did not want to change. "*Allah does not change the condition of people unless they at least try to do so,*" he quoted the Quran. He believed that the insatiable carnal appetite of some Muslims was the sole cause of the decline in religious practice not only in the UK but throughout the world. He wrote a short poem in Urdu on the subject and read it out to me. I can't remember the exact words but it went something like this:

*Hindu ko buhtoon ki Khudahi nay mara* – worship of deities humiliated the Hindus

*Yahudiyoun ko Musa ki Jodhi nay mara* – Disobedience of Moses humiliated the Jews

*Esahiyoun ko Essa kay wichhorhay nay mara* – Abandonment of Jesus humiliated the Christians

*Aur Muslamanoun ko inn kay lohrhay nay mara* – their uncontrollable cocks humiliated the Muslims

Ali Baba said that he could not understand why the Muslims were hell-bent on building mosques when they urgently need to build *an ummah, a community* that would live every day, every hour, every second according to the humanitarian principles propounded by the holy prophet. Except for a few Shia mosques that were managed for the community by the community, not so Sunni mosques, which were run as family enterprises rather than communal centres and only opened at the prayer times.

"Sharia says, there should only be one mosque within a three-mile radius, but I counted at least ten in Estone ward, all within walking distance of one another. After Eid and Jummah prayers in the Broadbent Mosque," Ali Baba noted, "the head butters were not even permitted to talk, shake hands, or embrace one another." He called worshippers head butters. He told me that Muslims today did not get their prayers answered because they were headbutting, not praying. After every prayer, I too had heard the Mullah cry, *"Silence in the house of Allah."* Prayers other than the *fard* should also be recited slightly louder than a whisper but never in silence, according to hadith, Ali Baba told me. As I talked to Ali Baba, I saw Jitu enter *the den of iniquity*. Irfan was already there. What were they up to now? I asked myself.

The vast discotheque room's ceiling lights cast vibrant patterns on the floor. The room was filled with a deafening boom of music as the DJ encouraged everyone to dance to bhangra music as Jitu entered. Young people were everywhere. Jitu watched, as scores of women in scant clothing contorted and twisted around their boyfriends or by themselves into different forms and sizes, their arms, legs, and boobs flying in the air. Some were curled up on the floor like pythons as if suffering from the ill effects of hallucinogenic substances while others writhed on the floor like snakes; the discotheque lights, frequently changed the colour of their skin. There was no rhythm or synchronisation of body movements. Twisting bodies covered the floor, and some severely inebriated individuals who were barely able to stand pretended to dance to the ear-splitting bhangra music before collapsing to the ground. It did not surprise Jitu to see Irfan already in the den sitting at the small bar in the corner, smoking and drinking lager. One, continuous narrow mahogany shelf was fixed to all four walls and encircled the entire room, ending at the door. More young men and women sat on stools, foreheads pressed together as if they were glued, drinking beer or other alcoholic beverages from glasses perched perilously on the shelves. Despite the clamour of the deafening sounds of the bhangra music, they seemed unaware of their surroundings as they chatted passionately and laughed and giggled. Neighbours didn't seem to object to these obscene late-night gatherings. Paul's relatives occupied the houses on either side. In the renovated terraced dwellings, the den of iniquity appeared to be more of a small hall than a chamber. Many young Muslims who were unable to enjoy life at home due to parental control and disputes over money and bills found social and psychological relief in the den. They engaged in card games, drank, smoked, fornicated, and used drugs without fear or favour. A plaque, hanging from the ceiling, just above the bar read:

*Boldly I say to all my Muslim friends*

*Those who wish to follow modern trends*

*And those craving an alcoholic drink*

*Or those from adultery don't shrink*

*Then enter my temple of acuity*

*Known to all in Estone, as the den of iniquity.*

In the den, tempers over women frequently erupted under the influence of drink and losses in card games. An unbroken line of visitors, professionals during the day and taxi drivers at night, kept the den running around the clock, making Paul Ali and his sister Naila very wealthy. Jitu spotted Irfan chatting to a group of friends and went over to him and sat next to him. Irfan handed him a drink. "Let the fuckers do the leaflets, let's enjoy ourselves," Irfan said turning his back to Jitu and continued talking. Jitu laughed and sipped his drink, staring at the boobs and buttocks of gyrating women. Jitu's blood pressure spiked when he saw erotically moving bodies, and his phallus stood erect like a mongoose on guard, creating a bulge in his trousers. Looking around, he sighed with relief; no one seemed to be paying any attention. He quickly covered it with a scarf lying on the seat next to him. It proved to be a big mistake. Moments later an intoxicated girl grabbed her scarf and although drunk, she realised what was in her hand beside the scarf, and jerked it, forcing Asif to stand up; her nails penetrated the spongy tissue. Asif screamed in agony as waves of pain, mingled with pleasure sent shivers through his body. "Let's go upstairs," he whispered, his lips touching her ears. A drunken youth next to him started yelling, "Eh, Sultan... that suit... suited and boo...booted man kissed your girlfriend." Sultan, despite his inebriation, sprang at Jitu and slapped him so hard on the left cheek , he was thrown back against the wall. He dropped onto the chair, sluggishly, still dazed. The man swore and shook as he snatched the girl by the arm and dragged her away. With his head in his hands, Jitu sat for what seemed like an eternity as he tried to recover from the ordeal. The only consolation for him was nobody noticed anything, not even Irfan. He was engrossed in conversation with a group of men and women, chatting to them about the election. Jitu, unsettled by the slap looked viciously at his friend.

Only a few years ago, he thought, Irfan was an unknown entity in Estone. Taking advantage of the Iraq and Afghanistan wars and many Muslims' hatred of Estone Socialists and their perception of the Democratic Party as a Muslim-friendly party, he joined it to be its candidate from the ward. Having risen through the ranks of the Democratic party due mainly to the favours from JB, Irfan ignored Jitu but continued to use him to achieve his long-term ambitions. Irfan's fertile, conniving and deceiving mind had already planned, to see himself in Westminster in the next general election. Many politicians and media outlets held these qualities to be necessary to achieving 'success' in their political life. The Democratic party had lost a lot of ground in the political arena of the country and looked for ways and means to regain the lost ground to avoid eventual extinction. The war offered them an opportunity to side with millions of people protesting the war. Unknown to its leader, his decision to oppose the Iraq war landed the democrats in the good books of not only Muslim voters but also other justice and peace-loving British Citizens opposed to the war. The local Democratic party leader, for the gratification of his carnal desires, took a liking to Irfan and called him, "a promising young politician". If by this he meant Irfan was a good liar and deceiver, then he was right. Irfan knew about Jitu's notorious background but willingly colluded with him for his long-term political gains. Unknown to me, Jitu and Irfan planned to turn the tables against me and transform me from a hero in the eyes of our political leaders into a zero-rated political untouchable. For the time being, however, his target was winning the election and destroying me politically, to the extent that it offered an opportunity for his friend Yoda to win. My total banishment from the political arena, he left for a later date. So, they listened to JB and Paul Ali and set about appeasing me but at the same time planned to destroy me by ruining my reputation and popularity. How they would set about achieving this aim, I did not know. But I was certain that I will soon find out. To fulfil their wretched dream, they unashamedly sought the help of Yoda Khan, one of the Socialist Party's most notorious and ruthless candidates. He assured the duo that he was with them as far as my destruction was concerned. But Yoda was a cunning politician and cleverly delegated the task of destroying me and helping Jitu and Irfan to his two cronies, Kalbi Jat and Himar Rajah. Kalbi Jat, an Indian national, middle-aged, with unpleasant body features was an exponent of Darwinian theories. He had earned this name not only for his looks but also for his beliefs and for perpetually laughing and baring his teeth like a chimp while talking. Himar Rajah was a Pakistani national; also middle-aged, skinny and had earned his name for 'living in sin' (unmarried) with three women – a Pakistani, a white girl and a Moroccan, not treating them equally and displaying a coercive and controlling behaviour towards them. He was also a regular visitor to the

90

*den of iniquity*. Like many other Muslims, he used verses of the Quran about concubines to his advantage, legitimising his carnal desire, like Jitu and Kalbi. Years ago, Jitu was a member of the Socialist Party and a major player in the group, the deadly trio, comprising himself, Himar and Kalbi formed an unholy alliance and were the chief practitioners of Himalayan politics within the Socialist Party. Some officers of the regional Socialist party joined the trio to practise Himalayan politics too. In the Estone ward, it was common knowledge that Kalbi, Himar and some Gora Sahibs- regional officers of the socialist party, acquired the skill of Himalayan Politics from Jitu. He did not deny practising dirty Himalayan politics but maintained it was passed down to him by his predecessors who gained it from the Gora sahibs when they ruled India. They taught the same skill to all other politicians in the Indian subcontinent. From there it spread to Europe through migrants from the subcontinent. He failed to mention his grandfather as the chief proponent of this diabolical manipulative system. Like his grandson, Sardar Chore took no prisoners in the practice of Himalayan politics in the district of Neelogonj. At election meetings, he made passionate speeches asking the audience to vote for his best friend Sardar Ashiq but after the meetings, he visited the voters in their homes, telling them he did not mean what he said in the meetings, they should vote for Sardar Biman. Some pious men in the district gave Sardar Chore the nickname: *munafiq*. Some Bengali residents of Estone ward said, only a handful of pious people lived in the district.

They said Paul Ali was related to Jitu through Sardar Chore as he was credited with having a one-night stand with Paul Ali's grandmother. If true, I fear for the future of humanity. It does not look rosy.

Amid the deafening noise, Irfan asked Jitu to leave the *den of iniquity* and return to the campaign office. They met Paul Ali at the exit. "What are you two doing here? Shouldn't you be leafletting?" Paul Ali asked.

"We've finished leafletting Paul. Just came in to have a drink," Irfan said sheepishly. "I told you two to stop playing dirty politics with Sufi. I just saw him walk past the den, without even looking this way. Come into my office, it's quiet there."

# Chapter Eleven

Paul paced around in his office while he told Jitu and Irfan to take seats. He seemed agitated. He asked them if they knew that his father and I were friends. They looked at each other in surprise. He told them his father was Pakistani and his mother Irish. Ali Ahmed was a good friend. We participated in local elections as candidates and knocked on doors and distributed leaflets in the national elections. Pakistan Election Commission sometimes invited Ali Ahmed as an observer through the auspices of the Pakistan Think Tank (PTT). Paul told Jitu and Irfan that his father always praised the fair conduct of elections in the UK, compared with open fraud in Pakistan. Fraud, vote buying, coercion, military intervention, shootings and assault on rival candidates were normal political activities in the Indian subcontinent, especially in Pakistan. The import of Himalayan politics to the UK coincided with the massive migration of workers from the Indian sub-continent during the 1950s and 1960s because of abundant work opportunities. Originally, immigrants were men only. But once settled, their families joined them and the early 1970s saw the creation of "ghettoes" or inner-city areas, around industrial zones like Estone ward. Election candidates chosen by the main political parties in inner-city areas had to be from the Pakistani, Bangladeshi or Indian communities. Interest from the West Indian and African communities was rare and spasmodic. The white indigenous people moved away from the inner-city areas, making exclusive white areas such as Littlefield and Coldfield their homes. The political vacuum created by such social displacement of people gave rise to a distinct Asian political class, not only versed in the art of the dreaded Himalayan politics but ambitious and greedy to the point of destroying community cohesion through the establishment of an additional exploitative network of baradari system.

The Himalayan Politics and the baradari network ensured the selection of prospective parliamentary and council candidates belonging to the baradari with the highest number of members in a particular ward or constituency. A distinctive feature of these two undesired political networks was spreading false information about the opponents and engaging in corrupt and illegal practices not only to ensure selection but success in elections. As the industry closed and job opportunities faded, unemployment rose rapidly and for many immigrants, dependency on the welfare system became the only means of survival. The Estone Socialists, during their tenure in office, go on a spending spree and the nationalists, when they are in office impose cutbacks that lead to economic difficulties for those on benefits. It was necessary for every nationalist party government that followed the socialist one to take such action to reduce the budget deficit. With no jobs and reduced benefits, many families lived in virtual poverty. Because of deprivation, lack of school places and employment opportunities, the residents of inner-city wards became susceptible to fake political promises made by politicians to gain votes. The majority of immigrants from the sub-continent were illiterate, falling prey to accomplished liars and practitioners of vicious Himalayan politics who did not hesitate to win elections by any means, legal or illegal. For them, the victory took precedence over legality. In the inner-city areas, telling the truth and conducting elections in a civilised manner became a thing of the past. Feeding the electorate false information by activists like Yoda, Jitu, Asif and Irfan became the norm. They were not alone. Some Socialists, Democrats and National Party activists from the sub-continent were not far behind in telling lies and spreading mischievous and baseless propaganda against each other in inner-city areas. It went something like this: *No one will get any benefits if nationalists win. They are racists. It's the Socialist party which welcomed immigrants to the UK. Don't vote for the Nationalist Party, they will send us all back if they win. The Democrats have only a few seats and they can't promise you anything.* The socialist party's female activists were no better as they told the same lies against their opponents and made absurd promises, which they knew could not be kept.

Paul remembered his father standing as an independent candidate years ago when the Socialist activists and candidates made several attempts at his character assassination: *Ali Ahmed is a womaniser. He is a straightforward person; he has no political acumen and doesn't understand politics. As an independent councillor, he'll have no power in the council chamber and cannot solve your problems. He keeps changing parties. He will not allow any grant applications to go through.* They told every Sunni Muslim that he was a Shia and they told the Shia, he was a Sunni. The Estone Socialists freely invoked the caste and baradari system, telling the lower caste voter: *Ali Ahmed is a Jat, do you want to vote for a Jat? Are you mad?*

Paul Ali's father lived and worked in the Estone ward for forty years and most residents knew him well. In the May 2001 local election, he got over two thousand votes against the socialist party stalwart, the sitting Councillor Adah Ram. On the day of the election, Ali Ahmed discovered massive vote rigging, by the socialist party, which was a major factor in his defeat. He immediately wrote to Mr Weno, the election officer, calling for re-election but Ali Ahmed received only a single-line reply, "*Your comments have been noted*". No criminal charges were brought against the perpetrators of electoral fraud. Ali Ahmed received threats from thugs telling him to "stop destroying the honour of the community, keep quiet or face consequences." He was told: *If ever you go to Pakistan, we'll boil your balls and skin your family alive.* Paul remembered his father telling him he was not worried about threats against his person but threats against his family forced him to take no further action on electoral fraud and personations. Ali Ahmed had always wondered if the regional and national leadership of the Socialist Party knew or was ignorant of the antics of their inner-city wards party or whether they carried the illegal activities out with their tacit approval. Ali Ahmed was sure that regional Socialist leadership was involved in favouritism and nepotism. Both Jitu and Irfan knew local Socialist Party leadership had not been fair to Ali Ahmed or me as we were not allowed to enter the selection process on one pretext or another. The sitting councillors, realising that they could be defeated by us in the selection process, conspired with local party officers and told the regional leadership lies about us. They told them that the candidates standing against them in the selection process were 'left wing' and 'antisemitic.' In response to such blatant lies, and without carrying out an investigation and amid vociferous complaints by members, the regional leadership closed the ward, suspended voting by members and declared the sitting councillors as 'selected'. Ali Ahmed and I were forced to leave politics until the advent of the Iraq war. Some members and officers of the local and regional Socialist Party refused to support me and Khan because they said, we were "too straightforward, hated Himalayan politics and didn't tow party line."

Ali Ahmed died on the day the war began. Asif asked him: "looks like your dad and Sufi were close friends, so why are you opposing him?" It was a good question and Paul did not answer it immediately. He was cautious in case he said something that he may later regret. Paul was not my supporter, but he did not want to oppose me openly in case I won and ask the authorities to act against his ill-gotten wealth. Also, Paul was confident, he could manipulate Irfan and Asif but persuading me to support his clandestine wealth creation operations would be impossible, but he did not want to tell them that. So, he said, he hated the Estone Socialists for what they had done to his father. "Sufi wants to rejoin the Estone Socialists and that's why I hate him." The answer was only partially true. Just before Ali Ahmed's death, and despite massive opposition from the socialist party members, Yoda Khan invited him and me to rejoin them. I refused but Ali Ahmed agreed. At a secret meeting of the Estone Socialists' regional and local officers, Yoda hatched a perfect plan to destroy him. "Don't be stupid," he told them, interrupting the debate on Ali Ahmed. "Like Sufi, he has a forthright manner, honesty and integrity. Democrats and nationalists won't have him either. So, let him rejoin us and we'll then destroy him. He'll never be able to fight a local election again."

Some members present at the meeting showed dissatisfaction with the plan and asked: "How will you do that? We can't stop him from coming onto the selection panel; he is an experienced councillor and well-spoken and highly knowledgeable." Yoda was furious: "I know. Don't tell me something I already know about Ali Ahmed and Sufi and there isn't much you can tell me. This is what we'll do," he paused for the effect. All Sixty local Socialist party members and regional officers like Rajah Moodie and old Mr West, a corrupt regional organiser who allegedly took bribes from Asian members before allowing them on the selection panel, fixed their eyes on him. "We'll promise Ali Ahmed a seat for the following year's election," Yoda continued. "His support for our candidate will lead to his two thousand votes transferring to us. We'll win with over five thousand votes majority. We'll get him onto the selection panel and then deal the killer blow!" Rajah Moodie jumped to his feet: "How the hell, are you going to do that? Once he's on the panel, he has the right to put himself forward to every ward for selection." Yoda smiled and tapped his nose. "I'll get Himar Rajah and Kalbi Jat, here to complain against Ali Ahmed to Mr West who will remove him from the panel." Again, someone protested: "Surely, he'll appeal as we've allowed several former Democrats and nationalist candidates and activists to join our party and the panel." Yoda agreed. "Of course, he will appeal, you morons. But the appeal panel will be pre-selected and they will accuse him, just as we accused Sufi, of supporting communists and of antisemitism. He'll stand no chance." Yoda explained further that no one will listen to him and, "even if he complains to the NEC, a Miss Black will reject his complaint. Knowing him he may ask for a judicial review but we have some Judges who are socialist sympathisers and they'll reject his application." They all clapped and cheered Yoda for a perfect plan.

Paul Ali told them that he learned a lot from his father. Like Jitu, Ali Ahmed, had one good habit that everyone in the Democratic party admired. He was a tireless worker and regularly campaigned well into the early hours of the morning —often up to 2.00 am. From Irfan's point of view, this was an extremely useful habit of Jitu because many Bangladeshi voters did not get home from work (their restaurant jobs) before one 'o'clock in the morning! Paul Knew Jitu was not an idiot, he had kinky ideas of his own. He was helping Irfan only for a reason: *to keep closer to him as he and Asif did not trust Irfan and suspected him of possible foul play after the election.* Paul suspected them both of planning something evil against me, but like me, he did not know what. "You two need to make sure that you don't antagonise Sufi, you understand?" They nodded vigorously when Paul told them that in his view my days, like his father, as a political activist will soon be over. I was disappointed that Paul, the son of my friend, was working against me but I think it was his perception that if elected, I will complain to the authorities about his illegal activities. Politics in the Cosmopolitan city were fast becoming a nightmare for straightforward political workers.

The Socialist party leadership and the Democratic leaders both wanted people who would agree with them as councillors, people they could control. Somehow, I did not fit in. Establishments and vested interests all over the world have rarely allowed aspiring politicians, possessing qualities of selflessness, integrity, objectivity, accountability, openness, honesty and leadership to become successful politicians. Having lived in the Cosmopolitan City for the last fifty years, I noticed many Parliamentarians, of all political parties, were honest and decent people but a section practised deadly Himalayan politics. Under no circumstances, should freedom of speech be sacrificed for political expediency or an excuse to destroy other countries. I am a stickler for a world government; through education of the masses and political campaigns, not by imperialistic means.

"We need to destroy Sufi's political career once and for all, Paul. We've waited too long," Jitu said. His tactics were simply to curse and complain about me to anyone who would listen, putting blemishes on my character, like a dirty spot on a pure white cloth. Female activists of Estone socialists, like Adie Gore and her sister Poore Gore told blatant lies to women voters about my marital life telling them I practised polygamy, and warned them their husbands might copy me and get another wife.

Some illiterate women believed them. "Oh, no, no, God forbid. We won't vote for him." They hoped these rumours would help in eradicating my popularity among female voters. Clever women asked them, "How many wives Sufi has?" The deadly trio's calculated response was: 'he has three wives.' Although Islam allows polygamy, it is illegal in England and the Asian culture frowns upon it. Pakistani and Kashmiri women oppose multiple marriages, fearing insecurity and loss of prestige. British law does not allow polygamy or recognise marriage or a nikah ceremony under Islamic law as valid in England unless the marriage was solemnised in a registrar's office or in a country where such marriages are a norm. A web of complex legal principles governs Islamic marriage in England and is beyond the understanding of ordinary people. Paul told Jitu that such rumours will not 'damage Sufi's reputation. My campaign, however, for clarity of law in this area had the full support of most electorate but not from the evil trio who feared my increased popularity will mean that the number of votes for me will be greater than theirs.

Rogue activists from all parties, paid between £5 to £20 to young junkies to spread rumours and lies about the opposing party and for personations. "By midnight on 5th May, if we become the councillors for the Estone ward, we'll make sure that the council builds houses on a massive scale. That's our promise". The pathetic liars knew they were making false promises. Only the victory mattered; the truth did not. They planned to amass extra votes to ensure that I came third or better still lost the election. They preferred Yoda to come third. Under their agreement, Yoda, acknowledged his own and his colleagues' position to be precarious. He agreed to ask for three votes – for himself, Asif and Irfan, and they for their part would do likewise. Such was the height of treachery that they knew it may pay. They knew I was working hard to get three votes and if they worked hard to get only two for themselves and a third for the Socialist candidate, then I would lose or I could come poor third and then I'll only have a couple of years as a councillor.

"It's noisy here today," Paul said, "we'll speak tomorrow. There's not much time left for the election. Again, I'll advise you to work with Sufi. Don't antagonise him and don't trust Estone Socialists. I leave you with this thought: *what if the Estone Socialists are using you to amass votes, for their candidates, not for you and Asif?"* Shudders ran through Jitu as it occurred to him that Yoda may be using Irfan and him to gather more votes for the Estone Socialists. The end would be as the Estone Socialists planned: *winning all three seats*. But they will get help from the Estone Socialists to destroy me, that was agreed and nothing could change that. Paul Ali asked them to sign a declaration that he had written for them, not to antagonise me.

When Paul looked through his draws for the declaration, Irfan tagged at Jitu's arms and pointed towards the ceiling. After a few seconds, he realised what his friend was trying to tell him. They signed the declaration, took Paul's leave and exited his office.

# Chapter Twelve

Outside the room, in the corridor, it was a little quiet but Jitu still whispered, "Why d'you want to go upstairs? What if someone sees us? Plus, I don't want to catch fuckin' AIDS!" Irfan slapped him and ran upstairs. Momentarily dazed, Jitu recovered sufficiently to run after him, taking two steps at a time, rubbing his cheek and swearing at Irfan. "Why you bastard slapped me for?" Irfan knocked on a door and quickly went in closely followed by his friend. "What the fuck...." Jitu stared; his mouth wide open. The sight of a beautiful woman standing to his right, in front of the mirror combing her shiny shoulder-length black hair sent his testosterone rocketing sky high. Dressed in a one-shoulder ruched crop knit top and black shorts, the colour of her scintillating dark brown skin seemed to accentuate the golden glow of the artificial incandescent light fixed to the centre of the ceiling. *She is stunning* he thought. *What a gorgeous girl. I've never seen such a pretty black girl before. That's what you call: black beauty.* A big bulge formed in his trousers and Jitu smiled as he stared at it. He turned away from Irfan and walked gingerly towards the woman. She stood with her back to him and noticed his approach through the mirror. Her big, almond-shaped eyes returned his gaze but Jitu felt it go through his heart. He took a sharp breath and moved closer to her and stood just behind her. He could now clearly see her perfectly round and firm breasts reflected in the mirror. Without thinking, he placed his hands on her shoulders and let them slip down and cupped her breasts, his thumbs making circles around her nipples. "You are not Sufi, are you?" She asked him looking at his smiling reflection in the mirror. His smile subsided immediately, and he almost shouted, "No!" She swung around on her heels and slapped him hard. He was shocked and so was Irfan. "Why the fuck is everyone slapping me around today? And what's this about Sufi? Is she Sufi's girl? Does he come here?" Jitu screamed. "Hush, Hush. Calm down mate and I'll explain." Irfan said. "This is Jennifer.......and .... Jennifer this is my friend, Jitu, I was telling you about." Jennifer nodded and saw that he was still messaging his left cheek. "Jennifer was my class fellow in Broadbent School", Irfan continued. "She is a nurse in the city hospital and has kindly agreed to sort Sufi out...you know what I mean!"

"No, I don't fuckin' know." Jitu retorted, still rubbing his cheek.

"Well...." Irfan began.

"Let me explain," Jennifer interrupted Irfan and opened her bedside drawer. She took out an election leaflet and held it up. "This is your leaflet, right?"

"Ye...ye. It's a good one," Jitu stammered, moving back; terrified that she might slap him again.

"There is a phone number for each one of you recorded on this leaflet...." She put her hand up to stop Jitu from interrupting. "I'll, within the next few days, ring Sufi and tell him I'm his supporter," she sounded so sweet and Asif continued to stare at her boobs. "Are you listening, Jitu?" He jumped and stood to attention, focusing his eyes on the floor. "So...sorry!" "Look at me. As I was saying, I'll tell him I need to know what his policies are and what he can do for me and the general development of the ward. I'll tell him about my West Indian and African connections and tell him that if he satisfies me...," she winked at them cheekily and continued, "with his answers, I'll get him about five hundred juicy votes-how about that for a plan?" "What fuckin' plan? Jitu said angrily. "Five hundred votes! That's no plan. He'll win you morons!"

"No, you moron! I haven't finished," she said, throwing her head to one side in a gesture of defiance. She continued to explain that if, "Sufi falls for it," she will invite me to her house on Love Lane. Once in the house, she will do the rest. "I still don't understand," Jitu looked puzzled. "Take this moron out of here Irfan. I've got no time for such an imbecilic shithead," Jennifer shouted.

"No... no... no, I think I got it! Marvellous! Fantastic!" He jumped around. "That'll be the end of his career, the end of marriage and family life! Wow! You're a genius, Irfan!"

"I can't take credit for it. The credit goes to Jenifer and Yoda. It's their idea", for once in his life, he spoke the truth.

"I've got a question," Jitu said thoughtfully. What if Sufi finds out or asks who's behind all this?" I wish I had known about their cowardly plan but alas, I didn't at the time.

"I'll blame it all on the Estone Socialists of course", Jenifer said without hesitation. "All this will cost just five thousand pounds", She said. Jitu's mouth opened in surprise. "How the fuck, are we going' to pay you that much?"

"It's been sorted," Irfan said triumphantly and to circumvent Asif's next question added, "As long as JB is with us, money is no obstacle. Right?" Jitu started to tap dance and sang:

Oh, what a beautiful world this can be

If good friends stick together, you see

Now surely against Sufi, we'll turn the tide

All will be well with John Boyes on our side!

"I hope Sufi isn't Queer like you Irfan?" Jenifer interrupted.

"No, No," Irfan quickly answered. "The Bastard is a womaniser. He's got four wives already – one here in the UK, two in Pakistan and one in Morocco!"

"Hmmm, interesting," Jenifer said, dismissing them with a wave. She already knew about my past life more than these scumbags did. She knew the story about my "wives" was fabricated, spread by Socialist activists. They are all the same – *petty liars*, she thought.

"Marvellous plan eh, Irfan...Well done. How did Jenifer know you are you know...," Jitu said as they rapidly descended the stairs and went through the partially opened front door out into breezy but sunny and busy Wilson Street.

"Queer? She was my neighbour and class fellow remember, and we never lost contact even after leaving school! And when JB did some damage to me, and I was hospitalised; she was my nominated nurse."

"So, she's trustworthy? She'll do what she says she will?"

"Absolutely! Forget about that now, let's go back to the campaign office and see what that bastard Sufi is up to."

# Chapter Thirteen

Irfan and Jitu scrambled up the flight of stairs as usual, two steps at a time, from street level to the first floor and entered the campaign office just as I was asking the activists to sit down. The room was crowded. At least a hundred people competed for about sixty seats. "Apologies for the shortage of seats. JB told our two morons to get a decent size room for the campaign office but this is all they could find," I said smiling. The commotion subsided. Many activists had not finished their food and were still holding their disposable plates, containing a *samosa*, some *pakoras* and a roast chicken leg. Old "Dr" Iqbal, however, had his plate crammed full of a mountain of samosas, several chicken legs and pakoras. Some members of the public, entering the campaign office, carried a plate of food from the restaurant across the road. Electoral Commission rules prohibit political parties to supply food during election meetings because it could be interpreted as 'bribery'. It was not from the party or any candidate or activist, I was certain. It would be unreasonable to ask them not to eat, but the Estone Socialists could complain to the electoral commission accusing us of providing food. I politely asked each person about the source of the food. They confirmed it was provided by the restaurant owner across the road, celebrating his son's first birthday. I got a few of them to stand outside the restaurant, and hold the food plates while I took the photographs.

I saw Dr Iqbal had stuffed some *samosas* and chicken legs in his duffle coat pocket. Even during warm weather, he always had the coat on, despite his wife telling him off but she also knew its usefulness as the low level of benefits forced them to live on handouts. "Dr" Iqbal's motto seemed to be: *when hungry, wear a duffle coat*. Residents knew about his idiosyncrasies and left him to his own devices. He was a straightforward person. He was not a medical doctor or a PhD, but had gained the title for the privilege of sharing his name with the illustrious sage, poet and philosopher of the east: Dr Sir Allamah Muhammad Iqbal.

"He didn't tell us about this meeting, did he?" Irfan asked.

"No, the bastard. He's got over a hundred men here. I know most of them. They'll do anything for him".

"Look he's got Asif on the rostrum as well. I won't ask for votes for him again."

"We have to silly, otherwise Sufi will win easily."

Most activists had taken their seats by now and Sufi was reading the real Dr Iqbal's poetry in Urdu about democracy, as a filler to give everyone time to settle down. His translation of the stanzas went something like this:

*iss razz ko ek marde firangi nay Kiya fash* – An Englishman once divulged this secret to me

*Har Chand k daana issay khola nahi kartay* – Though before public such secrets are never laid

*jamhuriat ek maghribi tarz e hakumat hai k* – That democracy is a Western form of government

*jis mein bahndu ko gina kartay hain, tola nahi kartay* – In which people are counted, never weighed!

The poem clarifies that the honourable doctor was not in favour of democracy for the Muslims. He was in favour of the return of the caliphate. Such an ambition could not possibly be in the West's interest, especially America's. No one forgot what happened under previous rightly guided caliphs. The Muslims ruled countries from India to Spain. They destroyed mighty Persian and Roman empires in no time. Reunification of fifty-seven Muslim countries under the banner of a Caliphate could lead to unwanted trouble for the *infidel West*. The caliphate could emerge as a military and economic power to be reckoned with. If a mad Mullah became a caliph that could lead to revenge for the extensive damage caused in Iraq, Afghanistan, Libya, Kashmir and Syria. Under a Caliphate system, Muslim countries will instantly die a nationalistic death; their borders will no longer exist, leading to the free movement of people, a single economy and a single army. The old enmity between the Aramaic religions could re-ignite leading to a third world war. A governor appointed by the Caliph in each country would replace all fifty-seven puppet regimes. Orders or more appropriately perhaps, 'requests' from Washington may well be ignored.

The tiny American patron may have no place to hide even though the divine books say the holy land belongs to the small but invincible master. Attempts to install a caliphate in Afghanistan, Nigeria and Pakistan were quashed by the American state apparatus, with tacit support from Singh and Olmert. Political analysts believe that under no circumstances would a caliphate be allowed to exist; quite understandably so. An anti-Muslim organisation, *the axis*, has been working day and night to prevent such an eventuality and protect the little master at the expense of human rights in Muslim flashpoints, such as Kashmir. However, the situation may well have been different if the attempt by early Muslims to occupy France was successful. But instead of a mad mullah, if a sane person could be placed at the helm of the caliphate, then peace, prosperity, truth and justice could prevail. Admittedly, discovering a sane person among the Muslim leadership nowadays would be a herculean task because of their internal animosities and sectarian divisions. At this moment, in time, there is not a sane person among the Muslim elite but one is due to appear anytime now – a Mr Mahdi. His precursor is hiding among the Salafis, Shias, Sunnis, Deobandi, Brelvi, and many other sects and sub-sects but there is no guarantee. I recall an incident (true or false, I am not sure) that occurred in the city of Multan in Pakistan in the late 1990s when a Mullah tried to stop a young man from committing suicide. When attempts to persuade the youth to come down from the tower failed, the Mullah climbed up and sat next to the man, and continued to discourage him by saying that Allah has forbidden mankind from committing suicide, and if he goes ahead with it; he will burn in hell. But the young man insisted on going ahead with his plan to end his life, saying that no one loved him. "Trust in Allah, my brother," encouraged the Mullah, "and he will solve all your problems. He loves you seventy times more than your mother."

"Are you a Muslim or a Hindu or a Christian?" Asked the Mullah.

"I'm a Muslim."

"Are, you a Sunni or Shia?"

"Yes, I'm Sunni."

"Me too," The Mullah said. "Are you Sunni Hanafi, Maliki, Shafi or Hanbali?"

"Hanafi Sunni."

"Me too. Hanafi Deobandi or Brelvi?"

"Hanafi Brelvi"

"Me too. Tanzeehi or Takfiri?"

"Tanzeehi."

"Oh no. Then die you damn infidel," the Mullah said and pushed the young man off the wall.

On the balance of probability, there is no chance of Muslims coming together even after the kingdom comes. The forces of the Patron and Protégé, I think, should calm down too and allow poor countries to develop so that they can at least make life easier for their people. What they are doing now, in the name of self-preservation or national security, is economically destroying countries that they perceive as a potential threat. I believe that recognition of Israel is a need of time and those Muslim states reluctant to go that way stand to lose everything in the long run. A nudge from Asif brought me back to the present.

Activists now occupied all seats and were asking me to repeat Dr Iqbal's poem. Even the old "Dr" Iqbal sat quietly in the front row but there was a reason for that; his mouth was busy munching a samosa. I repeated the poem and started the meeting. "Friends, thank you for coming to the meeting. Last year's local election in Enstone ward saw only a 28% voter turnout, that's not good for democracy. If everyone sitting here get their family members and friends and so on and they all vote on Thursday, we could achieve at least 45% turn out if not more, which will not only be good for us but also good for democracy." I informed the activists that the Democrats were confident they have around three thousand votes confirmed and only require additional five hundred votes to seal the victory. It was not easy convincing voters to come out and vote. There was a trust deficit between the politicians and the voters. This ever-widening gap needs to be closed, otherwise burial arrangements for democracy will have to be made soon.

I estimated the Democratic party vote to be near five thousand, well above the target of three thousand.

"Many people are fed-up with politicians and that's why they don't bother to vote Sufi," a young man named, Mark, interrupted from the back row. I took that point further by highlighting the antics of some politicians. "You're an intelligent young man Mark and you know most politicians are honest people interested only in solving problems faced by the public but a few morally corrupt and dishonest people have brought the profession into disrepute and others continue to do so but increased turnout at local and general elections will enable right persons to take seats in parliament or the council. Increased turnout will also keep the miscreants out and a measurable change in people's lives would be a real possibility."

I spotted Irfan and Jitu standing at the back of the room looking distinctly uncomfortable. I saw them before but ignored them. I let them seethe for a few minutes, and swear at me. I now beckoned them to come to the front and join me and Asif. Jitu was not a talented speaker and I saw the opportunity to expose him. "Jitu, d'you want to add anything to what I've just said in response to Mark's comment?" He hesitated and shook his head but suddenly wrenched the microphone away from my hand as Irfan secretly delivered a vicious blow into his ribs. I felt proud when the activists started shouting: "Sufi! Sufi! Sufi!" They knew about Jitu's character anomalies and had seen him go into spontaneous convulsions at the sight of the lectern and microphone. His voice now trembled and his hands visibly shook as he said: "I'm....I'm fee.... ling happy to.... say a few.... words. Everyone should.... shou... should.... vote like Sufi said ....to ....to keep corrupt people out...."

"Ye, corrupt people like you!" Tariq, a young local solicitor, standing at the back of the room interrupted and everyone laughed. "No, no... sir, we are nice people," Irfan said, snatching the microphone from Jitu and changing the subject. "We like to help you and that's why we need your votes. The Socialist Party is not worth talking about and you know what their leader has done to Muslims in Iraq and Afghanistan, so who is on your side? Yes, we are... the Democrats! The democratic party is the best." Salman, in his early sixties, sitting in the middle of the third row stood up and threw his plate, containing the remains of food, towards Jitu and Irfan. The plate and samosa crumbs fell short but the chicken leg, completely stripped of flesh, flew true and smashed into Jitu's right eye, sending him reeling backwards. Fortunately for him, Irfan broke his fall with his outstretched hands. I caught the microphone, which had flown into the air and was heading towards the floor. "We're not interested in your lies," Salman was seething with anger. "We want to hear the truth, not lies, so let Sufi answer our questions." Convinced that they were being cornered by my supporters and will lose votes, Irfan came up with an unbelievable but cunning story as he knew this story might turn the tide because most people present were from the Pakistani and Bengali communities. Many were not only illiterate but given to superstition and supernatural beliefs. He grabbed the microphone from me and pretended to be full of piety and self-righteousness, playing on the superstitious beliefs of the audience. "Last night," he began, "The great Pir Sahib (holy man) from India blessed me and Jitu in the Broadbent Mosque and predicted my and Asif's victory and Sufi's defeat." The audience, somewhat taken aback, partly believed the prophecy to be true, and became silent, listening intently. "Listen to this, he made the prediction when the Pir sahib was in a holy trance and you all know what that means," he glared at them. Some simple, superstitious and gullible people believed him and shifted awkwardly in their seats, while others asked him searching questions. "I'm only telling you what the Pir sahib said to us in front of at least a hundred people." Looking satisfied by the confusion on many peoples' faces, Irfan and Jitu walked out of the room, smirking. I knew they pulled a fast one and there was nothing I could do about it. I desperately sought a solution. Many Bengalis, Indians and Pakistanis were superstitious and had become willing fodder for the unscrupulous Pirs, roaming British Streets and dishing out lucky charms and talismans for this illness or that, for this worry or that. They made a lot of money.

Many Pirs in Britain owned several properties and large sums of money in bank accounts in the UK and abroad in Bangladesh, India and Pakistan. To make matters worse for me, Mr Doom Wala, an elderly Gujarati man from India, sitting at the back of the room stood up and confirmed that he was in the Broadbent Mosque when, in front of about a hundred people, the Pir sahib did predict Irfan and Asif's victory.

I now saw a way to discredit Irfan and Jitu; I was thinking of asking the audience if anyone was a witness to the Pir's prediction and asked the old man if Irfan and Jitu made any "donations" towards Pir Sahib's new mosque project, before his strange "prediction." Doom Wala confirmed this. Irfan and Jitu donated two thousand pounds in cash before the big prophecy. That was all I wanted to hear. It confirmed my suspicions regarding the Pir's prophesy. It was exactly like some Indian and Pakistani Muftis issuing Fatwa against any Tom, Dick and Harry after receiving substantial *Hadiya or recompense* – a civilised term for bribery! After hearing Doom Wala's testimony, supporters gathered around me and assured me of their support. "Those two scoundrels have paid the fake Pir, otherwise he wouldn't have dared to make such an outrageous 'prediction'. Don't worry Sufi, we're with you all the way." I thanked them all for their support.

The next day I made further astounding discoveries about my two cunning and lying compatriots –they had been up to no good. I cannot expect anything good from the duo. Evil was in their nature and that is what they exhibited at every opportunity. Irfan and Jitu campaigned only for Irfan and Yoda. They excluded Asif and me. So, they had been pulling even more fantastic stunts than Pir Sahib's prediction. "Only Irfan and Yoda will win so don't waste your votes on others," Jitu had been saying. A local shopkeeper, Noor Khan, argued with him: "But Sufi and Asif are also your party's candidates and everyone has three votes, so are you asking people not to vote for them?" Jitu admitted that he was only concerned about, Irfan and Yoda. "They can go to hell", he told him. "Noor my friend, all I'm doing is saving people from wasting their vote."

"Sufi was here this morning," Noor told him. "He was asking for three votes, one for each of you as well."

"Well, he is an idiot then, isn't he?" Jitu retorted.

"I think that word fits you and Irfan. Do you think Estone Socialists are on your side? They're collecting postal votes for themselves, not you, you morons." Noor Khan related the antics of my colleagues to me and expressed anger and disappointment at their treachery. I responded by saying, I too was disappointed but not surprised to hear Jitu's outburst.

"You do so much for them and they still hate you."

"That's their treacherous nature," I shrugged. It was getting close to one o'clock in the afternoon, time for Friday congregational prayers so I headed for the Broadbent Mosque.

After telling lies and walking out of the meeting, Irfan and Jitu knocked on every house on Hilton Street, Fenton and Frisby Roads handing leaflets and extolling Yoda's and Irfan's virtues to everyone who answered the door. In the same breath, they praised the leaders of the Democratic Party for their foresight and good fortune in selecting Irfan as the candidate. Oblivious to the insults and shaking of heads, Jitu continued to shower praises on himself, and Irfan.

"Anyway, it's Friday, aren't you supposed to be in the mosque?" Most voters knew Irfan and Jitu were thick-skinned, shameless politicians who had no scruples but ruthlessly pursued their goal of becoming councillors by hook or by crook. "I've just seen Sufi heading towards the mosque," Javed Khan told Jitu.

Jitu reached the top of Park Lane when he realised Irfan was missing. Yoda told him JB picked Irfan twenty minutes ago. They must have switched to a different street, Jitu thought. He urgently needed to tell Irfan and Asif to meet him at the Broadbent Mosque.

Tucking the remaining small bundle of leaflets under his arm, Jitu quickly dialled Irfan's number and spoke conspiratorially, "Go to Broadbent Mosque immediately, Sufi's there and he'll ask the Imam to endorse us as Muslim-friendly candidates and to oppose Estone Socialists. The bastard is thinking well. Javed Khan just told me. There'll be over a thousand people in the congregation, it's Friday, remember? Go quickly and I'll see you there!"

"I....I... I'm .... busy...." Irfan began as if in agony, but Jitu cut him short. "You stupid bastard, are you getting ......is JB with you?" Asif's blood was boiling as his face turned crimson. This was no time to dish out sexual favours, he thought. Estone Socialists were standing outside mosques, dishing out leaflets and he was getting... oh I do not believe it. "Sufi is still showing firm support despite our attempts at his character assassination. Get your arse to the mosque." True, according to polls, they were no threat but the Estone Socialists were a crafty lot. For them, winning elections was only a child's play. They could be extremely convincing and charming, turning lies into truth and truth into falsehood, just as they were doing against me. But they were no match for Jitu; except Irfan was getting on his nerves. "You've got no sense of fuckin' time and space, have you?" He shouted. "I'll explain to JB later." Replacing the phone in his pocket, he extracted the small bundle of remaining few leaflets from under the armpit and started posting them through the letter box of houses on Littlehook Road and then quickly made his way to the Mosque.

111

# Chapter Fourteen

It was a blustery but partially sunny Friday afternoon, just under a week before the election on Thursday, when I saw hundreds of worshippers making their way to Broadbent Mosque off Wilson Street. It was a good opportunity to ask the Imam to support me. The previous week, he declined to mention Irfan and Asif's names and only mentioned my name. I didn't want Irfan and Asif to appear at the mosque. I feared they might take revenge on the Imam for not supporting them. I approached the octogenarian, Bashir Hussein, supported by his son Muhammad Majid at the entrance to the mosque. Their progress was slow because of old Bashir's arthritic knees and back. The Imam led the congregational prayer only after old Bashir read his Naat *(a type of poetry eulogising the holy prophet)* and for this reason, he was very popular. Even at eighty-nine, his voice was still melodious and heart-touching. Irfan, Jitu and Asif disliked him because he supported me. For old Bashir, standing up in prayer, kneeling and prostrating were things of the past. His doctor blamed the lack of sunlight, perpetual cloudy British skies, a lack of vitamin D and disaster for poor bones and joints. Conditions like osteoarthritis and angina permeated the Asian communities not only because of the lack of sunshine but also their sedentary lifestyle and reliance on fatty foods. I remembered old Bashir telling me about his first arrival in England with his friends. They told him and other new arrivals to the UK from the Indian subcontinent to remember two things at all costs: *always vote for the Socialist party and use Adam butter in cooking.* Irfan and Jitu used this advice to ridicule the Socialist Party, stating that many Asians had now realised that Adam Butter was dangerous for their heart but they continued to vote for Estone Socialists, even though they were more dangerous for Muslims than Adams Butter; considering the problems they created in Kashmir and other countries and the sinister part they played in the demise of the Ottoman Caliphate and their support for the American invasion of Iraq and Afghanistan.

I accompanied 'uncle' Bashir into the Mosque and he spotted Irfan and Jitu: "Look, Sufi the criminals are here." When they came nearer, he mocked them: "We see Sufi in the mosque most of the time but have you two started praying now that election is here?" Other worshippers, close by, heard this and chuckled at this remark. Hanging their heads in shame, both Irfan and Jitu moved quickly into the mosque. From the feedback, I got for the last two weeks, most worshippers were on my side. After the laughter subsided, 'uncle' Bashir said, "You're a good man Sufi son. Don't trust these snakes but keep an eye on them so you know what they're up to. Their treachery knows no bounds." Others nodded and every worshipper not only shook my hands but patted me on the back. I thanked everyone and sat on the floor next to old Bashir, who sat on the chair. Sharia law allowed disabled people to sit on a chair to pray and as there were no more chairs left, many had to sit on the floor. Thanks to osteoarthritis and rheumatoid arthritis, the number of disabled worshippers had increased in recent years. Trustees at many mosques failed to provide extra chairs. I asked Broadbent trustees to supply more chairs but they refused blaming financial problems. I was surprised as thousands of worshippers donated between £5 to £20 just on Fridays. They could not account for the donations received from the public in response to my enquiries. The trustees did not produce detailed accounts. Many Mosques were well managed, but some had fallen to corruption, like the Gosia and Broadbent, the two largest in the Cosmopolitan City, where the management committees attempted to sell them as limited companies. Several worshippers complained about them being in a state of utter disrepair but the committees took no notice. Often the ceiling leaked, drenching the worshippers. All donations ended up in the pockets of some corrupt committee members and trustees. In the Broadbent Mosque, the lone trustee, supporting a long, wide beard but a narrow mind, refused to follow the constitution and to hold annual elections and misappropriated donations received from worshippers. No one complained, no one knew how or where to complain.

A committee member mentioned it to me, and I wrote to the Charities Commission but they took no action. In the cosmopolitan City, some trustees managed their mosques as family businesses, transferring excess funds to their accounts and leading a luxurious life.

Many mullahs never practised what they preached and never preached what they practised. During sermons their long beards always shook with anger at Americans, British or 'Zionists' but never at themselves. Practising deviations from original teaching was not their fault, nor was spreading hatred and discord in the community or creating schisms. That was the West's doing of course. There were hundreds of Masjids in the UK belonging to different denominations or *Maslak*, each led by an Imam more venomous than the other, defending his territory, calling each other liars and infidels and assigning gardens of Eden for themselves and hell for their opponents. The illiterate worshippers knowing a little about the Quranic teachings fell fodder to the priests and believed whatever they were told. God, it seems, listens to the Muslim priests. He is at their mercy. Many Mullahs unashamedly speak about God as if they know him personally, his thoughts, and his planned actions against the unbelievers and naughty believers. God says he loves to forgive; Mullahs says God will punish the man who wears a tie to a mosque, or he stands in prayer without making a fresh ablution or has wiped the top of the feet, rather than washing them during ablution or frequently raises his hands in prayer (*Rafah Yadain*) or he wears long trousers, covering the ankles; but it matters not if he tells lies, fornicates, backbites, sells drugs, parks his car inconsiderately, eats haram (forbidden) food, earns money by illegal means, hates other humans and blows himself up along with innocent people. Mullahs of different Maslak endlessly argue with each other about minor variations in the Muslim dress, ablutions, prayers, and beliefs in God, Prophet and Saints but they always sideline major issues confronting the Ummah. Many Mullahs hated me when I said that they need to build communities, not mosques. In the UK, even more in Pakistan, Muslim youth appeared to be sliding down the slope, having no clear goals to achieve apart from making money by hook or crook.

The Imam of the Broadbent Mosque, Imam Shami, was different. Educated at Medina University, he had an excellent understanding of Arabic, sociology, psychology and pure sciences. Luckily, he had escaped rote learning of a few jurisprudence and hadith books, known as *DARS-e-nizam*; a narrow-minded and controversial curriculum taught to

Mullahs. Some madrasahs taught a broad curriculum but many taught *DARS-e-nizam* and the graduates had a divisive and dogmatic outlook which resulted in the creation of schisms within a religion that otherwise propagated unity. Maulvi Imam Shami was, what they could loosely term, a moderate Muslim compared with many of his venomous and narrow-minded colleagues who were the product of this soul-destroying curriculum. It stifled *ijtihad* (an ability to make rational decisions) and led to the imposition of dogmatic beliefs and practices which led to the creation of schisms and internal discord and disunity. Out of one hundred and ninety-five countries in the world, fifty-eight are Muslim, with a combined population of about one and half billion which is about 25% of the total world population. Over 70% of the Muslim population is illiterate, thanks to the Mullahs and corrupt and inept politicians. Uninformed and illiterate masses are nothing but fodder for priests and politicians. Democrats and Socialist politicians were no different in Estone ward. Their popularity was rapidly diminishing, and they were falling from favour with voters and that was the only consolation for me. I was not in Imam's good books either, having debated with him on some aspects of his dubious teachings on Islam but the Imam now saw me approaching him, shook my hands, promised to support me in the election and ascended the pulpit to deliver the Friday Sermon.

Broadbent Mosque, on the corner of Wilson Street and Broadbent Road, was a comparatively large mosque with a capacity of just over seven hundred worshippers. They did not use top floor accommodation except on Fridays as during other prayers, the ground floor was barely half full. So, getting a space in the mosque on Fridays was the key priority and the reason for getting there early.

I attended last week's sermon and the Imam had encouraged worshippers to arrive early and promised them high rewards for doing so, including paving the way for a quick entry into heaven. Booking a place in heaven was becoming very easy nowadays for the believers so much so that many seemed determined to create problems for others while going to headbutt in their respective mosques. Worshippers parked cars erratically and inconsiderately drawing the wrath of the residents, the Imam and that of God but their narrow minds concentrated on getting a place in the mosque and in heaven to the exclusion of everything else. No wonder, the help of God was not there for them. Many had given up the teachings of the prophet to be a human being first but they replaced it with an irrational dogma of their own making. They gained nothing from prayers other than a little exercise and head-butting the ground, losing the true meaning of prostration. Lies, deceit, backbiting, selling drugs, and preaching good but practising evil were evident in the lives of many Muslims.

The Imam having sat on the pulpit, began his sermon in Urdu while his deputy sitting on the first floor above translated it in English. Imam Shami began with the recitation of Arabic verses from the Quran and then explained them in Urdu. Drones of worshippers began arriving and squatting on the floor wherever they could find a space. Some volunteers, eager to get more rewards, directed the incoming worshippers to the first floor as the ground floor was now full but some ignored their pleadings and continued to push and shove their way, upsetting many worshippers. I always criticised the devotees for being negligent of their responsibility to their fellow worshippers and other people. I could not understand how they came to pray, to do a good deed and yet ignore everyone else's rights by abandoning their cars anywhere on footpaths and roads, causing havoc outside the mosque, instead of parking properly. What is the point of being nice to God when you cannot be nice to his creation? Unfortunately, many Muslims nowadays lacked discipline and did their own thing, to hell with everyone else. Bombs were exploding in Mosques in Iraq, Afghanistan and Pakistan killing hundreds of innocent people; all in the name of their version of the belief system. Yet, it is a fact, that many Muslims and indeed some non-Muslims believe suicide bombing and nine-eleven were not the work of Muslims but other sinister forces involved in creating a new world order minus the Muslims and other peace and justice-loving people throughout the world. It looked as if justice, peace and truth were no longer valued.

That is what the Imam was preaching now. He was blaming others for the folly of his kind. "If anyone believes that nine-eleven, seven-seven or the so-called suicide bombings and murders of innocent people is the work of Muslims, then he, she or they need to see a psychiatrist. Terrorism has no religion, why then some Muslims, who objected to Islamophobia, and protested double standards of the West, were labelled by Western media as, Islamic terrorists? Simple," the Imam was answering his question, "To destroy political Islam and to prevent the unification of Islamic countries and to move the boundaries of Israel to the Euphrates, which would legitimise the formation of a world government!" This is where I differ from the Imam, and I told him so. I believe in a fair and just world government, and I believe that suicide bombing is most likely to be the work of Muslims because of their hatred for each other's Maslak. The Imam was merely regurgitating the so-called conspiracy theories spread throughout the world regarding the expansion of Israel to the Euphrates and the formation of a world government or a new world order! No one knew the truth. There was some truth in what the Imam was saying. Wealthy individuals, businesses and international conglomerates siphoned off world resources. This small, but powerful group controlled not only the means of production of everyday necessities but possessed extremely advanced technology and a war machine with weapons of mass destruction that could obliterate the world in seconds. They controlled the banks, the international monetary fund, the big pharma, aeronautical, motor and other industries to name but a few. Through meticulous planning, they now controlled the fate of every nation in the world through the international monetary fund.

Some residents displayed a considerable interest in politics and often asked for my opinion about the new world order and where were we heading. I thought that if they formed a world government based on truth and justice, it should receive immense support throughout the world. A world government is necessary to use world resources not only for the betterment of humanity, and alleviation of poverty but for the conquest of the universe. There was a lot of enmity and political polarisation between nations so it would be impossible to agree on a world government but they could narrow the differences on the conquest of the universe. Positive steps taken now could prove fruitful in the long run. Kashmir and Palestine were political flashpoints that contributed to the polarisation and could lead to the third world war. I believe God gave the land occupied by Israel to the Jews as mentioned in the bible and the Quran! I had many arguments about this with Imams and politicians. An understanding and acceptance of this truth, as stated by the scriptures and implementation of united nations resolutions on Kashmir would solve all problems and the world could move together to peace and prosperity on a scale unknown up to now.

The Mosque was full now. There was hardly any space left on both floors. Some people were still coming in. Rows and rows of devotees squatted on the beautiful green carpet; the majority had their heads covered with a topi (skullcap) but some were uncovered. They listened intently to Imam's sermon. "Vow to the liars and cheaters, for they will burn in hell", the Imam was saying. I noticed Irfan and Jitu enter the hall, looking for space. Threading their way through the worshippers, occasionally stepping on their toes and drawing sighs and curses. They aimed to get to the front row to let the congregation see that they were good Muslims. But they never prayed regularly, apart from Fridays. However, the frequency of their visits to all the Mosques in Estone increased during election times. "Sanctimonious bastards," old Bashir muttered upon seeing them forcing their way to the front row.

The Imam was waving his finger to emphasise his point. "Go to the internet, buy books and study history," he continued, "And you will find out the facts. Read books. You know the major problem with us Muslims today is that those who can read, don't read books! That's why most of us depend on a minority for information and guidance. Some sinister forces are working in the world today to disrupt our daily lives and they are planning to enslave us. Some of my fellow imams have warned me not to deliver political sermons as freedom of speech does not apply to Muslims. But I tell you, Islam cannot be separated from politics. It is a way of life not just a faith. I know the authorities can interpret my sermon as inciting hatred but I cannot change the Quran nor my beliefs or the *dean* for the sake of the American and British governments or anyone else. No amount of scepticism or a ruthless denial by world powers can erase the fact that the war on terrorism is nothing but a war on Islam. It is a Seyonic war to stop the spread of Islam in Europe and to occupy oil-rich Muslim lands and create a greater Israel." The Imam paused to allow what he said so far to sink in and took a sip of water before continuing, "without oil the Seyonic armies and their allies would be powerless. Brothers, it is important to distinguish between Jews and Seyonic forces. Many peaceful and Justice loving Jews agree with us that the prime cause of world instability and threat to peace is the Seyonic entity alone! Opposition to the Seyonic cannot be equated with anti-Semitism. It's not the same no matter what anyone says. They want to create a new world order, which means a world government without Muslims! That cannot be. Like Sufi here, I will be the first one to support a world government based on truth and justice but not on selfishness, expediency, exploitation and plunder. Alleviation of poverty, the conquest of the universe and finding God must be the basis of establishing a world government. Not for occupation or oppression but for genuine freedom and the rule of law. United Nations will be extinct under a world government; a good thing for the Kashmiris. Its failure to ensure freedom for the Kashmiris is a criminal offence. Replacement of the United Nations with an alternative international scientific research organisation, with increased resources, to extend the frontiers beyond the furthest galaxies would be good for the future of humanity. Planets of gold, rubies, and other light and strong, precious metals exist.

Space ships and time travel can be a reality. Humanity must unite and seek knowledge or be extinct. Knowledge is power; God is powerful, omniscient, and omnipresent because he possesses immense knowledge. *Knowledge is God.* The destiny of humanity is to find God, and gain knowledge. God says: *I'm a hidden treasure, find me."*

The literate among the congregation were enthralled but the deep meaning of the sermon went over the heads of others. I was in two minds: *to believe or not to believe what the imam was saying?* Conspiracy theories were rampant regarding the causes of nine-eleven, seven-seven and bombings in Paris. Jitu and Irfan not only believed that Mr Blair and Mr Bush were behind this war on Islam but they used it to gain votes. "There were no weapons of mass destruction in Iraq", they told the audience during their campaign meetings. "It was just an excuse to attack and occupy Muslim lands; all in the name of democracy and *our way of life.*"

What is their way of life? It is a Pandora's Box, full of deception and lies. There was and still is, an element of obnoxious behaviour and actions by a small group of extremists killing in the name of Islam. Or were they Muslims? The imam did not believe they were Muslims. They are the Kharijites who were expelled from Islam in the time of the rightly guided caliph, Ali. The question remains as to who was supporting this evil group. The Imam believed that Bin Laden and al-Qaida, the so-called terrorist outfit, did not have the capacity or the technical knowledge to carry out the September eleven atrocities. Another terrorist outfit, ISIS emerged, more dangerous than its predecessor. Analysts could be forgiven for thinking that certain nations or their agencies could be involved in creating such versatile terrorist outfits. Which nation(s) benefitted from their inhuman activities? Three countries stand out above the others. In their endeavours to destroy Islam, innocent people have paid with their lives. The Imam was saying that our response to the atrocities committed in New York was disproportionate and illegal, and a violation of international law.

"After the disintegration of the Soviet Union and their humiliating defeat at the hands of the Afghani Mujahideen, America became the undisputed world master. Blinded by its newly gained supremacy, it plunged headlong into Iraqi and Afghani infernos. A wise man has truly said: *those who wish to dig their graves, end up in Afghanistan.* Hundreds and thousands of graves from centuries past, contemplated by the mighty Hindu Kush Mountains, bear testimony to Afghans' valour and warrior spirit and confirmation that aggression against them does not pay. I do not support the Taliban or their policies; I am simply stating the facts," The Imam paused. "They are traditional fighters with fierce tribal loyalties and contempt not only for wealth and power but for death too. Death holds no terrors for them as they have no love for the world or its entrapments, so they've nothing to lose."

The Imam concluded his sermon by saying that earlier that day a worshipper asked him about the schisms and sectarianism within Islam. "These abominations," he said, "result from Satan and his followers, introducing innovation into God's revealed knowledge by misinterpreting it according to their whims and fantasy. It was also true," he continued, "That many Muslim priests or Mullahs or Maulvis prey on people's fear of the unknown and bribe them with rewards in the hereafter. Some young Muslims, fed up with life because of poverty and other issues, eagerly blew themselves up to get rewards in the hereafter. They've no compunction in blowing themselves up along with some 'infidels' and 'bad' Muslims. They believe that such inhumane action would give them a one-way ticket to paradise, where they would sleep with beautiful houris with almond-like eyes. Many innocent non-Muslims and Muslims have also been murdered by these deranged psychopaths. Do they expect to live in heaven with seventy houris? God is not unjust so how can he give reward for such diabolical actions? Some mullahs could always work something out – a fatwa here, a fatwa there accompanied by some baksheesh or more appropriately, a bribe.

Do they believe that no angels of hell will deal with such Mullahs? A sage of the East has truly said:

*Strange is the religion of Mullah, preaching enmity against the world*

*Stranger, even he reads the Quran but knows not the origin of man nor his ultimate abode*

*The source from which the night got its darkness; the stars got their light*

*That same source knows the secrets of man's existence and God's might*

*From, evil deeds the Mullah does not desist, but this sanctimonious Satan*

*sways and shakes as if spiritually intoxicated by the sound of the Muezzin."*

The congregation was now under his control so the Imam switched to local politics. "We Muslims must show unity in the forthcoming local elections," he said. "Observe and know each candidate before voting. Learn about his or her character, level of honesty and integrity. Never let those immersed in this immoral, God-forsaken, miserable world go forward as your leaders, because they will not represent you but only themselves." Jitu, as I later learned, drew a false conclusion from the sermon and he thought that the Imam was openly supporting me. He panicked: *I can't allow this. Sufi will win by a substantial majority.* Jitu,

121

clenching his fists, left the prayer hall and made his way towards the ablution area and as he expected, there was no one there. He dialled 999 on his Nokia and whispered: "The Imam of the Broadbent Sunni Mosque is preaching jihad and anti-Semitism."

Within minutes police surrounded the mosque just as the Imam descended the pulpit to lead the prayer. The congregation looked stunned and horrified as the police entered the mosque with dogs and wearing boots. They let loose two vicious K-9 German Shepherds among the terrified worshippers and arrested the Imam. The news of the Imam's arrest spread like wildfire, and more and more people came to the mosque. Police officers standing in the mosque's forecourt were attacked by the worshippers, angry at the disruption of their prayers. From their homes, only yards away from the mosque; two young men, Yousef and Jawed, were on their way to join the congregation when they saw the police with dogs. They retraced their footsteps, got the meat cleaver and a sword from their homes and came running to the mosque. Angered by the sight of the k-9s roaming freely in the prayer area, they picked their way through the frightened worshippers. When they reached the Imam, they hailed abuse at the officers: "Let him go you Islamophobic Nazis!"

"He is a terrorist," the officers retorted and instructed the k-9s to attack the two men.

Standing back-to-back, they launched a fierce counterattack that sent the officers and their animals scouring for safety among the worshippers. The officers barked further orders at the K-9s and the ferocious animals responded with more ferocity. This time the two angry worshippers pierced the animals' throats with their deadly weapons. The dogs just toppled over, whimpering in pain. Screaming worshippers pushed and shoved each other to reach the exit. Bright green prayer mats turned crimson as the blood seeped into the fabric of the carpet. The two police officers, backing away, shouted frantically into their walkie-talkies and within minutes, ambulances, fire brigades and a backup army of police officers arrived and surrounded the mosque, closing Broadbent and Wilson Street. Outside, I saw an injured police officer and recognised him as PC Davies from the King's Road Police Station. Shielding him from the angry crowd, I took him to the waiting ambulance. The officer thanked me and asked me to liaise with Superintendent Thomas to calm matters. I assured him, I was already thinking of doing precisely that but first, I had to find out how did all this begin.

I noticed, there was a sea of blue uniforms everywhere. Police cars and vans with flashing blue lights, ambulances, fire brigade and hundreds of worshippers, mostly residents thronged the area. There was hardly a space to move, chaos reigned where there was order minutes ago and lunacy replaced sanity. I watched armed officers and their dogs chase about eleven youths, including the two assailants, up Broadbent Street but to my surprise, five hundred yards down the road, they stopped and turned back. Why are they coming back? They should arrest the two assailants. What could be so important? I thought, and turned to face the Mosque.

My jaw dropped as I saw a large angry crowd coming up Wilson Street, other smaller crowds were coming up Newham Grove, Ashton Road and Barrington Street, shouting "Down with racism, down with islamophobia." Some were waving broomsticks, metal rods, and knives. Most were waving fists in the air. At the head of the crowd coming down Barrington Street were none other than my two lunatic compatriots, Jitu and Irfan! Asif stayed away. "Well, well, well," I said to myself, "What are they up to?" I had seen them in the mosque not long ago. Suddenly a horrific thought entered my mind. I dismissed it but it kept returning: *were Jitu and Irfan responsible for causing this chaos? Did they start all this and involve the police?* I had witnessed scenes like this during elections in the Indian subcontinent, specifically in Pakistan, but not here in England's Cosmopolitan City. Britain was the most peaceful country where people of all races, religions and beliefs were tolerated. *Bloody lunatics!* I thought. *They will do anything to win an election. Such monsters should be locked up and not tolerated, at any cost.*

Irfan was speaking into a large handheld loudspeaker. *Where did he get that from?* "Brothers listen for a minute," Irfan shouted into the loudspeaker as hundreds of men converged from other streets, onto a

123

large grassland area on Barrington Street. Judging from their facial expressions, I could tell that the crowd was highly charged. What lies have they been telling the crowd? "Friends! The mosque incident is the work of the nationalists and some Estone Socialists backed by Zionists. Only yesterday, their regional leaders made racist and Islamophobic remarks. They spoke of deporting Muslims to the countries of their origin thus confirming their parties' close links with the national front. Should we tolerate this blatant racism and Islamophobia? What do you say? Jitu and I say: *we should fight such bigots!*"

"We agree," the crowd replied and shouted: "down with racism and Islamophobia!"

The crowd continued to repeat the same mantra. However, Irfan put his hand up to quieten the crowd and shouted through the microphone. "Brothers the Estone Socialists are spreading nothing but lies among the electorate and we need to stop them. We need to make sure that our vote goes to the Democratic party on Thursday, May 5th. Our opponents tipped off the police and they violated the sanctity of the mosque." Irfan saw a large contingent of police move towards Barrington Street, having secured Broadbent Street and the area near the Mosque. Irfan and Jitu motioned to the crowd to backtrack along Anility Road towards King Street Police Station where they intended to further excite the crowd against the police. I thought how cunning they are blaming the nationalists and Estone Socialists when I was certain, it was one of them who called the police. The deadly duo had not expected the Police to clear the area so quickly. They suspected the police will put two and two together and work out who gave the police the wrong information about the Imam. Although some people still lingered around, just outside the police tape cordon, the attackers appeared to have eluded the police despite conducting the massive ground and aerial search.

Some police officers, encouraged by angry handlers of the dead German Shepherds, loaded police vans with unlucky bystanders, the majority had beards. They gave anyone with a long beard a vicious kick as a good measure and pushed them into the police vans. The prisoners now numbered about fifty – young and old, Asians, Africans and

Europeans but they all had one thing in common: *they were Muslims and wore long beards.* Men wearing black beards, white beards and red beards, among them the mosque Imam were all unceremoniously loaded into the vans and transported to the King's Road police station and locked up under the powers conferred by the Terrorism Act.

A group of teenagers, members of Al-Muhajir, a political group opposed to double standards in the UK foreign policy started gathering around the mosque. I repeatedly told them to desist from commenting on British foreign policy. "It's up to the government to plan the foreign policy in the best interest of Britain."

"No, they geared the British foreign policy to protect the tiny Zionist state by destroying Islam and Muslims. Just look at the United Nation's swift action in East Timor and the lack of it in Kashmir and Palestine. That's double standards. Don't you think? Your colleagues are better informed than you Sufi. Learn from them. You'll burn in hell."

"Rest assured, you'll be there before me. I'm happy with my little knowledge," I said sarcastically. There was no point arguing with these narrow-minded scoundrels. People like them act as self-styled religious brokers.

The two attackers who earlier ran away to evade police capture, now returned and began enticing young Muslims from the crowd to riot. They approached me and told me I was a coward. "How dare you support the Zionists. The British call themselves the bastions of democracy and justice, so why can't they do justice in Kashmir and Palestine? They've one policy for us Muslims and another for the rest of the world." Someone shouted that they had taken the Imam to the King's Road police station. A large angry crowd, headed by Jitu and Irfan, shouting and abusing police and the government moved towards the police station. To find out my notorious friends' motives, I joined the crowd. Now an army of Media men and women, having, learned about the incident, invaded the area. Reporters roamed the streets with their cameras resting on their shoulders with the camera lens giving the distinct impression of an eye protruding from their foreheads thus giving them the distinct appearance of having a third eye. A group of reporters from an Islamophobic TV news channel followed the crowd, interviewing anyone who would give the incident a terrorist twist. No one came forward except Chowdry Enam, a spokesperson for the Kharijites outfit, with a tendency to spew verbal diarrhoea against Israel and its friendly countries. Such outbursts gave the anti-Islamic forces an excuse to launch further attacks on Islam and Muslims. That is what the extremists, like the Kharijites, failed to understand.

When I reached the police station where the Imam was held, a large angry crowd had already gathered outside it and were shouting: *Release the Imam now, Down with Islamophobic Police* and *The Estone Socialists and Nationalists have sold Britain to the Zionists.* To my amazement, in the centre of the crowd stood Irfan with Jitu holding the speaker playing the role of the peacemakers when barely hours earlier they helped to create chaos on the streets of Estone ward. I was now convinced they created a dangerous situation just to prove they were the only ones defending Muslims. They seemed to have another card up their sleeve as I observed them encouraging the crowd to attack the police station! What evil game were they playing now? It was to show the voters that they were the only ones willing to defend them against racists and anti-Islamic elements. I believed by inciting the crowd, they were trying to force the chief superintendent to release the Imam so they can claim the credit for it and get the votes. *Cunning bastards*, I thought. Their focus was on winning the election by fair or unfair means. It did not matter to them. "Let me teach them a lesson," I said to myself.

I forced my way through the crowd, apologising as I pushed against a sea of bodies and got thrown from side to side like a pin Pong ball. Upon reaching the two idiots, I wrenched the microphone away from Irfan. "Brothers...Brothers...," I shouted and as the speakers crackled into life, hearing my voice, a large crowd forcing their way towards the police station stopped and turned to face me. The cordon of police officers, defending the police station, was relieved to see the crowd stop and this gave them time to reinforce the defence line. I said to the crowd that it was wrong of the two young men, to attack the police officers who were merely acting on information. The police accept that it was misinformation. "The question arises," I continued, "who was that person or persons who gave the police wrong information in the first place? That is the million-dollar question, isn't it brothers? Has anyone got the answer?" the crowd stood silent. There was no response. "These two men here, Jitu and Irfan can tell you how did all this start?" I said, "But I want you to promise me not to take the law into your own hands and when you find out who they are, you must hand them over to the police, nothing more." The entire crowd now appeared to be excited and surged even closer, trapping the escaping Jitu and Irfan. They looked pale and scared out of their wits. I smiled as I realised that the angry crowd blocked their escape route. "Jitu and Irfan here will help you find out who was involved in instigating this mindless violence. I'm going to request the chief to release the Imam," I said, handing the microphone to the shaking Jitu but did not directly name and shame them as I did not have the evidence. I hoped the chief will have it. The crowd lessened towards my right as some angry young men quickly moved towards the frightened pair. As I reached the entrance of the police station, I heard a crackle from the loudspeaker as they no doubt tried unsuccessfully to placate the crowd. I heard the clattering sound of the speaker falling on the tarmac above the clamour created by the crowd and was a sure sign that the two miscreants were in big trouble.

I left the crowd to deal with them and went inside the police station with the specific purpose of having the Imam released and calming the situation. I approached the reception and spoke briefly to an officer, who nodded, lifted the receiver, dialled a four-digit number, spoke briefly and replaced the handset. "The chief will see you in two minutes, sir," and went back to his desk. Superintendent Ricky Thomas was the "D" division commander, a much-respected officer who was known for his tact, fairness and prompt action. He was affectionately called the "chief" by his staff and members of the public alike. The Chief was a quiet, confident person, his taciturnity was often mistaken for stupidity by criminals. But he was a shrewd and forward-thinking officer and the criminals realised this when they ended up behind bars. He was a highly intelligent and down-to-earth man, committed to his job.

Exactly two minutes later the side door opened, and I was invited to see the chief. I followed a mature, bald officer into a spacious room with a black leather sofa set against the back wall and some reference books neatly arranged on the shelves above it. Behind the large mahogany desk sat the chief. A Dell computer, phone and an HP printer were the only items on the desk. "Take a seat Sufi please," the superintendent said pointing to the sofa. Before, I could say anything, the chief pre-empted me by saying that he was aware of the reason for my visit and thanked me for saving the officer's life earlier. The chief assured me he will release the Imam within five minutes. His officers had interviewed the Imam, and they were satisfied that he posed no threat to the safety of the public or the security of the country. The chief's unequivocal announcement that he found the Imam to be honest and frank pleased me immensely. "I'm, however, concerned about his anti-sematic views. He keeps attacking Zionists." I said in the Imam's opinion anti-Zionism is different from anti-Semitism. The imam genuinely believes that a vast majority of Jews also opposed Zionist policies. "Eh, chief be careful, they could also accuse you of anti-Semitism and that book could get you into trouble," I said pointing to a book on the shelf behind the chief. He looked horrified. "Which book? *Ulysses?* Are you talking about *Ulysses?* I've just started reading it. Just got to page 20."

"You're close to it now," I said gravely, "On page 28 this is exactly what James Joyce writes: *Mark my words Mr Dedalus, he said. England is in the hands of the Jews. In all the highest places: her finance, her press. And they are the signs of a nation's decay. Wherever they gather they eat up the nation's vital strength. I have seen it coming these years. As sure as we are standing here the Jew merchants are already at their work of destruction. Old England is dying.*"

"By Jove is that what it's said?" The chief exclaimed. "That's precisely what the justice and peace-loving pen of James Joyce has written," I said, "But the Imam doesn't agree with James Joyce. Old England maybe already dead, but it's not the work of Jews but other sinister forces. There is a difference between the two and that needs to be clearly understood. The Imam supports a world government by the Jews, chief but not by their unjust, relatives." The chief nodded vehemently and lifted the phone on his desk and dialled a number. A sergeant answered and in a thick, gruff voice said, "Sir."

"Sergeant, release the Imam, Mr Sahab is here to collect him."

"Yes, Chief."

"I think now I understand this anti-Semitism business in a new light," the chief said thoughtfully, replacing the handset. I was about to speak but a knock on the door interrupted me, and a bald head peeped, "Shall I bring the Imam here Sir?"

"Yes, bring him in here David".

The door opened wide and the youthful Imam, wearing a black turban entered the room. "Take a seat please *Maulana*," the Chief said politely and respectfully, showing that he had taken the trouble to know a bit more about Islam. The Imam appeared surprised at being called *"Maulana"* by a non-Muslim. Seeing the surprise on the Imam's face, the chief asked if he had said anything that the Imam did not like. The chief said he had done some reading on Islam (he knew a lot more than he admitted). He talked about the five pillars of Islam, the Quran and how the Muslims revered Jesus. The Imam smiled and seemed impressed but he took the chief and me by surprise when he said that he did not like being called *Maulana* because its literal meaning was: *our Lord*, and he regarded only Allah and his messenger to be worthy of such a title. "I prefer being called *Shaikh*." The chief smiled and said, "Thank you for that Shaikh sahib. I wanted to apologise for the mistreatment you received at the hands of some officers." This was an obvious reference to Imam's swollen lower lip and a deep cut to his nose. The Imam thanked him for his prompt release and a simple acceptance by the police that he had nothing to do with the disturbances but expressed his anger at dogs being let loose in the mosque. Acknowledging the error, the chief said that no doubt lessons have been learned and will be incorporated into the police standard operating procedures. But for the safety and well-being of the public and the security of the country, the police have the authority to act in a way the commanders deem fit. The Imam acknowledged this fact and asked the chief to deal with Satan Jitu and

129

his friend Irfan and asked his permission to leave. I also got up, shook the chief's hand and likewise asked him to deal with the two miscreants. The chief confirmed he was certain Jitu was involved but the initial call came from an unknown number. The chief said he prepared the initial details of police case (IDPC) to charge Irfan and Jitu but he could not prove the call emanated from his phone. "We'll arrest the devils but will have to release them once the crowd disperses. There's no way we can prove their involvement, as they possibly destroyed the phone and sim soon after calling the police." *Cunning bastards*, I said to myself again and could not believe how these two miscreants had created so much chaos, within minutes, for votes. I was happy thinking the crowd have taught them a lesson.

I walked out of the station, followed by the Imam and saw the chief looking down from the operation's room on the fourth floor onto the huge crowd that had now gathered outside the police station, still shouting at the top of their voices, cursing and waving placards and occasionally surging forward to break the police cordon. Had they succeeded in taking over the police station they would have damaged it and claimed revenge for the mosque attack. The chief had anticipated their moves and prevented the disaster. His rapid rise through the ranks was due to his uncanny ability to expect events and to prepare for them in time.

A group of demonstrators near the police station saw me and the Imam emerge from the automatic doors and surged forward, knocking part of the barricade down. For a moment, I thought the crowd would overpower the small contingent of Police officers protecting the left flank but the officers kept the barrier intact. I saw the chief peeking through the fourth-floor window with the walkie-talkie in his hand, barking orders. Within minutes Jitu and Irfan, along with the Kharijites ringleaders were arrested and taken inside the police station. The rest of the crowd followed me and the Imam along King's Road, back to the Mosque. Looking back, I saw the chief still standing on the fourth floor, smiling and waving.

# Chapter Fifteen

Following Jitu and Irfan's arrest, a spate of rumours circulated throughout the Estone ward like wildfire: *the police murdered the imam and attacked the worshippers, and Jitu and Irfan attacked the police and killed their dogs.* I gave up trying to replace them with facts. Practitioners of Himalayan politics in the Socialist Party continued to feed the public with further lies, not only about Irfan and Jitu but also about me: *Irfan and Jitu have also attacked Sufi, and he's on a life support machine* in the *city hospital.* There was chaos in the ward. No one knew what was going on. I had to turn my mobile off as I received call after call asking me if I was okay. Over the years, driven by an insatiable desire to win at any cost, activists of all parties acquired expertise in spreading rumours. This unnatural desire to win often lead to violence and this is especially true in African and Asian countries where activists kill and maim fellow citizens without compunction. Unscrupulous activists like Yoda, Irfan, and Jitu imported illegal election-winning practices into Britain, particularly in inner-city areas of England. Jitu and Irfan, however, blamed the British for leaving these skills behind when their special relationship, or more accurately, the colonisation of India, ended in 1947. According to Asif, the British, during their colonial rule, encouraged the use or misuse of the baradari system, bribery, corrupt practices, intimidation, lies, nepotism, character assassination, and murder of opponents to extend their rule. Some South Asian politicians coined the phrase "*Himalayan politics*" to describe the theory and practice of such an inhuman and evil form of politics. These evil practices still survive in the subcontinent, so I'm not sure to what extent the British were responsible for their perpetuity.

Such is the travesty of justice under the Himalayan political system that truth rarely survives for long. Under this despicable system, spreading lies enables crooked politicians to gain or regain the upper hand in elections. Recently, a European political party was re-elected with only 35% of the popular vote. So much for democracy and *"our way of life."* A parliamentary candidate and some council candidates and activists like Adie Gore, Jitu, Irfan, Paul Ali, Kalbi Jut, Himar Raja, and

Yoda Khan thrived under this unfair system in inner-city areas. What worried me most was the masterly way in which they escaped repercussions or punishment for fraud and personation over the years. During elections in inner-city wards, activists of all parties of Asian origin, particularly socialist activists, took full advantage of the baradari, or clan system. They reminded the head of every clan about the favours conferred on them and demanded a vote of the entire clan. If anyone refused to vote for the Estone Socialists, they victimised and alienated them from community events and reported them to various government departments like DWP and HMRC for real or imaginary fraud. The overseas political parties with branches in the UK may have been used to punish those refusing to vote for the Estone Socialists. Membership rules of all British political parties discouraged members from joining other political parties, but the local leadership of socialist, nationalist, and the democratic parties ignored these violations. Many Pakistani and Bangladeshi activists in all major British political parties held concurrent membership in the parties from the subcontinent. Such membership served a dual purpose. They received VIP protocol on visiting the countries in the subcontinent and could use their influence to bring trumped-up charges against opponents. Many voters understood these threats well and took them seriously, and because of this, the Estone Socialists always won in inner-city areas. These threats became a reality, only when the socialist candidates faced "good" candidates from the opposition parties, and they perceived an obvious danger of them losing seats to the opposition. Socialist candidates and their activists then resorted to unfair tactics to win. Strong opposition was rarely tolerated in inner-city areas. About me, they told the clan leaders as sweetly as possible, pretending to like me:

*Sufi is a good man, but he's no politician; he's too straightforward and too honest, so you won't get any grants, and he will inform the authorities about benefit fraudsters and drug dealers. Don't make the mistake of electing him.*

The candidates in the Cosmopolitan city council election and activists from the socialist party used another simple method, side by side with Himalayan politics, to win votes. They targeted the most vulnerable groups, the elderly, disabled, and illiterate migrants, and told lies about their opponents. A party that pursued a policy to reduce welfare benefits or limit immigration, bore the brunt of Himalayan politics. Even parliamentarians, like Adie Gore and Lenin Bourne, lied in their speeches during election campaigns. "If we don't win, remember that the Nationalists will deport all immigrants and stop or reduce welfare benefits. On hearing these lies, the inner-city voters got the impression that their presence in the UK and payment of their benefits depended on the Socialist Party's victory. I was worried about the threats of violence against Bangladeshi, and Pakistani voters. There was a risk to voters of arrest under false pretences when they visited their country of origin. The voters took such threats seriously, especially when made by well-known community leaders with affiliations to corrupt politicians and police officers in Bangladesh and Pakistan. Every year, since 1998, I wrote to the Cosmopolitan City Council's election office about these threats, but they took no action. I was convinced that neither the electoral commission nor the council's election office knew about rogue activists' threats to voters while travelling abroad. Branches of the Bangladesh Awami League (BAL), Pakistan People's Party (PPP), and Pakistan Muslim League (N) (PMLN) existed in the major cities in the UK, and some activists held duplicate membership. Co-operation existed between the members of the overseas and the local UK political parties. They helped and assisted each other in all matters of mutual interest, including electoral fraud. My supporters consistently argued that, like other communities, Asians should only become members of British political parties and ignore overseas parties. In my view, the activists and the candidates holding dual membership were committing a moral, if not a criminal, offence.

"Oh, to hell with them", I said to myself and Asif as we left the campaign office. Asif looked a bit worried and I asked him if he was feeling okay.

"Sufi, the long-range weather forecast is not encouraging. Rain is indicated on May 5th."

"Okay, Asif, thanks for that. Let's send an SMS to all our activists to be in the campaign office by ten o'clock tomorrow morning so we can plan for the polling day."

As we descended the stairs, we heard the call for the evening prayer. Asif wanted to pray as well. From our office, Broadbent Mosque was only two minutes away. We offered the compulsory three units of prayer, called the *fard* and left the mosque. My car had broken down so I asked Asif if he would drop me home. When I got into his car, my phone rang. It was Jane Grant.

"Sufi! Sufi!" She could barely control her excitement. I noted both fear and excitement in her voice. "Calm down, Jane. What's happened?"

"Its... Its Mirza... he's... "Oh, please just get here quickly."

Several thoughts passed through my mind, but it was not the time to speculate. Jane and Mirza were neighbours and lived in Druid's Lane, only a couple of miles away. I asked Asif to drop me there.

# Chapter Sixteen

Jane was already waiting for me outside No.11 when I arrived. I asked Asif to ensure that Jitu and Irfan finish delivering the leaflets. And complete the door-to-door campaign on the three remaining roads in the triangle. Jane briefed me about events so far. Mirza was holding two police officers, a PC Wood and a PC Evans at knifepoint. The officers came to arrest his brother, Yousaf, for the mosque attack and for killing two police dogs. I told Jane that I knew about the incident as I was there at the time. She asked me if I could persuade Mirza to release the officers. An armed response unit was on the way and they may kill him. "Things are bad already Sufi. There's an Islamophobic police officer here. He's the one standing by the gate, Sergeant Jones. He was swearing at all Muslims and vilifying Islam and the prophet. Luckily, Inspector Smith, the one standing next to him is a bit sane and has told him to shut his, gob. It was the sergeant, who summoned the armed response unit. The captive officers are also to blame for the way they approached the whole thing."

"It may be the officers' fault Jane, but Mirza has no right to threaten them with a knife. But knowing Mirza as I do, they must've done something terrible to get him so mad."

I thanked Jane and went over to talk to the Inspector. I told him that Mirza was my friend and I wanted to try to resolve the situation. I asked for ten minutes. The sergeant told me to get lost as I had no business there. "ARU will sort the bastard out. All Muslims should be dead." I suggested to the inspector that it may be wise to remove the sergeant. As his presence may infuriate the crowd that had gathered. I notified the Inspector that the police officers, Tracy and Richard were also my friends. That surprised him, but it made it easier for him to make his mind up. He gave me permission to go in and sort the mess out. I saw around a hundred Muslim youths standing around. It worried me that they may cause trouble. They had overheard Sergeant Jones's racist outburst against Islam and Muslims. The situation had the potential to get out of hand. The Inspector recognised the gravity of the situation and asked the sergeant to sit in the car and asked me to go in. "You've exactly ten minutes Mr Sahab. For your information, the ARU are on standby," he whispered, "I've not summoned them yet. Jane told me the captive officers may've brought all this upon themselves. Your friend seems to be more rational than I thought," the inspector winked. Most British police officers kept calm even under difficult circumstances. They made rational decisions based on available facts.

"Are you going to let the terrorists run the police department, Smithy?" The Sergeant shouted. The inspector glared at him and I shook my head in disgust. Mirza shouted from the bedroom: "If anyone enters the house, I'll stab the officers."

Druid's Lane was a small cul-de-sac and number 11, Mirza's house, was the end terrace house. Jane's house was number 9. The door to no.11 was open. I went inside. "Mirza, it's me I'm coming upstairs."

"The Armed response unit is on the way Sufi; you keep out otherwise they'll kill you too."

"Oh, shut up. I don't have to listen to you Mirza, I'm coming upstairs. We'll die together if it comes to that."

I saw him standing behind a mahogany desk. Tracey and Richard sat on chairs, with their hands tied at the back. I greeted them and asked them not to worry, no harm will come to them. "You know them Sufi?" Mirza got more agitated.

"Yes, I know them. What Happened?"

"They were aggressive from the moment they entered my house, Sufi. They shouted at me to produce Yousaf. I told them that unknown to me he had flown out to Pakistan. They said I was telling lies. You know I don't lie Sufi. They got me mad. They think I'm Yousaf. Can you understand that?"

"Officers, I know Yousaf. I also know Mirza. He's not a liar. There has been some misunderstanding."

"Sufi, we told your friend that we made a mistake. We did ask for his identity but he didn't listen."

"That was a reasonable request from the officers, Mirza. Why didn't you show them your passport or driving license?"

"How could I? They got me down on the floor and were about to handcuff me when I released myself from their clutches and turned the tables on them."

"We accept, our actions weren't exactly fair but to hold us at knifepoint is not the way forward."

"They're right Mirza. You should release the officers immediately." Mirza placed the knife on the table and moved to untie the knots. I picked up the knife and threw it on top of the high wardrobe. Mirza kept venting his anger. "Why do some Politicians and mass media, hold all Muslims responsible, for the actions of a few? The extremists are the Kharijites. Yousaf got with the wrong crowd. So, why blame me? I didn't attack the police in the mosque. Can anyone blame all Jews for the actions of Zionists? Or all Christians for the actions of neocons? Or all Hindus for the actions of RSS thugs? So, no one should lay the blame at the door of a Religion for the inhuman actions of some of its so-called adherents."

"I wouldn't take this line of thought too far my friend, these are dajjal times and the truth is not valued. You may end up in jail, or in Guantanamo bay, lose your life or become one of many victims of pandemics. Such incidents, will increase in frequency and lead to considerable loss of life. There'll be more concentration of wealth in the hands of the few. It will lead to a final move towards a world government, led by you know who."

"Why don't they understand that we love the prophet more than our lives? And if anyone insults him, the pain disintegrates the very core of our being. And an inevitable violent reaction ensues. That causes terrorism. Aren't they intelligent enough to understand that?"

"Yes, my friend. They're super intelligent. Make no mistake about that but the destruction of Islam is part of the plan. When we react with anger or violence, it gives our enemies an excuse to attack Islam. They want to portray Islam as a radical ideology, and Muslims as violent. All I'm saying is that there's no need for us to defend Allah, the prophet or Islam. Look, at what has happened throughout the Western world after September eleven. Despite the persecution, there's been a sharp rise in conversions to Islam. Leave it to God my friend. What does God say in the book? *Makaru wa makarallah, wallaho khairulmakayreen* – they plan, Allah, plans too, and he's the best of planners. Today, Islam is the fastest-growing religion in the world. And within a short time, it'll overtake Christianity as the largest world religion. So, sit back and enjoy. What's written in *Kitabun Mubeen* (the open book) will happen. No one can change it."

"They want world government Sufi. Or a new world order, whatever, but why vilify Islam and Muslims?"

"Theirs is a reason for that but I support a world government, it's the need of the hour."

I asked everyone to go out. The police officers came out first followed by me and Mirza. A heated discussion ensued outside when the waiting police officers moved to arrest Mirza. I asked the officers not to arrest him as it would be unfair. The two police officers accept there was a misunderstanding. The officers confirmed this and asked the inspector not to arrest Mirza. Sergeant Jones was livid and blasted the two officers as cowards. They responded by telling him to resign as he wasn't mentally fit to remain in the force. The sergeant left the scene in anger. Inspector Smith called the armed response unit and told them they weren't needed. Satisfied with the fair outcome of the incident, the youths dispersed. Peace and tranquillity reigned in the area.

I left Jane and Mirza chatting together, said goodbye to them and asked Richard and Tracey to drop me home. "Why can't humans live in peace and harmony?" I asked no one in particular. "Aren't we all the descendants of Adam?" I rang Asif and asked him to make sure that all activists come to the office in the morning. I went to bed. It took mere ten minutes to restore sanity in the area, but it left me tired and anxious. Anything could've happened.

# Chapter Seventeen

Almost all activists except Irfan, Jitu and Paul arrived on time and I began the meeting without them. I wasn't worried about Paul, but I couldn't understand why both Irfan and Jitu were absent. They got released from police custody without charge. JB and one other "high-ranking" council leader had asked the police to release them without charge. They didn't even receive a caution. This was unusual and made me worry a bit. People like that should receive punishment. Otherwise, their criminal activity will not stop and their ego become more inflated. They pulled a fast one by destroying the evidence of the phone call. Their meticulous planning deceived even the police and they escaped punishment. Salman and Sharma, my spies in socialists' camp, said that while they were out leafletting in Fenton Road, they saw Jitu, Irfan and Yoda enter the *den*. They met Paul and discussed discrediting me. All three had a lot to drink and danced with Miriam and Anne, the local prostitutes. They then went to the campaign office and sorted some leaflets out. But Irfan told them to go home, "Why should we work, while Sufi's out enjoying himself. I'm going to a meeting." I wasn't enjoying myself; me and Asif were conducting a door-to-door campaign at the time. Irfan told them he had a meeting with the election agent in the council chamber. "Don't yield your lovely body to Martin, my darling Irfan, otherwise JB will never forgive you," Jitu teased him and Yoda laughed. Irfan didn't take the remark kindly. Jitu and Yoda realised this and ran down the stairs. Irfan threatened to smash the bundle of leaflets over their heads. All three finally stopped by the front garden of Tania's house on Fenton Road. She'd overheard some of their conversation. She phoned me and warned me to be vigilant and not to trust the trio. To my disappointment, she couldn't tell me exactly what the trio said. She had seen them sitting on her front garden wall. She could hear them through the open window of her front room. But her mother, unfortunately, interrupted her. All she heard was something to do with my arrest. And the end of my political career. It did sound as if they were planning something big.

I dismissed the thought. Whatever they were planning will become obvious soon. I carried on with the meeting. Around sixty pairs of eyes now focused on me, awaiting instructions for tasks on the polling day. I selected ten activists to act as polling station agents. I assigned seven activists to pick up disabled voters. And fifteen volunteers to distribute last-minute leaflets. The magnificent fifteen will also knock on doors to get the voters out. Four volunteers agreed to take charge of the public address system- Asif Kazak and Hasan Ali to take turns to make announcements in Urdu and Bengali. Leroy and Nawaz to drive the cars for them, mounted with loudspeakers. It was a good way of reminding voters to go out and cast their votes. I saw Jitu and Irfan standing at the entrance. They were late. I beckoned them to come to the stage. My phone rang. During election time, it always rings at an inappropriate time, one could be sure of that. The pair brightened and lifted their eyebrows when they heard it ring. I asked the caller to hold for a minute. "Where have you guys been? You look thrilled. Oh, I know you got away without charge. Congratulations." They nodded but said nothing. I pressed the secrecy button on the phone and asked them to continue with the meeting. "I've got a caller online, asking me to meet her and she may get around five hundred votes for us."

"Oh, that's great. Good luck Sufi," they said. They behaved as if they arranged the call. Did they arrange it? I contemplated seeking clarification from them about the call but decided against it.

I noted the caller was not on my contact list. I resumed the call as she was offering to get around five hundred votes for us. I didn't recognise the voice, but she identified herself as Jennifer Jackson from 33 Love Lane. She asked me to see her and she will get around five hundred votes from the Afro-Caribbean community. She said she has some questions for me about housing and other matters of concern to the community. I was sure I heard the name before, but memory failed me. There was no harm in seeing her as five hundred extra votes would lead to our victory. The trio agreed to continue the meeting, so I went out.

It was only two 'o'clock in the afternoon and I wanted to see Jennifer as soon as possible. I didn't want the Estone Socialists to get her on their side. I didn't know what was in store for me. I knew something was being planned against me but votes mattered most. If anyone promised votes, I went there without hesitation. I paid no attention to warnings from friends to be extra vigilant. When visiting strangers' homes, "take precaution Sufi. Wear a small body camera or keep a small USB recorder in your pocket."

Unknown to me, the evil plan was set to activate as soon as I reached love lane and entered Jenifer's house. They planned to end my political career at that time. Unless I could change the direction or minimise the damage. My analytical mind will have to come up with an urgent and viable solution. I had tried to understand what form the plan could take. The arrest would mean, instant disqualification. I wasn't sure what was the aim of the plan. Was it to discredit me? Or was it to get me disqualified? Discrediting me would mean, I won't get the required number of votes to win or get fewer votes and come poor third. In that case, the following year they would deselect me in favour of Jitu. They also had another plan. A rumour circulated, in Estone ward and neighbouring wards about a second plan; plan B. Or was that plan A and the one against me was plan B? I couldn't tell but the source of the report was credible. It said the Estone Socialists had a foolproof plan to get votes by fraud and win all three seats. So, was the elusive plan to do with election fraud and not against me? But Tania said they were talking about my arrest. Whatever the truth, it would soon become manifest in one form or another. As the election was two days away, I dismissed the troubling thoughts. I got out of the office and headed for my car, parked around the corner on Broadbent Street. I met five of my supporters on the way and they greeted me with thumbs up.

"Are you still campaigning door-to-door Sufi?" Munir asked.

"Yes bro, off to love lane now."

"Oh, good luck Sufi. Are you after love or votes?"

"Both mate!" I said and they burst out laughing. They said goodbye and I got into the car. Before leaving the office, I saw Irfan, Jitu and Paul whispering to each other. I couldn't get the scene out of my mind. Then, to my surprise, they started dancing or what looked like a dance. They were trying to avoid activists from noticing the brief exhibition of joy. They rubbed their hands in glee too. This proclamation of joy was very touching, but what was it in aid of? Must be to do with their release from custody. That was a good enough reason to celebrate or was it for a more sinister reason? Only time will tell. It took me ten minutes to arrive in Love Lane.

# Chapter Eighteen

"I bet he's responding to the call from her," Asif said joyously.

"Yes, I think so too," Irfan was ecstatic. "The stage is set; the lovers will meet in love lane and Sufi will be no more. There will be no time to get a replacement for Sufi. So, I, Asif and Yoda should win. Oh, what a plan! Perfecto." And they started dancing again.

"Oh look, when the cat is away, the mice will play," Adam said in his loud and gruff voice, and everyone laughed.

The trio looked visibly shaken by the laughter. Irfan recovered sufficiently to grab the loudspeaker and continue the meeting.

The worshippers were entering the Quba Mosque on Love Lane for the afternoon prayer when I knocked on Jennifer's door. I thought of praying first but wanted to be on time for the appointment. There was still half an hour left before the commencement of the *Zohar* (afternoon) prayer. About twenty minutes would be sufficient for the meeting with Jennifer and I could join prayers after. *Perfect*, I thought and rang the bell again. I stood in the small front garden by the white PVC French doors. There was an extra door inside the entrance and I guessed the hall began thereafter. From the outside, the terraced house looked dilapidated, in need of pointing and exterior painting due to chipped brickwork and rotten windows. The roof carried old and broken black slates. I guessed it was rented. As I waited for Jennifer to open the door, Gul Khan passed me on his way to the mosque and greeted me, saying I looked smart. I returned the greetings and was surprised to hear Gul Khan's negative comment about Jennifer. I got the gist of what he said but couldn't understand the subtle message contained in Khan's remark.

"Hope you're only after her votes, not her other merchandise. You're a pious person Sufi, hopefully, you'll not come to any harm but be careful. Rumours circulating in the ward suggest that you're the target of a sinister plan. May your God protect you, my friend. Good luck".

Khan shook hands with me and made his way to the mosque just as Jennifer opened the door.

"Perfect timing Mr Sahab. I'm sorry I was in the bathroom."

I was momentarily taken aback by her looks but recovered immediately. She was no ordinary-looking African girl. She was tall, slim, light-skinned, curvy and stunning. It would not be an exaggeration to say that beauty seemed to ooze from every pore on her skin. Not only her facial features but her entire body was perfectly proportioned, and her beauty affected me to the core but I recovered from the shock almost instantaneously, which appeared to surprise Jennifer. The look on her face told me: *you haven't even noticed how beautiful I am.*

"No problem Miss…?" She hadn't told me her surname.

"Jenifer Jackson. But you must stick with Jennifer Mr Sahab."

"Well in that case you call me Sufi, please. That's fair."

She smiled, bowed and stepped aside to allow me to enter the house.

I passed through the second door into a spacious room. I had expected a hallway but there was none. I discerned a subtle and unexpected change in lighting. The small circular chandelier emitted an eerie diffuse crimson light around the room. I noticed the wall between the traditional front and rear reception rooms had been removed to create this large, tastefully decorated and furnished room. I was unable to pinpoint the exact colour of the curtains but they looked pale green in the diffused light. I frowned as I saw the curtains were drawn, shutting out the bright afternoon sunlight.

"Have a seat Sufi, please. I will bring tea and biscuits and we'll have a chat." Jennifer disappeared into the kitchen, shutting the door behind her.

Instead of sitting down, I decided to explore the room. From the centre of the room emerged a spiralling staircase that seemed to weave its way to the floor above. There were expensive black leather sofas to the left and a massive home TV screen with a glass cabinet next to it. In the furthest corner, a seven-shelf mahogany bookcase rested against the wall. Its bottom four shelves were empty. I was surprised to notice that in addition to various versions of the Bible (King James, American Standard and Twentieth Century New Testament) there was a copy of an English translation of the Quran and Bhagwat Gaeta filed side by side on the top shelf. There were philosophy books by Kant, Descartes, Rumi and Alama Iqbal – the poet-philosopher of the East on the second shelf. Nursing, psychology, anatomy and physiology books filled the third shelf. For some reason, my attention lingered on nursing books. My wife was a matron in the city hospital. I was sure I heard the name Jennifer Jackson before. Did Iram mention Jennifer's name? I decided against asking her about it.

Five Luxurious armless leather chairs were placed behind the table by the bay window, linking the Sofas and the bookcase. Curiously, one luxurious leather chair with some electronic gadgets protruding from it was placed in the centre of the room, facing the home cinema. A green light emanated from one of the gadgets, indicating that the chair was plugged in. It must be an electrically operated reclining or a messaging chair.

Jennifer emerge from the kitchen carrying a tray with a decorated China teapot, matching cups and saucers and a plate full of milk chocolate biscuits, slices of almond-walnut cake and viscount biscuits. *My favourite stuff*, I thought. *How does she know my likes and dislikes?* It was uncanny. *Must be a coincidence*, I thought.

"Here we're Sufi. Have a seat here please." Jennifer indicated the seat, next to her, on the sofa and placed the tray on the large glass coffee table and began pouring the hot, steaming tea.

"How's the campaign going Sufi?" Jennifer asked, handing me the cup, and moving the plate towards me.

"Better than expected Jennifer. And now with your help, I am sure we should win. If I know anything about psephology, five hundred votes swing from Estone Socialists to Democrats will mean a reduction of around one thousand votes for Estone Socialists. Over 90% swing to us is already ensured courtesy of nationalist and socialist blunders in Iraq and the fact that the sitting councillors are out of touch with the public!"

"Glad to be of some help! Is everything okay between you and other Democratic candidates?" Jennifer asked thoughtfully and continued, "Some voters think that they're colluding with Yoda against you?" Her up-to-date knowledge about the events and rumours circulating in the Estone ward surprised me. She must be seeing a lot of local people every day. I wondered what work she did.

"Maybe, they're working against me but I'm not so sure. I've plan B. I've got at least one thousand ardent supporters, who will only vote for me if these rumours are true. This will ensure my victory. This plan will only be implemented if Asif and Irfan go all out against me. My friends are keeping a very strict eye on them."

"Oh, that's good. You seem to have covered yourself."

"Hope so. The only drawback is that electorate in inner-city wards is divided into various *baradari*s. This makes it......"

Jennifer interrupted: "Yes, I've heard a lot about *Himalayan politics, the baradari system and influence from overseas.* How will these affect your election Sufi?"

"You've already impressed me and it seems to me you know a lot about Asian culture," I said pointing to her impressive collection of books on Asian philosophy and religion. "As I see it, the problem lies with some Socialist candidates and activists," I paused. "Over the years, they've developed a foolproof election strategy based on the Himalayan politics; whereby they select a head of each clan, do favours for them, and get them to collect votes from everyone belonging to that clan. It's like snatching votes or obtaining them by coercion if you know what I mean."

"I know exactly what you mean Sufi," Jennifer said sweetly, placing her hand on my knees. She looked from head to toe, and appeared to be admiring my athletic body "I've closely studied the psyche of many of these so-called community leaders from the Indian subcontinent based in the inner-city areas and honestly can't see how they can live with their conscience."

"I don't know either. But I do fear for the future of many people from the Indian subcontinent. They don't hesitate to tell lies, stab you in the back and exaggerate. They'll do anything to win elections and make money. Stealing, drug dealing, fraud, deception, they'll stop at nothing. Their motto seems to be: *make money come what may!*"

"Majority are Muslims, aren't they? Would you agree Sufi?"

"I think to some extent you're right. But religion doesn't tell them to lie, cheat, steal or commit fraud. I hope you're not insinuating that?"

"No! I'm not. No religion tells anyone to do those things. Islam is a way of life and it hurts me to see its followers completely lost these days. There appears to be no appreciation, especially by the Muslims, of the immense scientific, mathematical and social contributions made by their religion for the advancement of humanity." Some biscuits were remaining on the plate but my tea had finished. Jennifer smiled as I stared at the teapot. She poured some more.

"True," I said munching a viscount, "but I believe, it's due entirely to the fact that currently out of around a billion Muslims over 70% are illiterate. It seems to me that they've been deliberately kept that way. The illiterate often become the fodder of the priests and *lotas* of the politicians. The remaining 30% are the rich ruling class. Opposition parties in Pakistan and the government accuse each other of acting as nothing more than American and European *poodles*. The very people who brought knowledge and prosperity to the rest of the world are now the living dead."

"Yes, that's one way of looking at it Sufi but I thought it was because they don't follow the Quran," Jennifer said moving her hand from my knee to the top of the thigh and back again. She was talking about the Quran and Islam so I assumed she knew about the limitations placed by sharia law on intimate interactions between men and women. "Muslims are specifically told not to take disbelievers as friends and helpers," she continued, "but look at the leaders of every Muslim country; are they not friends with Europeans and Americans?" She carried on to say that around fifty-eight countries call themselves *Islamic* but they are mostly poor and powerless to even defend themselves. They regard their enemies as friends and seek their help daily and display an uncanny hatred for each other! Murdering and maiming men, women and children, their brothers, sisters and future generations without compunction; without a hint of humanity in them. How sad is that? The holy book is full of wisdom and knowledge; the first welfare state was established in Medina but the Muslims. You people have handed all good things over to the West. What remains are dozens of sects, each at the other's throat. I don't understand what's happening with Muslims?"

"I agree with your analysis, Jennifer. I also think, one reason for the decline is abandoning scientific research and replacing it with despotism and nepotism, living a life of luxury and extravagance and destruction of the Islamic state on the first of November nineteen twenty-two; the other being the direct interference of the European states in carving up the Middle East into smaller states and installation of puppet regimes to eradicate opposition and to exploit and plunder their resources and keep the masses illiterate. You only have to read Tom Fromkin's book: *the peace to end all peace!*"

"Yes, I've read it and many others. I read in the hadith that gaining knowledge is the duty of every Muslim. So, what happened?"

"You see Jennifer, the masses haven't been allowed to gain knowledge. That would've put the mullahs and the ruling elite out of business. For instance, there's supposed to be no priesthood in Islam. Every Muslim who attends a mosque to offer prayers is expected to be able to lead the prayer if needed. In Christianity, Hinduism and Judaism, priests, pundits and rabbis are expected to lead the prayers and interpret the religion for the masses, not so in Islam."

"So, you're saying Sufi that in Islam the so-called Mullahs or Imams are not necessary?"

"Precisely. As you said, gaining religious knowledge as well as knowledge of the sciences, humanities and the arts is incumbent on every Muslim, male or female."

"Oh, my God! I think I understand now Sufi. As the *Uma* is dependent on the mullahs for the interpretation of Islam so it's easy for any rogue mullah to manipulate the masses and interpret Islamic teachings, including the Quran to fit their whims and desires. Am I right?"

"Absolutely. You've got it, Jennifer. But let's not dwell on these matters as I don't combine religion with politics. International politics, democracy and the rule of law are outside the domain of local government and fall within the authority of the Parliament and foreign affairs. I don't think any political party will select me to stand as their parliamentary candidate."

"But we can't forget the current turmoil looming over the world due to demands from an unknown and powerful entity for coercive compliance with the so-called *new world order*. Anyway, I thought in Islam religion and politics can't be separated. Don't some of the world powers fear political Islam more than anything else?"

"Maybe Jennifer but secularism is the champion of the day in the West and we alone can't preach integration of religion and politics."

Despite my reservations, Jennifer Jackson went on to consider the fateful events of Tuesday the eleventh of September two thousand and one. No peace and justice-loving person, the world over, could forget the tragic events of that fateful day. September eleven, she thought, would be remembered throughout the world as *a day on which a brutal and barbaric attack was launched on America* leading to the alleged loss of some fifty thousand lives as it was first, claimed. The figure was changed to twenty-five thousand, then nine thousand, then six thousand and CNN finally settled for *around four thousand innocent lives lost*. Whatever the figure,

149

no doubt it was a world-changing event, whether planned by internal or external forces only time will tell. First reports suggested the evil deed was committed by a group of Muslims, largely of Saudi Arabian descent, described by the biased Western press as *Islamic* terrorists. Terrorism has no religion, then why say so? That question will go unanswered for many decades. The culprits were thought to be Saudi Arabian, so why attack Afghanistan, Iraq, Syria and Libya? Jennifer thought. That September eleven should also be remembered in the Muslim world as the beginning of an unprecedented attack on their religion and way of life. For the evil acts of a few, the entire leaderless, helpless Muslim *Uma* was held to ransom by the so-called Democratic, free and civilised world. Soon after the attack, the entire Muslim Uma was labelled as barbaric and uncivilised by politicians and the media. The two Bs set about dismantling the *Muslim Uma* and teaching them a lesson they will never forget. Words like *"Islamic terrorists"*, *"crusades"*, *"infinite justice"*, *"Socialist Islam"*, *"evil ideology"*, *"extremist ideology"*, *"our way of life"* and *"reactionary Islam"* were freely dispensed as a bitter medicine for the Muslims to swallow. The forces of "democracy", "free world" and "civilised society" set about the task of avenging the loss of innocent American lives by spilling the blood of innocent Iraqis and Afghani Muslims as if their lives didn't matter. By using weapons of mass destruction, they blew many innocent men, women and children into smithereens, calling it, *collateral damage.*

"I can't disagree with your analysis Jennifer. The simple fact is there is too much injustice and falsehood in the world. Unless truth and justice prevail, humanity is doomed. I believe nationalism is a disease that should be eradicated. No more national boundaries. No more interference with the natural movement of people, goods and services. A world government is needed to pool the resources to eradicate poverty and seek new frontiers; it's time to conquer the universe, not each other."

"No doubt you've noble and lofty political and social aims Sufi for the new world order." She clapped and leaned forward like a lioness ready to pounce on her prey. "But what are your proposals for us ordinary folks in Estone ward? Housing? School places? Council Tax issues – housing benefit and council tax reductions?" She uttered the words slowly and in a measured tone that imparted to me a sense of aggression and a tinge of unfriendliness which to a degree, worried me. Why this sudden change in her demeanour?

"Okay, no problem. That's why I'm here. I will briefly answer your questions, now that we've sorted the world," I laughed, Jenifer didn't. "To tell you the truth there is very little a city councillor can do for the electorates. Let's take housing. A vast majority of the electorate are living in privately owned or rented houses with the local government housing stock utterly depleted by the Thatcher government's right-to-buy legislation. Sitting council tenants smelled an opportunity there and bought their homes immediately. Councils across England blame the central government for imposing financial constraints in terms of borrowing caps and prudential borrowing capacity on building homes and other investments. And...

"Oh, I don't get these technical terms Sufi. Explain to me in simple terms, why didn't the council build new homes to replace the depleted stock?" Jennifer interrupted

"I think it was nothing more than the successive governments' policies of not funding any large-scale council house building. It costs money and Councils have a significant role to play in dealing with affordable social housing but the government needs to financially unchain them to borrow money to build houses which can then be rented out. RTB needs to end to make house building a viable proposition."

"What is RTB? And, isn't there a severe shortage of school places in Estone?"

"Sorry, RTB is *right to buy*. And yes, you're right there are fewer places and long waiting lists in schools that have resulted from new residents settling in the area from the European Union and other parts of the world but resources needed to expand schools and build new ones to mitigate the shortages never materialised."

"I also want to ask about drug trafficking in our city, particularly in this ward. If elected, what are your plans to eradicate this rapidly spreading social evil?" She continued to complain about large groups of boys constantly hanging around on the street corners using drugs and being targeted by drug dealers. Young lives are destroyed beyond belief. The communities must be saved from unscrupulous drug dealers.

I promised her if elected I would regularly bring the issues discussed to the notice of respective cabinet members and the police. Alleviation of Estonians' concerns is my priority. I emphasised that I couldn't possibly guarantee there would be positive responses from the relevant local or central government departments.

Jenifer appreciated what I was trying to do. She couldn't understand why councillors and Parliamentarians were impotent to do much for their citizens. "What's the point of electing councillors and MPs if they can't solve our problems?" Some councillors say that the faceless bureaucrats run the show. They're the real rulers."

Everything costs money and money is a scarce commodity. They know this and yet most politicians promise the moon. It's the poor suckers, the voters, who fall for the false promises. "Didn't Churchill once say that the best argument against democracy was a five-minute conversation with an average voter?"

"True Sufi. And someone also said that *Politics is the art of looking for trouble, finding it everywhere, diagnosing it incorrectly, and applying the wrong remedies.* Everything is changing. People are taking their comedians more seriously than the politicians."

Jenifer went on to vent her anger on politicians and said politics is pointless without religion. Without religion, politics can become like a misguided missile that can unleash havoc on the world. Religion was needed to instil compassion into political decisions.

Capitalism, communism, socialism and secularism were nothing more than veils behind which tyrants and oppressors hid their ugly faces. I agreed to some extent but on a more personal level I believed if capitalism was imbued with care and compassion, it would go a long way to solve social, economic and political issues confronting humanity today. Jennifer said, there was no compassion left in the world. For the last two years or so she had been trying to get her landlord, Midland Housing, to repair her house without success. She said even housing associations were masters unto themselves and didn't care about their tenants. Midland housing was the worst social landlord in Cosmopolitan City, she thought. Jennifer confided in me about Asian voters who always abused and insulted the Socialist party candidates for failing to represent them in the council, failing to take up their routine enquiries about housing, council tax and waste collection and yet always ended up voting for the *same failed* candidates and re-elected them. *What the hell?* I said that in my opinion, Asian voters easily fall prey to practitioners of Himalayan Politics and were largely governed by their hearts, not minds and simply followed the *baradari* or *clan* system and acted on the erroneous belief, spread by some Socialist Party activists that it was the Socialist party which not only allowed the immigrants to enter UK for settlement but also dished out dole money to them and as a result of this generosity, they were obliged to return the favour and show gratitude to the party by voting for its candidates; good or bad! Jennifer reminded me of what a famous politician once said: *her function in life was not to be a politician in parliament but it was to get something done and called upon the voters not to elect urchins to parliament.*

We burst out laughing. "Are you thinking the same as me? There are far too many urchins in city councils and the parliament nowadays," Jenifer said.

"I don't know about Parliamentarians," I said, "but there were certainly some urchins in the socialist party who relied heavily on the baradari system to get elected and managed to become councillors from time to time. They're part-timers, nothing useful has ever been done by such people."

Very few parliamentarians and councillors match the criteria of perfect public servants. Sovereignty belongs to people under a true democracy. So why do people continue to suffer? That means there's no true democracy. The power lies in the hands of the few and the number of dedicated Democrats continues to dwindle. The three countries in the Indian subcontinent were ruled by those, indifferent to the suffering of their people. They sat in Parliament all day long, twiddling their thumbs, rising occasionally to briefly utter some rubbish; clap or laugh at someone else's sick joke and sit down again. Some manage to even rob the public purse and laugh all the way to the bank, not even bothering to thank those who made all this possible for them!

"Jennifer, there is a saying I came across the other day about the relationship between the public and the politicians. It goes something like this: *The thieves choose members of the public to rob them but the public chooses some politicians who not only rob them financially but rob the future of their children too!*"

"Right Sufi, good point," she clapped. "Thieves like Irfan and Jitu are always on the lookout for victims, like residents in Estone ward to further their agenda! Talking of agendas, I've heard Irfan and Jitu promise Muslim voters that they'll support the Palestinians against Israeli occupation, oppression, plundering and exploitation of their resources. I promise," she said, raising her hands, "this is the last discussion topic Sufi and then we get down to business."

"I think there are currently two major flash points which can start the third world war. One is Kashmir, and the other is Palestine. In Kashmir, the entire Indo-Pak subcontinent can undergo total annihilation as the warring countries have a considerable nuclear arsenal which the loser will not hesitate to use. In Palestine the situation is different. The two nations can exist side by side provided all Muslim countries recognise the state of Israel. Understandably, the Israelis are apprehensive about their security and fear for their existence and have refused to go back to the June 1967 borders. This is their prerogative.

All holy books of the Aramaic religions, including the Quran, contain references to the holy land being given, *in writing*, to the Israelis by God Almighty......"

"Wow I didn't know that," Jennifer interrupted. "I think not even many Muslims know about the Quranic assertions regarding the holy land. Amazing! Extraordinary! That's enough of politics for today, Sufi. Let's play a game."

"Game Jennifer? What game? Sorry, I don't have time for games. I need to carry on campaigning. I was thinking if you are free to come with me to see your friends and ask them to vote for the Democrats."

"You're a very noble person Sufi. Here you're asking for votes for your evil compatriots as well, while they're beseeching every voter not to vote for you! However, the game I'm talking about has been paid for by your party members and I think the Estone Socialists made some contribution. Yes, Yoda has something to do with it. So, I'm obliged to play the game which will lead to your disqualification as a candidate."

I was shocked. "Oh, so that's their evil plan. But why are you helping them, Jennifer? I didn't expect you to sink so low to their level."

"I'm afraid it's my job Sufi. I'll do anything if the money is good."

"But haven't you got another job? I've heard your name before but can't remember where. There are principles that one should have Jennifer, money is not everything."

"To my way of thinking money is everything Sufi. Nothing can be done in this world without money."

"Money is not evil per se but the use to which the money is put must be legal, moral and honourable. So, I take it there are no five hundred extra votes? It was a con all along! I can't believe it." I rarely raised my voice, but my temperature was rising now and I felt sick. What treachery!

"Legal? Moral? Honourable? These are mere words Sufi, no one pays any attention to them. As far as votes are concerned, I can still get some for you but it all depends on how you play the game", she beamed.

I laughed nervously. "What? You're joking! Whatever they've put you up to can be sorted amicably, Jenifer. Let's play this game: you make

155

a lovely cup of coffee or tea, I don't mind which, and while I sip it you tell me how much they paid you and for which game. I'll then show myself out and leave you in peace," I said, trying desperately to change the subject. "But if you don't have time then I understand, I'll just leave."

"I've plenty of time for you Sufi. Please don't worry. I'll prepare a steaming cup of coffee for you but first let's have a steaming sex session as they paid me five thousand pounds," Jennifer said, removing her skirt and blouse.

I moved quickly towards the door. But Jennifer was quicker. Now stark naked, she placed herself between me and the door. For a moment I was struck dumb. I stared at her curvy, attractive, saffron-tinted body that glowed in the diffused light. She pursed her soft, pink lips invitingly. *She's so beautiful* I thought. *She looks like a hoor. I didn't see her like this before. Guess I was too preoccupied with the election campaign.* I hadn't imagined any girl from the African continent to be so beautiful. Jennifer was no doubt a *true* black beauty. Her attractive stem-thin comely figure was tantalisingly accentuated by her curvilinear waist. The saffron tint to her complexion complemented by her luminous white teeth and elegant nose bore witness to her physical perfection. It was as if God almighty made her with his own hands instead of engaging outside contractors, such as angels or devils. But her soul was certainly devilish. I knew many other women who, like my neighbour, Ms Amy Brown appeared to have been outsourced by the Almighty! It had been truly said: *beauty is in the eyes of the beholder.*

Jennifer raised her eyebrows and moved towards me as she saw the rising bulge in my trousers; a known male weakness for which I was no exception. I moved back. "They paid you five thousand pounds to have sex with me? It doesn't make sense."

"No, no, no. They paid me the money to call the police the moment you entered my house and have you arrested for raping me," she laughed clapping at the same time. "Having sex is my idea. I'm being kind to you. I've heard a lot about you. You've got a nickname, *Mr Dangler*. I want to see if the nickname suits you," she said moving closer to me.

"Please don't Jennifer. It's sin." I was doing my best not to lose my temper. It would be disastrous if she calls the police.

"Oh, come on Sufi what's sin? Don't bring religion into this. It's business. I got paid five Gs to enjoy myself with you. Don't get me wrong, you'll enjoy it too." She made a face in mock annoyance. "I know you're a big boy. I waited a long time to get you inside me. Am I not attractive Sufi?"

"No that's not the point Jennifer," I said somewhat calmly. I was so shocked by her behaviour that I couldn't make my mind up whether to be angry or diplomatic with her. This was blackmail. "Of course, you're extremely attractive…"

"That settles it then. It's just you and me. No one else is here," she interrupted.

"There's always someone here Jennifer, watching us all the time."

"You mean God? Oh, darling don't bring him into it. He's an old spoilsport. Let's have some fun."

"It's a sin, Jennifer……"

"You keep saying that," she interrupted me again, raising her voice. She was becoming more and more agitated. I could see her nipples expanding and redness between her legs. There was a painful stirring in my trousers too. If I'm honest; it took a herculean effort to stop myself throwing on top of her. "They wanted me to have you arrested, I'll let you go once I'm finished. If you try to leave now, I'll just call the police…"

"That's blackmail! Police are not stupid!" I said, visibly angry now. I've never let the anger get the better of me in the past.

"Maybe not but you know they'll arrest you and ask questions later. And that'll be the end of your political career. Do you want that?"

"Ah, so that's their evil plan? *The question is how do I get out of it?*" I muttered…

"What did you say? Stop muttering Sufi you can't get away darling just move to the chair in the centre of the room. That's going to be the stage for today's drama. It's all set. You're the star of this show," She beamed.

"Put your clothes on Jennifer. You'll catch a cold. I'm not going to participate in this immoral act. It's fornication and my religion, as well as other religions, forbid it. The Sharia punishment for the fornicator is burial up to the neck and stoning to death. You…"

"I've said Sufi I have no alternative but to fulfil the "contract". So please come to the stage." Still standing by the door, I shook my head and refused to entertain Jenifer's wishes. Realising that I will not play the game, she decided to remain calm but firm, making me realise the sheer hopelessness of my situation.

"Sufi whatever you do please don't force me to contact the police. All your hard work in the election so far will come to nothing within minutes."

"For five thousand pounds you are blackmailing me and destroying my career. I fail to understand this…. I",

Jenifer interrupted me again. "You don't understand Sufi. Financially, I must survive. My salary is insufficient to meet my needs. I was looking to buy a house but the Estone Socialists have promised to get me a council house. I want to move away from the scoundrels in the Midland housing………."

"I can't believe Jenifer that you could sink so low as to blackmail me and force me to commit adultery. You're trying to rape me, it's a very serious offence. You'll never get a council house. They're just using you. You just told me most politicians promise the moon so how can you believe them? No new council homes are being built and there's no stock left."

"I'll need to buy a house if I couldn't get a council house. So now you understand why I need the money?"

I went on to say I didn't understand her at all and that I couldn't possibly commit fornication as the fear of God was instilled into me since childhood. My Arabic teacher in the mosque called it *ithmun Kabir* -great sin. The chance of being stoned to death was non-existent here in England but my inner being rejected going down that sinful route and even the thought of it made me sick.

I suspected, from her fidgety behaviour that Jenifer didn't wish to continue to force me to succumb to her desires as it would drive me to be cagier and temperamental. Unknown to me, she moved to her plan B. If only she could get me to sit in the armless kinky chair or even come close to it, so she could push me into it, the automatic containment mechanism will be triggered, and I will instantly become her prisoner. My hands would become tied to the side of the chair and the legs grabbed by the powerful airbags which worked on Newton's principle of motion - to every action there is an equal and opposite reaction. The Veyron cocoon massage-style chair was built on NASA's principles of zero-gravity seats. In action, the chair mimicked the weightlessness experienced by astronauts in space. The legs remain higher than the body to optimise circulation and blood flow, allowing the most relaxing massage chair experience. Jenifer procured it to impart true comfort, excitement and a titillating experience to her clients and called it *the pleasure trap*. The zero-gravity experience of the cocoon promoted overall well-being, reducing heart rate, soothing stress, and calming both body and mind. But when she took control of the chair with a poor soul trapped in it, his heart raced, blood pressure shot through the roof and calmness replaced screams of pleasure.

She stood behind the chair. I was anything but calm. I picked up her clothes and moved towards her, fuming with anger, telling her to put her clothes on. That was a bad move. Jennifer waited like a lioness, ready to pounce and push me into the chair. She moved further away, to draw me closer to the chair. I told her angrily; I was in no mood to further tolerate her excesses and I was leaving. I threw her clothes on the chair and turned to leave. As I turned my back to Jennifer, she pounced, leaned over the back of the chair and held me firmly at the shoulders, pulled me down with sufficient force. I collapsed into the chair, triggering an automatic containment mechanism, trapping me in seconds. Jennifer laughed triumphantly, clapping her hands.

"What the fuck is this thing? Jennifer Release me immediately from this trap. What you're doing is illegal, to say the least. What do you want?" I was furious, more at myself for not thinking straight than at her.

"Sufi you should know by now what I want," Jenifer said, laughing loudly, looking more arrogant and carefree than before.

I couldn't keep the shock out of my voice. "You can't do this Jennifer", there was a hint of a plea in my voice as she knelt in front of me, her naked heaving breasts displaying round, dark hard nipples, which brushed my lips as she loosened the belt around my waist, pulling my pants and trousers down to knees. My struggles came to nothing as my hands and legs were firmly encapsulated by *the pleasure trap*.

"Oh, I can do what I like Sufi. You're in no position to bargain. I've waited a long time for a ride on you and now I got you where I always wanted you," she said throwing her head to one side and sliding her hand along my impressive length. I moaned with pleasure but at the same time screamed at Jenifer, calling her a whore.

"Just relax and enjoy Sufi," Jenifer said smiling. "You want it as much as I do. Look down Sufi. You are so hard and swollen."

"I'm not enjoying it at all." I lied and begged the Almighty's forgiveness. "It's sin you..." my body convulsed with excitement and I moaned and hissed with pleasure through gritted teeth as she swallowed me and tightened her mouth around me.

"You pray five times a day Sufi," she said, regurgitating me. "I don't know why you're worried. All your sins are forgiven five times a day! That's what mullahs say, don't they? So just lean back, enjoy now and ask forgiveness after your next prayer. You're hissing and moaning with pleasure Sufi. See I told you; you'll enjoy it."

"To hell with you," I retorted, "I'll burn in hell I know but at least you will be there before me. That's for sure."

"There is no life without sin," Jenifer said swallowing me again.

"You cruel … bitch," I gasped with pleasure.

"Look at your holy book," she said releasing me again and circling her tongue on the tip which sent shivers down my spine, I began thrusting frantically but all I managed to do was wiggle my bum in the chair. "One hundred and thirteen chapters out of one hundred and fourteen chapters start with your God being merciful."

"My foot. It's not that easy to gain forgiveness or paradise," I said angrily, trying unsuccessfully to free myself from the clutches of the Veyron. I moaned with pleasure but then swore as she brought me back again from the brink.

"Jenifer you fuckin' bitch. Either stop for the love of Jesus or finish me off. I've got campaigning to do. I only have seventy-two hours left before the polling day on Thursday. Not much time left. A lot of voters need visiting yet. Estone Socialists have a lead in postal votes. I've got to get as many voters as possible to physically go to the polling stations and vote to overturn Socialist's postal vote lead."

"Just think of erection now Sufi, not election. I'll campaign with you tomorrow and get you the five hundred or so votes; maybe more," Jenifer said winking and swallowing me again. I moaned with pleasure but continued to yell at her, calling her a blackmailer and a greedy bitch devoid of all morality.

"As I told you before Sufi, just ask for forgiveness from your God after the next prayer and you will be forgiven. That's what Mullah Fazlur says. Right?"

"You and your bloody Mullahs. Yes, they tell their congregation to pray five times a day and all their sins committed between one prayer and the next would be forgiven! Armed with this false promise of forgiveness, many Muslims the world over, happily screw other peoples' wives, sisters and daughters. Men freely engage in illicit sex and fornication day and night and just go to the mosque to pray and believe that their sins would be forgiven. In some rich Muslim countries, they import young girls from India and Africa and leave them to fend for themselves when they get pregnant. Teenage girls with babies slung over their shoulders or tied around their waste, beg for food and money."

"Don't put me off darling by talking negatively, I haven't come yet. I'll climb on top now and when I'm done, I'll let you go. I promise darling." Jenifer said, kissing me passionately.

"You're going to burn in hell not me."

"I don't mind burning in hell. You just calm down Sufi. I'm wet now. I was hoping you will lend me a finger or two but you're just a moaning mini, aren't you? *Moaning* mini you got it Sufi? *Moaning*....", she started to laugh explosively.

"Fuck you, Jennifer, it's not funny."

"That's what I'm asking you to do Sufi," she said sitting astride on my thighs.

"Don't put it in. It's a sin. Let me go."

"No Sufi can't let you go. Told you, haven't cum yet."

"You don't cum, I cum you stupid......"

"But I cum too. Women cum too you know. You don't know much about sex, do you? Oh, my dear Sufi, she hasn't taught you much, has she?" Jenifer teased.

I was thinking frantically now, who hasn't taught me? From Jenifer's expression, it was clear that she didn't want to say what she said. Who was she talking about? I needed to think quickly. Eating pork is forbidden but there's no sin if one is forced to eat it. That's it! I'll have to sacrifice my religious belief to live and fight another day.

Irfan, Jitu and their socialist thugs will not have the pleasure of seeing me arrested. The painful look on their faces to see me free would be my reward.

"Who hasn't taught me what? I don't know what the fuck you're talking about. Put the fuckin' condom on me, you whore I don't want to get AIDS."

"Ah, no problem. See?" She spread the gel on the palm of her right hand and moistened me thoroughly. She then held it and rubbed the tip against her in a circular motion sending shock waves not only through her own already tense body but made me gasp and moan with pleasure too.

"So, you want me now Sufi?"

"Yes, yes…No, No I don't…. oh, just finish me off bitch for God's sake. I've campaigning to do."

"Make your mind up Sufi. Yes, or no?" She asked giggling.

"It's not funny, you fuckin' whore."

"I know darling. It seems I've known you for so long. We're getting on well and now I'm going to get you, my dear. Just a minute…here, we go."

Suddenly, I realised that anger will not solve my problem. Was she talking about my wife not teaching me? Oh God, I've been an idiot. I couldn't believe how stupid I'd been. I must placate Jenifer with some kind words. I'll have to do some acting. Under no circumstances must I allow her to call the police. That would put an immediate end to my candidature and give my opponents free ammunition to destroy me as they wish. What she was doing was not only immoral but illegal and challenged my principles at the core level but I had to keep calm and escape unscathed from this disastrous predicament. Why didn't I think of something sooner? Anger took over my reasoning. Events took a wrong turn too quickly; I couldn't turn an adverse situation in my favour, I had done that successfully many times in the past. I'd heard her name and seen her picture before, but I couldn't remember where.

I decided to exaggerate the pleasure and started yelling. Jennifer looked amused.

"Oh. So, you want me now? For your information, I'm about to reach a climax. Your timing is out."

"It takes me at least sixty to eighty minutes."

"What? Fuck me!"

"Ok. Release me and I will fuck you like no man before! You call yourself whore? Slayer of men? And you can't take my eleven by six, can you?"

"Oh, so you think you can defeat me? Think again darling," and with that, she pressed the mechanism release button. Her mouth opened wide as she saw me fully erect and rock hard. She looked at it wide-eyed. What was she thinking? That I could do serious damage to her if I wanted to? She shrugged, and I heard her muttering to herself. I heard her say, 'he's too kind. He would be gentle.' I was overjoyed to be free. Jenifer didn't expect what followed. I lifted her in one sweep and moving to the sofa released her from a height of six feet. She landed face down with her bum stuck in the air. Perfect doggy position. I moved quickly, pinning her down and ramming her. She screamed with much pain and a little pleasure. My thrusts became a wild frenzy as if I was taking my revenge on her for raping me.

"You are killing me Sufi. Please stop".

"Now you know how it feels. How many times I asked you to stop? Did you? No! You didn't. Why should I?".

"Oh, please I think you hurt me badly. I'm bleeding. I didn't think it was that big." She was in pain and crying.

I noticed some blood as I hastily pulled out. Jenifer slumped down on the sofa, her bum and thighs were covered with blood. I noticed a sizeable tear just below her clitoris.

"You will be ok nothing to worry about. You'll need a few stitches, and you won't be able to see your clients for at least two weeks," I said sarcastically. "But then you've been paid handsomely haven't you by those bastards, Irfan and Asif?" I said, pulling my trousers up.

"You Muslims have to have a shower don't you after sex?" she said still moaning in pain.

"What do you know about Islam you bitch?" I said throwing a cushion at her face. "I'm going to…." I stopped abruptly. "I know where I've seen you before. With Iram. I saw your picture with Iram. You're a nurse."

"Oh no please don't tell her about this." She said speaking as if in great pain.

"I'll have to tell my wife if she asks. I can't keep this a secret. We tell each other the truth."

"No please don't tell her Sufi. She's, my boss. I'll lose the job."

"Good! I'll tell Iram to get you the sack. She has a picture with a whore like you! What sort of company does she keep?"

"No. You don't understand. I don't want to lose my job. She's, my boss. I'm a staff nurse and she's a Matron. She thinks I'm a nice person. You see she taught me all about Islam," she said still sobbing.

"Well, well. What a small world. So Iram taught you about Islam?" I asked incredulously. "She hasn't done a good job has she?"

"If you don't tell her I won't report you to the police. I will make some excuse and tell Asif and Irfan some story."

165

"Now you're learning. If you call the police, I will tell her. I'll go now, I got so much to do…" I said patting myself down and making sure everything was in order before I left. Satisfied that there was no bulge in my trousers, I moved to the door.

I looked at her briefly. Jenifer was still slumped down on the sofa and her face reflected nothing but pain. She was sobbing audibly with tears flowing freely down her cheeks onto the sofa. *I shouldn't have done that to her*, I thought. *She appears to be a nice person.* For a fleeting moment, I had a strong desire to embrace her and apologise but controlled myself, recalling her atrocious behaviour. I had an even stronger impulse to beat the shit out of her. With a glance, mixed with anger and sympathy, I let myself out of her *den of iniquity* with a sigh of relief.

Outside the weather was dismal and the road was deserted. I spied a small group of men standing on the corner of Trinity Street and Felton Road. From the distance, I couldn't see who they were but I noticed they were in animated conversation and as I approached them, I knew my guess was right. Jitu and Irfan together with Yoda, Ratman and ten other Socialist party activists stared at me as if they'd seen a ghost. They looked questioningly at each other.

"What the fuck are you lot doing here? Are you campaigning with Estone Socialists? Does Johnny Boy know of this?" I asked angrily, pretending that I didn't know about their plan.

"Oh, you don't have to mention it to him Sufi, do you?" Jitu and Irfan stammered.

"Of course, you don't". They answered their question

I wanted a shower, I felt dirty and sweaty. I didn't expect Jenifer or any sane woman to collude with these low-down entities from the Democrats and the Socialist party but morality is often sacrificed for financial gain. Shortage of money and morality don't go together. Having sex with a stranger or outside of marriage is a sin. Such action was unforgivable under Sharia law. I decided to examine my actions in detail to ascertain whether I could've avoided the whole unpleasant incident thereby saving myself from this major sin of fornication. The conclusion was swift and easy: *Jennifer had trapped me through deception*. Surely it wasn't my fault. There was nothing I could've done to avoid it. It was fortunate that she knew my wife and I was saved from a certain disqualification. The *Shaitans*, Irfan, Jitu and Yoda were to blame for this. Mercifully, their evil plan had come to nothing. Was God really on my side? I thought so.

I fixed an angry look on Asif and Irfan, before turning right onto Wilson Street and heading home.

# Chapter Nineteen

"What the fuck happened do you think? Where's the police? Why wasn't Sufi arrested?" Jitu asked, skipping around frantically. Addressing no one in particular, he glared at them all. They all looked angry, frustrated and disappointed. No doubt everyone was waiting to see Jennifer keep her promise and expected me to pass them having a ride in a police car. They imagined waving goodbye to me and then heading off to Jitu's house to celebrate the end of my political career with samosas, kebabs, and biryani which his mother and sister prepared for the occasion. The pain of failure was evident on their sunken faces which they intermittently buried in their hands. After what seemed an eternity, Yoda Khan, towering above others, considered most cunning of them all because of his age and experience, spoke slowly and conspiratorially, his white beard shaking with anger. He beckoned them all to come closer to him. They were all alone, standing on the corner of Fenton Road. They did not need to whisper; but the shock of seeing me walk away, free, affected their sanity.

"You morons should've realised by now that somehow, Sufi has escaped from the clutches of eh… whatever her name is and will win with flying colours unless we stop him."

"But what can we do? All our plans have failed." They chorused.

"We've plan B. Unlike you Democrats, we've been in the game for a long time. We always have plan B. This is going to be the best plan, it'll not fail. Listen carefully. This one is foolproof," Yoda said taping his long hairy nose.

Fifteen men surrounded Yoda like vultures around a carcass and intently listened to his master plan for victory in the election! Yoda told them he knows at least thirty heads of various clans in the Cosmopolitan City. He'll need at least fifteen more volunteers. There'll be thirty of us so one of us will go with the clan leader into the homes of postal vote holders and remove the entire envelopes containing the postal votes from them. "Victory will be mine and Irfan's. We'll decide the fate of the third candidate later. Forget Asif, he always goes campaigning with Sufi," Yoda said, "and defeat for Sufi will depend entirely on the number of postal votes we snatch." They settled on the round target figure of three and a half thousand postal votes. Yoda told them, he contacted Haji Habibur Rahman earlier, and it's agreed, the postal votes will be opened and identity details completed at his warehouse on the eve of the election by only a handful of trusted activists chosen by him and Mr Rahman.

"So, it's all set. I want all fifteen of you, to pick a volunteer each and be in the campaign office tonight at ten 'o'clock sharp. We've twenty-four hours to collect the postal votes and on Wednesday night we'll meet in the warehouse. We may have to stay all night to finish filling in the postal vote forms. First, we need to collect…"

"No snatch," someone interrupted.

"Ok snatch for God's sake, whatever," Yoda snarled. "Just don't get caught. Many voters will give you the envelopes because they can't fill them in so they'll be happy for you to do the honours. Others, more knowledgeable and non-Socialist voters will refuse. In that case, tell them Sufi sent you or you belong to their clan. Invoke the baradari system always. And if all else fails bribe them or buy the votes. Most voters will settle for a twenty-pound note."

"What if bribery doesn't work?" They asked.

"Then use Himalayan politics' other potent weapons - intimidation and threats. These will work on most residents from the subcontinent. I've managed, in the past, to have many people arrested and fake cases started against them in Pakistan and Subash Miah has done the same in Bangladesh, so they know the score. They'll willingly hand over the ballot papers to you. All collected, snatched or bought postal votes should be taken to the campaign office and we'll move them to the warehouse, in black bags, after dark on Wednesday night," Yoda said and paused for emphasis. "On Thursday morning, we'll need a hundred volunteers to take thirty completed postal votes each and put them in the designated bags in the polling stations for them to be counted on the following day.

Do you still think Sufi will win? No way!" They all clapped. Yoda continued: "We need to snatch or steal the postal votes between now and Wednesday night. On average, there're four votes per household so between thirty of us, we've to visit only twenty-five or so houses each. Five Royal Mail post bags, full of votes, have already arrived at the campaign office. We bought or snatched these from postmen. Two postmen 'willingly' handed them over because of threats and intimidation. You must only resort to threats and intimidation if you're sure that the voters will not speak to the police. Luckily, elderly Asians are terrified of police, because of their experience of Pakistani police. Anyway, we mustn't involve the police at any cost. Is that understood?"

"What if they catch us?" Irfan asked.

"You're always fuckin' bearer of glad tidings, aren't you, Irfan?" They all laughed and jumped on him. They froze on hearing Paul Ali's voice. "Oh, we've got a lot of hyenas here wasting time and not campaigning."

Yoda told everyone to keep the plan secret from Paul Ali. They nodded.

"What's going on here? Are any last-minute plans being made to oust Sufi? My advice is don't try anything illegal. Sufi is sharp. No doubt he's keeping a close eye on you all."

"Oh, don't worry Paul, he won't catch us," Irfan said.

"You're in a chirpy mood, Irfan. What are you hiding?"

"Oh, no, no nothing," he said rather too quickly. Paul's suspicion changed into certainty. He glared at them. Slowly circling them as they stood still with hands folded and eyes downcast like schoolchildren in front of their teacher. He spoke slowly and menacingly. "I'm telling you all again: *do nothing illegal or harm Sufi. He's very shrewd and I know he's got you all under some sort of surveillance.*"

"Don't worry Paul," Yoda intervened. "We've got everything under surveillance too."

"I sincerely hope so," he said, looking over his shoulder as if he will not see them again. He paused at the door of the den of iniquity and saw them disperse.

"Forget him, he's gone to his den. Paul always worries too much. Let's collect, no snatch, some postal votes," Yoda said, punching the air.

# Chapter Twenty

"I'm on Hunters Road now," Ratman whispered, into the phone. "I'm about twenty behind them. You're right Sufi. I think they're up to no good. According to my postal votes list, they're knocking on the doors of postal voters and rudely pushing past them. Looks as if they're not invited in. I can see them emerging with black carrier bags, tucked under their arms." Ratman was my number one spy in the enemy camp. I often told him he'll do well in MI5. He provided extremely useful information to me and useless one to the Estone Socialists, during the past few weeks.

"Check the list again. Are they only entering the homes of registered postal voters? Are you sure Ratman?"

"Yes, I'm sure man. I'm not blind. I have seen Raja Belal, Chaudhry Arif, Khawaja Adil, Irshad Bhatti...."

I interrupted: "Oh my God Ratman. They are clan chiefs. The Estone Socialists are using them to snatch the postal votes. That's why they're pushing past. Have you seen Kalbi and Himar?"

"Yes. They're working with the clan chiefs. Himar and Khawaja on one side of the road; Chaudhry Arif, and Kalbi on the other with Bhatti. Yoda is here too driving a black Prado Land Cruiser at a snail's pace along the Road. They're all working at top speed; placing their pickings in the boot of Yoda's car and running back to knock on the next door. Oh, I can see a piece of paper in their hands. It's a voter list, I think? They've two black bin bags full of something", Ratman whispered excitedly.

"Full of Postal votes of course, what else? Can, you remember the door numbers they've entered?" I asked sensing, personation being organised too.

"Ye. I've just written them down randomly. 4, 7, 8, 12, 16, 17, 23, 24, 33, 38, 43 and now Kalbi is going into 44 and Himar into 53. Kalbi entered numbers 38 and 43 with a key. Proxy votes, do you think?"

"Okay wait," I said and then looked through the absent voters' list. "Stay with them Ratman. Don't lose them whatever you do. Keep me updated every five minutes, please. Oh, my God, they're not only stealing postal votes but also collecting poll cards; numbers 7 and 23 don't have postal votes, they're absent voters. No one lives at numbers 38 and 43. Both houses are empty since six months; they're in Pakistan. They've filled proxy forms for them. Looks like they've postal vote fraud, proxy vote fraud and personations in mind, triple trouble for us. Jesus what are we going to do?"

Reports kept coming in from all over the ward and I nominated five more activists to monitor the movements of the opposition candidates and activists. I was sure that they were planning the biggest postal vote fraud and personation ever! I couldn't understand the mentality of the local political parties, their candidates and activists. Hell-bent on flouting all rules to win at any cost. The Cosmopolitan city was truly turning into a banana republic. Did the NEC of the Socialist Party know what their local candidates and activists get up to? I was certain, at least one person on the NEC, a Ms Black, knew because I had written to her. I wasn't sure about the rest of the NEC members.

I began to collate some facts and figures. The government introduced postal votes to combat voter apathy and to increase electoral participation, but it did not put any stringent anti-fraud measures in place. The government and local councils were in constant denial of electoral fraud and repeated their mantra of the system working well; when there was no system in place! Could postal vote fraud make a material difference to the outcome? With an increase of around five thousand postal votes this year, it could. Even with 10% wastage, the odds were in favour of a false 'victory' for the Socialist Party. That would be unacceptable and unfair.

In the event of Estone Socialists "winning," the election petition will have to be started in court, to overturn the election result and call fresh elections, maybe across all inner-city wards. And that would be a waste of public money so it was incumbent on all parties to ensure that the elections were free and fair. It was increasingly obvious from the antics of the Socialist party activists during the previous weeks' campaign that they aimed to win by whatever means. They spread disinformation to malign my character and to divert attention from their plan to steal postal votes and polling cards from voters. This signalled the take-off of Himalayan politics to the next level. Paying Jennifer to discredit me was an evil plan that mercifully backfired on them.

Last week, Ratman saw the Socialist party activists exchanging twenty-pound notes for sealed postal vote envelopes, ironically, on steel lane. Their activists had increased the tempo in all inner-city wards by resorting to fraud. I saw such illegal and immoral election practices in the subcontinent but didn't expect them to take place in the UK; the mother of all democracies.

Alongside fraud, sectarianism and caste systems were invoked to divide the electorate and gain votes. They labelled me as Shia and placed me in a lower caste than my actual caste. I was neither. This was a low, morally unacceptable level to which the Socialist Party candidates and activists had sunk to gain votes. Asif and Irfan aided them in this unholy alliance to con the voters. The situation was looking bleak and we had to be prepared for all eventualities. I was certain that the events were now heading for an all-out war where every rule was there to be broken and to my obvious distress the election officials were turning a blind eye to the complaints against all types of fraud from most inner-city wards. Several residents saw BME postmen handing Royal Mail post bags to the Socialist party activists in the Estone and adjoining wards. They also saw envelopes change hands. My lengthy letter to the elections officer Mr Weno elicited only a one-sentence response: *your comments have been noted!*

I knew I must re-organise my team and collect evidence to bring the fraudsters to justice. Irfan and Asif could not be taken on board because of their agreement with Yoda. Asif had brought some important information about their joint plan to steal postal votes. I hoped once my fellow Democratic candidates realise the extent to which they'd been deceived by their trusted mate, they would see sense and stop playing the game with us. On the available evidence, it looked as if there was no chance for me and Asif to win. If the Estone Socialists play ball with Irfan and Jitu as per their agreement, then two Estone Socialists and Irfan will win. Without losing further time, I rang Irfan and Jitu against my better judgement and explained the situation to them. They responded by saying there was no evidence of postal vote fraud and that I was worrying for nothing.

Asif said he believed that both Irfan and Jitu learned their lesson and have broken their agreement with Yoda and the company. I knew how the Socialist mind worked. I was certain they were using Irfan and Jitu. The Estone Socialists would only vote for their candidates, not Irfan. Following Asif's revelations, only one thing was certain: *All three of us will lose.* "What makes you think that they've learned their lesson, Asif?"

"I know for certain that they looked worried yesterday, and I asked them what was bothering them. They surprised me by saying, "The Socialist bastards are making our life difficult by breeching the agreement." I asked them, "What agreement?" But they didn't respond and walked away."

"Well, well, you know Asif that's the best news I've heard for a long time now. Looks like our two musketeers have discovered a Yoda plot to ignore them and go for an all-out Socialist victory. Let's call all our trusted activists to the campaign office, get them together and increase the discreet surveillance of the Estone Socialists, at least tenfold and collect evidence at the same time. Let's beat the bastards at their own game."

"Sufi, is it worth involving JB?"

"Good idea Asif but I don't think it'll be wise to involve him at this stage. Let's wait and see. If what you say turns out to be the case, then we can bring him on board. At the moment, he'll believe whatever Irfan tells him."

"I think you're right."

"Ring everyone on this list Asif," I said passing a typed sheet containing around fifty names and phone numbers. "They need to be in the campaign office tomorrow by 10.00 am sharp. The ones with a cross by their names are already on surveillance, so don't call them. I'm going to speak to our colleagues in adjacent wards. We might learn something useful," I said smiling. Asif said that he couldn't remember when I last smiled.

# Chapter Twenty-One

Asif and I walked to the campaign office slowly and in deep thought. We were glad to see all forty of our most trusted activists in the office. The surprise was Irfan and Jitu were also there with five of their most infamous cronies. I knew them well. They were sharp and cunning. For years they evaded arrest from the social security and the tax investigators and received no punishment for benefit fraud and tax evasion. They were experts at not being caught.

I saw Irfan and Jitu in an animated conversation and suspected Asif was right. They may have fallen out with their socialist co-conspirators. There was never a doubt in my mind that their criminal collaboration will one day fall apart. Politics to them was nothing but deceiving others, self-fulfilment and not hesitating to step on other peoples' necks, if needed, to become successful. They perceived success as amassing material wealth, social status and extravagant lifestyle. Success to me was spending life in the service of humanity and living by the seven principles of public life. Here, in Estone ward, as elsewhere, honest people who worked tirelessly for their political parties; leafletting, canvassing, and campaigning for them got nothing in return. They got little or no opportunity to become candidates. Whenever it came down to a choice between service to the party or the electorate, the honest chose the latter, which proved unpopular with the party hierarchy. The good guys never liked the way the socialist regional party selected its council candidates for the forty wards. If the regional leadership sensed a victory for a candidate that they didn't approve; they promptly closed the ward and suspended the selection process, and imposed a candidate of their choice. So much for democracy.

In Himalayan politics, the poor have always been considered, from time immemorial, to be a burden on the state. It was this injustice and exploitation of the poor that gave rise to Marxism. But more recently, they made the poor work even harder to pay taxes to the state for tolerating their very existence. So that the rich could enjoy and the poor suffer. Why wouldn't they suffer? Even the almighty appeared to have abandoned them. God claimed to create them in his own image and with his hands but then left them at the mercy of tyrants, the world over. Wailings, prayers and supplications of the poor flew past his omniscient, omnipresent and all-powerful self. God appeared to be listening only to the rich, and cruel rulers, the devils disguised as humans who ruled from generation to generation. Failure to recognise others' efforts and good works often led to hatred and enmity. Most Muslims blame Christians, Jews and Hindus for their bad times except themselves. Yes, the Ottoman Caliphate was destroyed by creating discord and disunity through deception but the traitors within allowed it to be torn apart. Muslim rulers' Sybaritic behaviour was to blame for the demise of the Islamic empire. Over the years they fell from God's grace and the position they occupied as world conquerors was lost. David Fromkin, the great American historian tells us in his book, *peace to end all peace,* how some European nations planned and executed the destruction of the Islamic empire, and carved out tiny states between 1914 and 1932, which hate each other to this day; so there can never be peace in the area.

When out canvassing, Jitu and Irfan played on the emotions of the Estone ward voters for their support of Palestinians. The duo rarely missed an opportunity to brainwash the voters into thinking that I was opposed to the Palestinian cause. At the start of the election campaign, the Democratic party held a massive meeting in the Fairview meeting hall. And Irfan spoke to hundreds of voters and activists, telling them: "We must never forget that some Christians and Jews will never rest until they annihilate Islam and Muslims. I'm not saying this, the Quran says it. And this man Sufi is their best friend. Just think, where do we Muslims stand today? The favours of the Almighty have transferred from us to Jews and Christians causing me deep grief. I cannot understand why Sufi is supporting our number one enemy, Israel. Like the Almighty, he favours the enemy, as if divine favouritism isn't enough. I perceive intense rivalry and enmity between the three great Semitic religions. In the Quran, the Almighty tells the Israelis: *remember our favours upon you and we chose you above all nations.* What a travesty of justice! I can't believe it. Even our Allah favours the Israelis! I feel let down as my prayers to the almighty to foil all Jewish and Christian plans against us have remained unanswered. Our despotic leaders have fallen prey to political deception and economic destruction. Himalayan politics, the economic and military power of the tiny state propped up by their American benefactors have wreaked havoc in the Islamic world within a short time. The ill-fated participants of the 1974 Lahore Conference have disappeared from the face of the earth, one by one. Some have been hanged, others murdered or blown to Kingdom come. Sufi says the holy land does not belong to the Palestinians. But they have inhabited the area for over a million years. Aren't the Israelis illegally taking over their homes? Even Some Muslim thinkers and politicians like Sufi, support Israel, based on the Quranic revelation in 5:20-21, which says that the almighty Allah *wrote the holy land over to the Israelis.* Some Muslim countries, like Saudi Arabia and UAE, I believe now subscribe to this notion and if we accept this, it means that the holy land belongs to the Israelis and the Palestinians are mere tenants. But the world needs to understand that many Jews oppose the creation of Israel, insisting that only Zionists wanted it, not Jews. Sufi says the so-called Zionists are Jews too. But there is a tacit animosity between them. But they forbid open argument because the Zionists take offence. They cry anti-Semitism and the entire media and their supporters demand blood. They've taken over the world and yet they want more. Sufi wants them to head a world government. World government! No way! Be very careful of Sufi, he's not what he seems. I say he doesn't deserve your vote." A burst of subdued laughter, imbibed with sarcasm circulated the meeting hall because majority of those present didn't subscribe to such openly fallacious propaganda against me.

Irfan and Jitu didn't see me enter the meeting hall until I was on the stage. I had heard some of their propaganda regarding my support for Israel which I regarded as a vicious attempt at my character assassination. They had tried to excite the crowd on the most sensitive Palestinian issue, highlighting my "immoral" support for the Zionists instead of their victims. Character assassination slogans like, "*he supports the oppressors rather than the oppressed.*" And "*everyone in Estone ward should refuse to vote Sufi,*" were in circulation in Estone ward. I merely stated the facts.

"Oh, pray why should they not vote for me?" I asked angrily. Irfan and Jitu swung around, red-faced and profusely apologetic. "And what's this about, 'immoral' support? I think you were referring to my support of Israel. If so, what's immoral about it? Don't you idiots read the Quran? I'm only saying what God is saying in the Quran regarding the holy land being written over to the Israelites thousands of years ago."

"No Sufi we weren't talking about you. We were just making general comments on the plight of the poor Palestinians." I told them angrily they were doing much more than that. Arif, Salman and others, sitting closer to the stage spoke up: "They were slagging you off Sufi."

"Thank you! Now what do you have to say?"

No one knew these miscreants better than I did. In Estone ward there was widespread condemnation of the duo's attempt at maligning me, spreading rumours and disinformation about my support for Israel. Non-Muslim, left-wing politicians and many Muslims in Britain opposed Israeli actions against the Palestinians as inhuman and uncalled for. Whether their actions were brutal was secondary to their right to be present in the holy land. Factually, as I understood it, the Israelis were the owners of the holy land, as stated in the bible and the Quran. Apart from Estone ward, other inner-city wards in England were no different where many Muslims and non-Muslims opposed Israel and supported the Palestinians. I agreed that sometimes the Israeli forces acted cruelly and inhumanly against unarmed Palestinians, particularly women and children. But the Israelis had the right to be there, and they were not the 'forces of occupation' as some referred to them. Missiles from the surrounding area have been fired at the Israelis. They have the right to respond. Those launching the missiles should know the consequences of their actions. I accept that a man with a stick or stones is at a disadvantage to a man with a gun, but he does not have an automatic right to attack the armed man.

Sticks and stones do hurt. So, persistent attacks even with such crude weapons may draw a response which may not be just, equal or proportionate. Aggression is forbidden in Islam.

So, in inner-city wards, rumours flourish in all sorts of shapes and forms and they deemed any activist or candidate showing support for the Palestinian cause to be worthy of their vote. One rumour, which angered me most and permeated Estone and adjacent wards and therefore, had the potential of irretrievably damaging me politically, was that I got paid thousands of pounds for supporting Israel, for inventing a lie about the holy Quran containing verses that supported the argument about the holy land belonging to the Israelis.

My thoughts were jolted back to the present as I heard a commotion in the campaign office. I saw some activists surrounding Irfan and Jitu and asking them angrily about their unholy alliance with the Estone Socialists. Embarrassed and red-faced, thinking that they were unwelcome, the duo decided to leave the campaign office with their five friends. Realising that Asif was right and they did appear to have learned their lesson and the importance of keeping the enemy closer, I asked that they should take part in the proceedings if they wanted to win the election. The invitation from me was music to their ears, and they sat down in the back row. I asked the rest of the supporters to take their seats as there were developments regarding postal votes which they all ought to know. Confident that if the duo attempted to compromise our plan by disclosing any information to the Estone Socialists, they'll be held accountable, I called the meeting to order asking everyone present to keep whatever they were about to hear from me, strictly to themselves. Leakage of any part of the information will give Socialist Party activists the chance to be extra vigilantes, making a discovery of the postal vote fraud extremely difficult if not impossible. The activists promised to keep things secret. Having got the assurance, I informed them of important facts and figures that I had gathered from Estone and surrounding inner-city wards. "We've seven, very sharp and highly intelligent activists on surveillance," I said narrowing my eyes and leaning forward. "Under no circumstances will I allow anyone of you to jeopardise their mission. So, listen carefully, please. Intelligence received from our activists shows that our opponents are planning postal vote fraud on an unprecedented scale. Our activists estimate around three thousand postal votes have already been removed or snatched by the

Estone Socialists from voters' homes or the postmen with or without their agreement. They have snatched a similar number of votes in the adjacent inner-city wards of Heartlands and Ashbrook." I paused for these facts to sink in and gasps of surprise and anger to subside before continuing. "The three candidates, local party officers, organisers and activists of the socialist party are seeking a safe place – a house, or an industrial unit or any other secure premises large enough to accommodate them where they can open the ballot papers, fill the information in and re-seal them and deposit them at the polling stations tomorrow. Posting the ballot papers to the election office is not a viable proposition for them. They'll have to complete the ballot papers tonight as the election is tomorrow." I paused again to allow the information to sink in. "I believe they're going to select the Seafarish warehouse, belonging to their two rich supporters on Wilson industrial estate, on the outskirts of our ward. A perfect hiding place to do their dirty work." I informed them about my earlier visit to the warehouse and my assessment of the suitability of the premises for carrying out this unprecedented and illegal task. "Put it this way," I said. "If I wanted to do postal vote fraud, I would choose Seafarish warehouse as it's set well away from the main road and only a narrow dusty road leads to the large car park at the back. The front door has a massive shutter which would be down as soon as all the culprits are inside. But the foyer and the offices can be seen from the perimeter of the warehouse. Luckily, the sides of the warehouse are all glass and obscured only by tall red-robin hedging plants. We can hide behind the hedge to observe the office area which they will use for completing the postal vote forms. The hedge has small openings at several places which we can use as spy holes using these binoculars," I said handing five binoculars to designated activists.

"We know Sufi, you think we're working with them. We're not. We don't trust them anymore. They've not only deceived us but used us for the realisation of their crooked plan," Irfan said. Jitu remained quiet; head buried in his hands. I noticed the word "anymore" and smiled. I was eager to place Irfan, Jitu and their five friends where they can't interact with any Socialist activists. That way, even if they were double agents, the damage they can do would be minimal or non-existent. I didn't trust them yet. Turning to Salman, Sharma and Asif, I asked them to monitor the warehouse from behind the hedge and to inform me immediately when the opposition party arrives. I asked Irfan, lefty and Payara to go to Rahman's house in Newtown, on the main Road, opposite the socialist party's campaign office. "I've spoken to him. He will allow you to observe the office from his attic. Any suspicious activity must be reported to me immediately. Is that understood?"

"No problem, mate," they all replied, making the thumb-up sign. After obtaining further assurances of care and discretion I asked them to leave and be extra vigilant. I was certain the Socialist Party activists will use the warehouse for postal vote fraud because of its location and inaccessibility. But I had to ensure that we also kept the other two places under surveillance so as not to leave anything to chance. Satisfied that I had covered everything, I remained alone in the campaign office and placed my iPhone on the desk in front of me with the ring volume at the maximum. The marked register showed a 30% turnout the previous year. Around 70% did not vote. This was not good for the democracy. No wonder a few undesirable elements, liars and cheats, practitioners of Himalayan politics got elected as councillors and MPs. This deadly form of politics was not confined to people of Asian origin as many Europeans and Americans practised it even more effectively. Lies, deception and treachery are part and parcel of the political spectrum throughout the world. Perhaps this is the reason many ordinary people stay out of politics. During our door-to-door campaign, hundreds of people opened their doors to us only to shut them again, saying, "We're not interested in politics." I know a UK government that came to power, receiving only 35% of the public vote. Is that democracy? I believe such governments have no legitimacy to govern. First-past-the-post is an outdated and unfair electoral system. It should've been replaced with proportional representation long ago.

Noisy footsteps disrupted my thoughts. Jitu and Irfan entered the office and before I could speak, they apologised and said they remembered an urgent matter which needed to be discussed with me. They were profusely apologetic about their attempts to get me disqualified and blamed the Estone Socialists for encouraging them to do so. I wanted to tell them that's a typical Muslim leaders' excuse blaming the Western powers for persuading them to commit treachery. Why let anyone encourage or persuade you do wrong? But I decided against it. I resolved not to trust them, but diplomatically said to them I had forgotten their attempts at maligning me and that together, we should endeavour to win the election. The duo said they wanted to let me know that they propose to unleash a string of deadly attacks on the Estone Socialists, regarding their war on Islam and to portray the Estone Socialists as Muslims' enemy number one. I said I have no objection to that but encouraged them to conduct the election campaign within the electoral commission's guidelines. I thanked them for their candidness and they left the office to resume surveillance duties.

Over the last couple of days of the election campaign, Irfan had spoken at several well-attended meetings, slating the Estone Socialists and the nationalists for waging war on Islam. They blamed the socialist leader for taking Britain to war on the pretext of lies and false information regarding Iraq possessing weapons of mass destruction. To rapturous applause from the audience, they called on the international court at the Hague to indict the warmongers for crimes against humanity. Because of the vicious attacks on the Estone Socialists and the nationalists, polls predicted a landslide victory for the Democrats in inner-city wards. To remove Saddam may've been a good idea, but the method used was violent and inhumane, and ordinary people suffered. Irfan said the decision to go to war was illegal.

The aim was to gain not only vast oil and mineral wealth for the West but also to make Muslim countries the testing ground for their vast sophisticated and highly destructive weapons. There appeared to be a policy of limiting progress in Islamic countries to keep them in constant turmoil, under control and at the mercy of the IMF. The insane destruction of Afghanistan, Iraq, Libya and Syria bore testimony to this. There's a deeply held belief among many political analysts that Kennedy paid the price for his refusal to allow private banking conglomerates, like IMF. He foresaw nations held to ransom under such a system. During door-to-door campaigns, the voters questioned me about these conspiracy theories. I declined to comment but informed the questioners, that the attacks on Iraq and Afghanistan were launched following the September eleven events and to my knowledge, there was no evidence of any sinister motives behind the tragic war other than self-preservation and 'national security' but calling the wanton destruction and death of thousands of civilians as 'collateral damage' was inhuman.

Under intense bombardment, buildings and bodies had simply vaporised, but this was considered, 'collateral damage'. Muslim blood was cheaper than American blood. Over four thousand people (reduced from fifty thousand initially) allegedly died in America on September eleven. But hundreds of thousands died in Muslim countries. The Americans had to be avenged. Why shouldn't the Muslims pay the price with their blood? Even a hundred-fold. That was the sinister thinking of the neo-cons behind unleashing terror on Islam and Muslim countries. For the sins of a few, many Muslims the world over paid the ultimate price, mistrust, loss of freedom of speech and vilification of the entire Ummah. Anti-Muslim rhetoric, Islamophobia and insulting the holy prophet were hailed as 'freedom of speech' and anything said in favour of Muslims and Islam became 'incitement to hatred.' I was only concerned about the loss of freedom of speech but otherwise had no real preference for either viewpoint. I wasn't in favour of the war but regarded it as an essential exercise to prevent further terrorist attacks in the UK and the rest of the world.

Why not scrutinise the *marked register* I thought, instead of sorting the World out as I waited for the phone call from my spies. Local councils produced this document after every election and a mark, placed against the name of each voter showed that he or she had voted, hence the name "marked register". It also contained the names and addresses of voters who, for years, didn't vote. Unscrupulous political activists from all parties used the register for voter personation. It was easily done. A personator could memorise the name and address of the absent voter; go to the polling station and give the details to the polling clerk. He or she would then be issued with a ballot paper with no question asked and the personator would mark the ballot paper and place it in the ballot box. Personation done. Through this method, many votes were stolen. The marked register was useful for targeting regular voters, but unscrupulous activists misused it to steal votes. I knew I had only one day to maximise my votes so the marked register should prove extremely useful. I gathered as much information as possible about the definite voters and decided that I will make ten teams of two supporters in each team and let them loose in the ward tomorrow, getting voters out of their homes to vote, I should do well. The idea was to target as many voters as possible using the data from the marked register.

The phone buzzed. It was Irfan and as he spoke, I detected an urgency in his voice. I strained to listen to barely audible words whispered by Irfan. "Looks like they've moved to other premises Sufi. There is no movement at all here. It's like a graveyard."

"Why the fuck are you whispering then? I can barely hear you?"

Change of venue by Estone Socialists was always at the back of my mind but the intelligence was reliable and it was early in the evening yet. I was certain that they'll make their move in the dark, late at night. Irfan was habitually impatient. He wanted everything done quickly. He often got into trouble with family and friends because of his impatience and thoughtlessness. I asked him to be patient for an hour until it gets completely dark. "Be vigilant. Don't go to sleep," I told him. Irfan didn't seem happy but grudgingly agreed and rang off.

# Chapter Twenty-Two

Exactly an hour later the phone rang again. It was Asif this time, whispering excitedly. "They're here Sufi. We didn't see them earlier. All of them arrived around fifteen minutes ago. They used the back entrance. I can see an enormous table laid out in the warehouse's foyer. The owner of the warehouse is standing by the entrance. It's a hub of activity. There are at least a dozen men. Three are arranging chairs around the table and the rest are opening the bags and taking out envelopes. There must be thousands of ballot papers Sufi."

"Ok, good work. Where's the rest of our team?" I asked.

"We're all here, a dozen of us watching them from behind the bushes next to Power Avenue. As soon as I spotted them, I asked everyone to abandon other sites and come to this one."

"Good work mate. Keep me informed. Two of you go to the back entrance and keep a watch. Take photos but discretely. Do nothing stupid to alert them. I'm going to ring the police."

I got through to *the Chief* on the third attempt and quickly appraised him of the day's events. "To be honest, I was expecting a call from you or someone else in Estone ward. We've received reports of postal vote fraud from your neighbouring wards and police headquarters tell me it seems to be a national phenomenon – Bradford, Leeds, Peterborough; you name it. We can't even fight elections fairly let alone each other," the chief said. And I could almost see, in my mind's eye, the chief smiling ruefully. "Didn't you mention something about the baradari system last year Sufi? That's what is being practised throughout the country, isn't it?"

"Yes, it is Chief. Baradari system or the Himalayan politics. It's an *Asian* thing chief. We adopted this imported and evil political practice without thinking." I was apologetic. The practice of Himalayan politics was widespread among all 'Asian' candidates whether they were from the national, Socialist or Democratic parties. "I have been trying to stop activists of all political parties from practising the Himalayan politics, chief, since 1970 but to no avail. I joined Estone Socialists, when I was only sixteen and a few years later was elected secretary of the Northend constituency......".

"I know Sufi," the chief interrupted. "The Honourable Sheila Wright MP, Clare Short MP, Jeff Rooker MP and those popular councillors like Saeed Abdi and James Hunt told me everything about you. You worked hard for the party but they always took you for granted and never valued your contributions. That's the political parties for you." I confided in the chief about the tremendous support I had received in the 1980s from those great Parliamentarians to prevent activists and candidates of all parties from practising Himalayan Politics but without success. At that time the fraudulent votes obtained by parties were in the region of five hundred. Faced with good opposition candidates, the Estone Socialists turned to Himalayan politics, illegally gaining hundreds of votes.

"Do you think Sufi that the National Executive Committee (NEC) of the Socialist party know about the antics of their local and regional parties?" The Chief asked.

"I think they do chief because I wrote to Miss Black, a NEC member about the wrongdoings of the local party in our Estone ward but she refused to act."

"Where's the justice, democracy and rule of law nowadays? Didn't Ms Short resign as a protest against the Iraq war?"

"Yes, Chief I think she did, but it changed nothing. Democracy is a system of governance, where people are counted not weighed."

"I read Clare Short's book, *An Honourable Deception*. This book is a must-read Sufi. It's an eye-opener. I have just finished reading it. It's on the bookshelf in my office. Pick it up any day you are free."

"Thank you, sir, but no need chief. I received a copy from the Honourable author soon after it was published. I've read it three times."

"Okay, Sufi. Leave this postal vote incident with me. I'll dispatch some officers to the warehouse. Don't worry, if any crime has been committed, we'll prosecute."

It was clear from Ms Short's book that her Party had lost some of its values under the leadership of the time as they concentrated more on the presentation of the party rather than substance and there followed a noticeable erosion of civil rights, especially for the Muslims, in the country and democracy in cabinet discussions. I believed the only good thing that party had ever done was the creation of the National Health Service in 1948 among other minor achievements. It created problems too. Most notable was the Kashmir problem. Since my arrival in the UK at thirteen, I heard many lies from successive leaders regarding their "untiring efforts" to solve the Kashmir issue. Not a single British politician made any effort to solve the Kashmir issue, behaving like true colonialists and turning a blind eye to the mass killing, forced disappearances, torture, rape, suppression of freedom of speech and ban on worship in mosques in Kashmir. India openly flouted United Nations resolutions and international opinion. The United Nations need to compare Kashmir with East Timor, a part of Indonesia. The Indonesians were accused of committing barbaric acts against the people in East Timor. There was a swift intervention by the United Nations which resulted in the independence of East Timor. So why has the UN failed in Kashmir? The answer is simple. In East Timor, the alleged oppressor of Christian inhabitants was a Muslim Country but in Kashmir, a fascist Hindu state, a friend of the West, oppresses the Muslims. There lies the answer, the double standards of those who run the UN. Truth and justice must prevail throughout the world for humanity to reach sublime heights. Someone should dismantle boundaries between nations. A world government is needed with the power to use all available resources to alleviate poverty from the face of the earth and make it a haven for all to live in peace and prosperity. There should be no need for the armed forces or weapons of mass destruction, saving trillions which could be spent on discovering the secrets of the universe. To build spaceships like star trek and go where no man's gone before and discover planets made of precious metals – gold, yaqoot (rubies) and Murjan (diamonds). That

189

isn't all. The intrepid searchers would find planets consisting purely of sapphires, amethyst, emerald and many others. The opportunities for humanity to truly become humans were limitless if only greed, lies, deception and a ruthless desire of some nations to become superpowers were replaced with generosity, truth, justice and international cooperation.

The piercing sound of the telephone bell suddenly shattered the hushed atmosphere of the campaign office, interrupting my thoughts.

"Sufi, It's Payara, the police have arrived! The Socialist activists are running out of the warehouse, using the back door. We caught two of them and handed them to the police. Three have run away. We don't know who they are. The police......"

"Thanks, Payara, good work. Where are you guys now?" I interrupted.

"We're just outside the main entrance of the warehouse. Asif and Irfan are inside, talking to Sargent Brown."

"Ok, good. Put one of them on."

"Ye Irfan's coming out. Here he's."

"Sufi bad news," Irfan sounded disappointed.

"What happened?"

"The police arrested all of them except the three who ran away. They also took all postal ballot papers into custody but then the Sargent received a call, apparently from the chief, ordering him to release everyone and take no action."

"What?" I shouted. I stood up from my seat. Angry. "How can the police do that? An electoral fraud has been committed, they've been caught red-handed, they should be arrested. Have the police confiscated the postal votes?"

"I've counted around seven black bin bags full of envelopes, some sealed and some opened. They've taken them away, but the sergeant told me that the bags will have to be handed over to the returning officer to be included in the count, tomorrow."

"What the hell? I'll contact the chief. You guys come back to the campaign office."

# Chapter Twenty-Three

Word of electoral fraud spread quickly throughout the ward. The election office was jam-packed. Hundreds of Democratic party supporters gathered outside the campaign office. I informed JB, and other regional leaders of our party, of the sorry events. Everyone wanted to know the complete story. Reports of postal vote malpractices emerged not only from neighbouring inner-city wards of Heartlands and Ashbrook but also from Bradford, Coventry, some London Boroughs, Huddersfield, Halifax, Leeds, Peterborough and Walsall among others. The Democrats and National Party local leaders, candidates and activists could find no plausible explanation for the failure of the police to arrest the perpetrators of the crime and confiscate bags full of illegal postal votes, including proxy votes, snatched from their legal owners. It was a travesty of justice and a license for the criminals to convert the Cosmopolitan City into a banana republic. Such electoral malpractices occurred in the past in Bradford, Peterborough and Tower Hamlets among others. No doubt many other instances of fraud went unreported or were reported, as in Estone ward, but the election office took no notice.

I knew such electoral malpractices were not the norm but successive governments did little to stamp them out. Elsewhere, in the UK, postal and proxy vote fraud was sporadic. In inner city areas, it was frequent. A blatant disregard for electoral commission rules and irregularities involving postal votes, bribery, personation, and intimidation could be seen in areas predominantly occupied by people of South Asian origin. I had read research papers published by prominent researchers like Drs Akhtar and Peace, highlighting such incidents and citing the baradari system, imported from the Indian sub-continent, as the primary cause of the electoral malpractices.

Irfan and I welcomed JB and James Watt (local National party leader) onto the stage and asked everyone present to take a seat wherever there was one available and explained how the postal vote fraud was discovered and the police informed. "The police visited the warehouse under the codename: *operation whine*. This demonstrates the casual attitude of the police towards the fraud. It hasn't been taken seriously. What concerns me most is they left some black bags full of postal votes with the fraudsters." I handed the microphone over to JB.

"I thank you, Sufi and your team for a job well done. We'll try to stop the postal votes from being counted tomorrow," JB said and James Watt nodded furiously, everyone else gave a thunderous applause.

"Is there anything pointing towards the involvement of the election officials, the returning officer or anyone from local or central government, Sufi?" Adam Asked after the applause died down.

"Maybe Adam, but there's no way to confirm who was involved because *the chief* refused to go into details about the phone call. Someone did phone him and told him that the police had no authority in the matter and postal votes should be made available for counting tomorrow. Was the caller from the central government or the local? My guess is we'll never know. My worry is the black bags full of fraudulently completed postal votes will be accepted as legitimate at the count. If these are counted there's no way we can win. For the life of me, I can't understand why the police left without arresting the fraudsters. We caught them red-handed. I may be wrong, but hundreds or even thousands of postal votes were open and spread all over the table and the unopened ones were in the bags."

"Is there any way, we can stop the count tomorrow and the returning officer asked to investigate?" Jim, a reporter, asked. I didn't realise the packed campaign office included some journalists. "Of course, we'll try our best tomorrow morning Jim. So, all counting agents should be there at 9.00 am sharp. I've got a transcript of the conversation I've had with *the chief*. His accusation regarding a call telling him not to interfere in the electoral process is recorded on my phone. This is a great mystery. One thing is clear: *the opposition wants to win at any cost.*"

"What happens if they count the votes in the black bags and we lose?" Irfan asked.

I said: "We need to ask our good friend, Barrister Khan that question. I guess that we'll have to take the matter to court. But before we can, we'll need a lot of evidence and a petition to have the election declared void under the Peoples' representation act." Several members raised their hands, offering to be the petitioners.

"Thank you for the offer. Please keep in touch. It looks like we'll need you. I can't see the returning officer agreeing not to allow black bags into the count. It all appears to be a fix." I felt dejected, tired and angry. I wasn't the only one, it seemed. Jitu, Irfan and Asif sat in the back row; face buried in their hands. They had been deceived, used and abused. They'd tried their best to have me arrested and my career ruined but for my part, I asked for three votes, never reported their treachery to the party hierarchy and never let them down.

"He has a good heart, that Sufi. Our so-called fucking friends beat us at our own game, and used Himalayan politics against us," Jitu said angrily, "I'm going to sort the bastards out, if it's the last thing I do."

"Do nothing rash Jitu," Irfan said but Jitu and Asif were already going down the stairs.

"Can I ask all counting agents to meet here, in the campaign office, tomorrow at 8.00 am? The count will take place at the Alex Stadium. We'll leave around 8.30 am in our respective cars and meet in the Alex Stadium car park and arrive at the count together. We should be there in time to persuade the returning officer not to count the stolen postal ballot papers. It's nearly midnight. Let's go home and have some sleep. See you tomorrow."

# Chapter Twenty-Four

Jitu and Irfan were already at the count when I, Asif, JB and Payara arrived. Only three counting agents were allowed beside the candidates. Irfan was in an animated conversation with the returning officer, Mr Moher and the election officer Mr Weno. I heard the returning Officer say: "It appears the votes were cast legitimately, and we have interviewed the candidates involved. They say the voters completed the ballot papers and not the candidates or the party officials. The candidates and activists took possession of the ballot papers for safety reasons and to ensure the votes arrive at the count in time as it was too late to post them."

"In that case why didn't they follow the electoral commission guidance by asking the voters to take their completed postal votes and hand them in at the polling stations? That's the electoral commission advice, isn't it?"

"Good point Mr Khar," I said startling them. "What is your answer to my colleague's excellent question, Mr Moher and Mr Weno?"

"Mr Moher has already answered your friend's question, Mr Sahab. We're going to include these votes in the count. Our decision is final," Mr Weno interjected rudely.

"It's not your decision Mr Weno. We want to hear from the returning officer. Before you make your final decision, Mr Moher, let me read to you last night's police log: 'Officers attended the warehouse on Power Road to a report of local councillors doctoring the postal votes. Six persons present with a table full of election forms…. none of the envelopes were sealed….' We have a record of around a dozen people initially present, so half got away. What further evidence do you need to exclude these *doctored votes* from the count Mr Moher?"

"As Mr Weno has already stated, we'll include the votes in the count. I see no reason to decide otherwise."

"What! With due respect Mr Moher, my colleague has already made an excellent point regarding the electoral commission's unequivocal advice that under no circumstances should the candidates, the agents or the activists handle post votes. You'll be making a big mistake by including these fraudulently obtained votes in the count. It would not only be grossly unfair and an illegal act but would make a mockery of the Democratic process. You'll be allowing these criminals to get away. You need to consider the police log and the numerous postal vote boxes and bags that have mysteriously turned up at the count, full of votes for the Estone Socialists. You need to consider that fraud has been carried out in all inner-city wards."

"Oh, whatever Mr Sahab."

Mr Moher spoke briefly, in the presence of local socialist leadership, to all deputy returning officers in inner-city wards, instructing them to include all postal votes in the count and left the Alex Stadium. Violent arguments ensued among the counting agents and candidates as the Estone Socialists were heading towards an unlikely 'victory'. So much for democracy and the rule of law.

After the 'count', the socialist candidates ridiculed Democrats and National party candidates, walking pompously and laughing in a derisory tone. Himar shouted: "Who said the Estone Socialists are finished?" The rest of them responded: "Oh, the Democrats, the Democrats-what a lot of rubbish!" To the obvious dismay and shame of Irfan and Jitu the Estone Socialists 'won' all three seats. They profusely apologised to me for being so naïve and accepted that the Estone Socialists succeeded in using and abusing them. That night the "winners" hired *the den of iniquity* and held lavish celebration ever seen in Estone ward. They 'won' in the neighbouring wards too. Rumour had it that over half of Estone ward turned out for the premature celebrations as the Democrats announced legal action against the socialist 'thieves' under the Peoples' representation act 1983 to set aside the election results in Estone and two other inner-city wards.

# Chapter Twenty-Five

A couple of weeks later, several newspaper headlines heralded the legal action against the Estone Socialists. Some headlines read:

HIGH COURT DATE FOR 'VOTE RIGGING' CASE

HIGH COURT TO RULE ON 'POSTAL VOTE RIGGING'

National Newspapers carried reports of a high-profile legal case, alleging postal vote fraud in Europe's biggest Cosmopolitan City. The high court Judge, Mr Justice Berrington ruled, to the delight of the victims of the fraud, that there was sufficient evidence for a full hearing to be held. The Honourable Judge ordered the city council to hand over postal ballot application forms and ballot papers. Newspapers carried comments from the local and national leadership of the Democrats, praising the Judge for taking the case to a full hearing. The petitioners talked of engaging handwriting experts to enable irrefutable evidence to be presented to the court to prove massive electoral fraud. A young Barrister helped organise the Estone ward petition and claimed to have received six death threats since the date of the hearing was announced. I believed the Barrister, as nothing could be put past the Estone Socialists. Desperate times call for desperate measures. And these were certainly desperate times for the Estone Socialists.

I learned about the fight between Irfan, Jitu and four Estone Socialists on the day of the count in the Alex Stadium. I had noticed that Irfan had a black eye and Jitu had a nasty cut to the lower lip and bruises on the knuckles of his right hand. Jitu said little in response to my enquiries but Irfan blurted out everything. In the Alex Stadium car park, Jitu accused the Estone Socialists of repudiating the agreement to vote for Irfan. An argument developed between Yoda and Irfan. Jitu continued to play the dirty game. He told Yoda had they included Irfan and made him 'win' too the matter would've rested there as the local Democratic leadership would've been satisfied with the result and there wouldn't have been talk of a court case. The local Democrats would've been content with winning only one seat. "They didn't give a toss about Sufi's or Asif's seat," Jitu complained to Yoda but he just laughed at him.

"Instead of apologising or displaying remorse for their treacherous actions, the Estone Socialists just laughed and ridiculed Jitu and me," Irfan explained. Tempers were then raised and Jitu landed a punch on Yoda's nose sending him reeling backwards; his fall broken by the boot of his car. While Yoda was out of action, other two fraudsters, Himar Rajah and Kalbi Jat attacked Jitu causing him facial injuries. Irfan received a punch to the chin and the left eye from Mr Patwari; it was a right-left combination. Two security officers of Pakistani origin intervened and stopped the fight. It was clear from Irfan's demeanour that he was still in pain. *Violence begets violence, and those who live by the sword, die by it.* Such riddles were difficult to conceive and painful to solve, I thought unless you're Einstein or a local socialist party leader.

I switched my attention to my mobile phone where hundreds of texts and voicemails cluttered up my storage space. Voice messages and texts were all scathing and brutal in their condemnation of vote-rigging. Comments like: *thieves will never prosper* and *the 'harames' ruined the reputation of our community* topped the poll. But thieves had already prospered. A supporter sent me a copy of the news report, containing a statement from a national organising committee member of the Estone Socialists, suspending all culprits from the party. She said that she will vigorously pursue a disciplinary process to inculcate a sense of public service into their members and that she expects the highest standard of honesty and probity from public servants. The campaign workers and all ward and constituency officers will receive training in the ethics of public service. She further said that Himalayan Politics will be uprooted from the Cosmopolitan City. "We'll not allow our city to be turned into a banana republic," she said.

Below the statement, there were many comments and pictures of laughing emojis: *"What standards?" "What honesty?" "We'll believe you when these crooks are behind bars."*

The high court judge appointed a special commissioner to investigate the postal vote fraud. Initial scrutiny revealed startling facts about how the fraud was masterminded. We also figured out the salient mechanisms and identified them in the petition. The Honourable commissioner described the warehouse as a 'vote-rigging factory'. Sophisticated methods to procure postal votes were utilised. Witnesses saw their activists and supporters standing on main roads, bribing local voters into handing over their postal ballots. Some envelopes containing the ballots got stuck in the letter boxes and children were sent to retrieve those. In Westwood Heath ward, a pillar post box was set alight, allegedly by the socialist party supporters to destroy postal votes believed to have been cast in favour of the opposition parties. Not only many householders were intimidated into handing over their ballot forms but they offered some postmen £500 to hand over their sacks containing ballot papers. A few postmen received death threats from a candidate for refusing to hand over the sacks. In the 'vote-rigging factory', many votes were altered with correcting fluid. It was a field day for Himalayan Politics.

As a witness, I attended the hearing of the trial daily and heard blatant lies given in evidence at the hearing. Many searching questions posed by the Honourable Election Commissioner indicated to me that he didn't believe the evidence given by the Estone Socialists. It was to the credit of the Honourable Commissioner that he caught their lies at the outset of the trial. A marked difference existed between the evidence given by the Democratic witnesses and the Estone Socialists. The petitioners adopted a simple approach. They alleged that the Estone Socialists illegally obtained thousands of postal ballot papers and then sat in this warehouse filled the blank ballot papers in their favour and altered those that were cast in favour of the opposition, using correcting fluid. Different men completed thousands of ballot papers was confirmed by handwriting experts. Any reasonable person listening to the trial proceedings would've concluded that the Democratic Party's witnesses gave clear, concise and credible evidence whereas the socialist party's witnesses' evidence was inconsistent and incredible. Indeed, one witness, a socialist candidate changed his original statement to 'fit the evidence' produced by the petitioners.

After the trial, the commissioner sent his report, together with the evidence to the Honourable Judge, who reserved the judgement for a later date. The Estone Socialists were 'confident' that the judgment will be in their favour. So, I analysed the evidence to see which way the Judgement could go. Will the Honourable High Court Judge declare the election void or accept the Estone Socialists as properly elected? From what I had heard in court, it was clear to me that the Judge will declare the election void. The evidence given by the petitioners and their witnesses was consistent and credible and corroborated by police officers and the documentary evidence provided to the court. The handwriting analysis showed postal vote fraud on an unprecedented scale. My summary of the evidence was not very much different to the original summation of the court. I summed up the evidence like this: *On the night of the election, the democrats believing that the opposition candidates and activists were up to no good, kept a close watch of their campaign office, on Wilson Street. The petitioners saw Himar Rajah and Yoda sitting in the Audi TT car outside the campaign office. Through the binoculars, from the attic of the house opposite, they saw some occupants looking anxious, so they left the house, got into their car and kept up surveillance from a distance. Soon after a Porsche 718 Cayman car arrived, driven by Raju Miah, with a passenger. They got out of the car and one of them retrieved several black bin bags from the boot and entered the campaign office. By this time, it became clear to the Democrats that the rumours about fraud had a factual basis and the opposition party was planning a massive postal vote fraud to retain the seats. Some five minutes later, the third candidate, Adah Ram arrived with three passengers in Range Rover Velar. And four men emerged from the campaign office, placed around seven black bags in the boot and got into Audi TT and drove off followed by the Democrats' surveillance team. They left Range Rover parked outside the campaign office. The Audi TT, driven by Yoda, arrived in the car park of the warehouse. From there the Democratic Party's second surveillance team took over and from their vantage point behind the shrubs observed the car park and the warehouse. Shortly afterwards, another Porsche and a Tesla Model 3 arrived and then an Audi A6 Avant arrived followed by Volvo XC40.*

*In all, a dozen men entered the warehouse with seven black bin bags full of postal votes. They spread the postal votes on the table and began filling them. They divided the tasks between them. Eight persons were assigned to fill the blank ballot papers, and two to alter the ballot papers already completed in favour of the Democratic party candidates. And two to seal them. Yoda acted as the adviser and rang other activists directing them to bring additional stolen ballots to the warehouse.*

*The petitioners said they then called the police. The police gave the evidence stating that five police officers under the command of a Sargent arrived at the warehouse around midnight in response to several calls alerting them to a vote-rigging taking place. They discovered several Asian men in the foyer of the warehouse. They identified the men as candidates and activists of the Estone Socialist party. They further testified that on a large oval-shaped table in the room, the police saw a lot of paperwork scattered on the table. They saw plenty of ballot papers, some with crosses on them and many were unsealed envelopes of A5 size. They remembered one man sitting on a sofa who was chubby, bald and wearing glasses and was very obstructive. They weren't sure if criminal offences had been committed so they referred the matter to a senior officer.*

*The Socialist Party's witnesses told an unbelievable story. They said they had collected thousands of ballot papers for 'safe keeping.' They had taken the ballot papers to the campaign office but didn't find it safe enough so they took them to the warehouse to put them in the safe. What safety issues were there? They didn't have an answer other than to say that they weren't sure royal mail would deliver the ballot papers to the election office in time. Asked why didn't they allow the owners of the ballot papers to take them to the polling stations on polling day? Again, there was no plausible answer. According to the police evidence they spread out the ballot papers on the table. So, if they were taken to the warehouse for safekeeping then why were the ballot papers not placed in the safe? Why were they laid open on the table? Again, an incredible response was given; they had decided to count the ballot papers before putting them in the safe. Why were ballot papers then open and being completed and altered? Again, the court received no credible response from the Estone Socialists.*

In response to the allegations against the returning officer, Mr Moher and the election officer, Mr Weno by the Peoples' Party and the Democratic Party, both accused gave no evidence but were represented by a counsel who maintained that there was no doubt in the returning officer's mind, he and his election officer made the right decision in the light of the information available to them. So, the accusation against the returning officer regarding allowing lax rules and admitting the fraudulent votes (secretly brought into the arena by the Estone Socialists) in the count was untenable. The presiding deputy high court Judge responded by saying that the court could not ignore the circumstances in which these boxes appeared and caused a major row at the count.

I was certain the returning officer may not have known about the full facts but Mr Weno knew as I told him in a detailed letter in the previous elections about such fraud. Mr Weno simply ignored the issues raised and I suspected he was fully aware of the circumstances of the acceptance of the fraudulent votes into the count as was the local leadership of the Estone Socialists.

To the delight of the Democratic party supporters, the postal vote fraud case took just under eight months to conclude, from start to finish. In an extensive report to the high court, the Honourable commissioner stated the polls in the two Cosmopolitan city wards were marred by corrupt and illegal practices and organised on a massive and systematic scale reminiscent of an election in a banana republic. The postal voting system was wide open to fraud, and the fraudsters knew this. The six fraudsters were suspended by their party and would've faced criminal charges if the police investigated the matter. I believed it was a travesty of justice that the fraud on such a scale wasn't referred to the director of public prosecution. In summing up one barrister identified over fifteen types of fraud carried out in the election in the two Cosmopolitan City wards. The dominant type of fraud involved theft of ballot papers followed by proxy votes and personation, where the ballot papers were sent to a unique address, completed and sent to the election office. Other types of election fraud identified, involved the Estone socialist party supporters standing on main roads and attempting to bribe voters into handing over their ballot papers.

They encouraged even children to steal partially posted ballot papers from letter boxes. And a royal mail cut-out street post box full of ballot papers was set alight, and they offered postmen around five hundred pounds to hand over the sack of ballot papers.

I and every other supporter of the Democratic party were confident of a victory after an executive summary containing all his findings were delivered to the high court by the learned election commissioner.

# Chapter Twenty-Six

In a hundred-and ninety-two-page damning Judgement the high court ruled in favour of the Estone ward petitioners and ordered re-election in the ward. The court had done justice in England but in countries of the Indian subcontinent, I recalled witnessing an election in Pakistan, where fraud was openly committed but no one took any action despite several complaints. I was told this was business as usual in this part of the world.

The Judge pointed out that similar concerns of laxity of the system were brought to the notice of the authorities in some English cities by some candidates and newspapers like *The Times*, but ignored by the returning officers and councils. The Judge noted the tendency of politicians of all Parties to dismiss these warnings as scaremongering. I applauded the Judge for exposing the system of postal votes and for calling the Cosmopolitan city *'a banana republic'*. I was extremely disappointed when a few months later, two members of the socialist party who were known to have taken part in the electoral fraud were acquitted on some elusive technical grounds. The evidence against them was overwhelming, but they walked free which sent the wrong message to potential fraudsters. The courts imposed no fines and no prison sentences. A mere disqualification for five years was insufficient to stop electoral fraud. It was a well-planned electoral fraud, discovered only by a stroke of luck and should've been used to punish the fraudsters to deter any re-occurrence. As things stood, it convinced me that the fraud will remain for years to come until heavy prison sentences were imposed for this heinous crime.

Years ago, I recalled, the failure of Mr Weno to respond positively to my complaints of electoral fraud was the root cause of current fraud. Had steps been taken to investigate my complaints, the situation now would've been different. At that time, I thought the failure to act was simply because of complacency but this election fraud and the government's inconsiderate response proved beyond any reasonable doubt that some responsible people were in total denial of the fraud, not just complacent.

In the re-run of the election, I won along with two colleagues, but fraud didn't cease. The Democrats never achieved the target vote, because the Estone Socialists gained around a thousand votes year after year, which weren't destined for them. Postal vote fraud, proxy and personation again played a major role. In the year 2000, years before many other election frauds, I arrived at the church road polling station at around 8 am and found two Socialist Party activists, Himar Rajah and Kalbi Jat already standing outside. "Oh, Sufi Sahab, good morning. You're too late," They boasted, "we've already done what we had to do." They smiled, got into the car, and drove off. I asked the clerks for a tally of the total votes cast so far at the polling station. The figure they gave to me astounded me. Over five hundred votes had been polled already in just under an hour. This was strange. I had expected only around fifty, maybe slightly more but the figure should've been under a hundred. I went to check other polling stations. It was the same story in all seven polling stations. What was going on? As I returned to the Church Road polling station, four teenagers met me at the steps going into the polling station. They stopped me and asked if I was a socialist party candidate. They looked somewhat intoxicated. I asked them how could I help. They produced four polling cards and told me they didn't live in Estone ward and never voted before in any other ward. They wanted to vote for the socialist candidates because a rich socialist supporter, Rehman, had given them the polling cards to cast the votes in favour of the socialist candidates.

"How much money, did he give you?" I asked.

"Ten pounds each."

I took the cards off them and led the boys into the polling station. The polling clerk, a female in her thirties, daughter of a local socialist party supporter asked them their names and address. They just shrugged, pointing to the cards in my hand. The poll clerk asked me to give them their cards. I told her that the cards were not theirs' as they didn't live in the ward.

After, some procrastination, she asked them their names and addresses which, as I had expected, didn't match those on the polling cards. I showed the cards to the polling clerk, stating that ballot papers shouldn't be issued as these were obvious cases of personation. The clerk looked for the names on the cards, in the register, ticked them and got her colleague to issue the ballot papers to the teenagers as I looked on in obvious disgust. "What do you think you're doing?" I asked angrily. "Forget it, Mr Sahab, you're just jealous they're socialist party supporters."

"It's nothing to do with jealousy. You've just allowed personation to take place, Mrs Hasan, you made it so easy." She told me to complain to the presiding officer. He was an elderly Indian man, in his early sixties, a council employee. He was all ears, but after I finished, he apologised profusely and told me there was nothing he could do. As they handed the poll cards to the clerk, we correctly issued ballot papers. I told him, I handed the cards to the clerk. They didn't even know the names or the addresses on the polling cards. He refused to listen and told me to leave otherwise he will call the police. "Please do," I retorted. The police were no help, and I contacted the election officer, Mr Weno. "I'll investigate the issue Mr Sahab and get back to you," he said. I'm still waiting for the response.

During the telephone call to the returning officer, I suggested Polling clerks, presiding officers and the returning officer should be recruited from a different city and there should be a requirement to produce identity details from the voters. A dedicated election officer and a police officer should be available at the end of a telephone line, if not in every polling station, in every ward to hear any complaints which should not be treated as mere 'gripe' but investigated with alacrity and due diligence. I noted several supporters of every party often hung around polling stations, harassing voters, and aggressively demanding that they vote for their party. This anti-democratic activity only occurred in inner-city wards. I asked the returning officer to ensure safeguards were put in place so that perpetrators of fraud and harassment could be punished with prison sentences, unless this was done, fraud would continue unchecked.

In the words of the honourable judge, *"The government believes the systems to deal with fraud are not working badly. The fact is that there are no systems to deal realistically with fraud and there never have been. Until there are, **fraud will continue unabated.**"*

There are only two ways to live one's life. One is to think, there are no miracles and the other is to think everything is a miracle.

# About the Author

The Himalayan Politics
(An affront to democracy)

Note about the Author

The author came to the UK from Kashmir in 1967 at the age of thirteen. He graduated in Biomedical Science and worked in various hospitals in blood sciences departments in NHS.

He took part in local and National politics from the age of sixteen and became the local constituency secretary a year later. He worked with prominent Parliamentarians like Hon Sheila Wright MP; Hon Clare Short MP and Hon Jeff Rooker MP. After twenty years, he became disillusioned with dirty politics within the local party and after September eleven atrocities and the Iraq war; he reluctantly joined the Democrats. He campaigned in local and parliamentary elections over the years and was himself a candidate in numerous local elections. In one such election, he and his colleagues were victims of a postal vote fraud. A high court Judge declared that election void a year later and ordered a re-run of the election. The author was elected as a councillor in 2005.

# Glossary

*Astaghfirullah* – God forbid
*Baksheesh* – alms for the poor
*Baradari* – caste system
*Gora Sahibs* – Englishmen
*Hanafi, Maliki, Hanbali, Shafi* – schools of jurisprudence in Islam
*Harambee* – unpleasant person
*Hooris* – beautiful women of paradise
*Jahil* – ignorant
*Kafirs/Kefirs* – unbelievers
*Kumi(s)* – menial workers
*Maslaks* – Mullah led religious belief
*Mirpuri* – resident/language of Mirpur, a city in Azad Kashmir, Pakistan
*Muezzin* – Caller to prayer
*Nakamee* – failure
*Nath/Nath* – a eulogy to the holy prophet
*Pakoras* – a spicy fritter
*Pir/Peer* – spiritual leader
*Quom (s)* – Race (s)
*Rafah Yadain* – raising of hands in prayers
*Rajput* – rich/kingly class
*Salafis, Kharijites, Deobandis, Barelvis* – sects of Islam
*Samosa* – fried south Asian pastry with savoury filling
*Shaitan* – Satan
*Shia and Sunni* – The two Major sects of Islam
*Yaar* – dearest friend
*Zamindars* – landowners

Milton Keynes UK
Ingram Content Group UK Ltd.
UKHW011044231123
433129UK00005B/439